# SECOND CHANCE

## (THE DEADMAN BOOK 5)

## LINELL JEPPSEN

WOLFPACK
PUBLISHING
— EST 2013 —

**Deadman's Revenge**

Paperback Edition
Copyright © 2019 Linell Jeppsen

Wolfpack Publishing
6032 Wheat Penny Avenue
Las Vegas, NV 89122

wolfpackpublishing.com

Paperback ISBN 978-1-64119-800-4
eBook ISBN 978-1-64119-801-1

# SECOND CHANCE

# FOREWORD

*The Trinity, 1907*

Three old men sat in an opulent parlor drinking brandy, smoking expensive cigars and discussing the merits of murder in commerce. They were all quite wealthy, born into an unbelievably lavish lifestyle, courtesy of their forefathers.

Edward Branson, a widower and the oldest of the three, was the son and principal heir of the Branson Bank of Boston family. He was and had always been decadent, cruel and entirely without conscience when it came to the acquisition of money—which was why, at the age of seventy, he was one of the richest men in the world.

He was also one of the greediest men on the planet. Having been born into "Old Money" with all of its shabby elegance, he yearned for disposable capitol like a thirsty man craves water. Nothing he owned, however, gave him pleasure...the minute he acquired what he wanted, its worth diminished, exponentially.

The second man in the room, sixty-eight-year-old Timothy Farnsworth, was the only son of a railroad tycoon. He had been groomed to take over the reins of his family's railway, but showed no interest or aptitude for business. At eighteen he was sent to Harvard University where he met his friend and mentor, Edward Branson.

From the moment Branson met Farnsworth he knew he'd found his right-hand man. Edward had never been a big man, or strong, and he knew that if he were to achieve his dreams of wealth beyond imagining, he would need a strong arm.

Timothy fit the bill, exactly. He was tall and built like a lumberjack. He was not intellectual, cared little for money, women or possessions but, like a faithful hound, he lived to serve. And serve Edward he had, for over forty years. He had only one weakness…his love (and hidden passion) for the third man in the room…Stephen Castle.

Castle was the youngest of the three at sixty-five. Although age was finally taking its toll, he was still tall and handsome, with wide gray eyes and a long, aristocratic nose. He came from the acclaimed Castle family, Attorneys at Law… a long line of august men (and women) who had defended presidents and kings alike for over a century. He knew the law, in all its myriad forms, like the back of his hand. He also knew how to stretch and bend the law like the sweetest salt-water taffy.

He was happily married to his wife of thirty-seven years (which spoke to some soft part of a heart which had long ago hardened against the rest of mankind), although the couple lived in separate abodes and had not shared a bed in over twenty years.

Stephen knew of Timothy's affections, and although he did not reciprocate in any way, he felt a certain sympathy for the man, and tried to shield him from Edward's more violent and nefarious schemes. Too often over the years, for autonomy's sake, Edward had demanded that Timothy do some of their bloodiest deeds by himself—with no back-up or protection.

These men stopped at nothing—ever—to get what they wanted. In spite of all Stephen's legal machinations, some things—like murder, blackmail and treason—were not to be tolerated by the law. That's where Timothy came in, and for all his loyalty, the man had suffered.

He had been shot—twice, and stabbed. He had served time in prison and had lost two young male lovers to retribution and revenge meted out by Edward's enemies. Still, Timothy knew no other authority in the world than the man he had sworn fealty to in his early twenties.

He was old now, though, and used up. Stephen knew that Timothy's usefulness was coming to an end and he secretly seethed at the man who sat across from him. More and more, he sensed the menace behind Branson's veiled glances, his knowing smirks.

It didn't seem to matter to Edward that Stephen and Timothy held as much dirt on him as he did on them. Both of them knew that despite a lifetime of loyal friendship and service, Edward would have them killed in a thrice, if they dared to defy his every wish.

They listened as he spoke into the twilight gloom. "I want that mine, goddammit!" Looking up, he stared at Stephen. "For all your fancy-pants lawyers, I'm still not seeing any progress on declaring Wallace's purchase illegal!"

Stephen gazed out the large, multi-paned windows running with sheets of rain, to the moss-covered gargoyles spewing green-tinged runoff from the mansion's eaves. Queen Anne Hill was one of the tonier neighborhoods in Seattle, Washington, but it was not immune to bleary blankets of fog that crouched over the region like a smelly gray dog, or the buckets of mud that came with the rainy weather.

He was heartily sick of Branson's assumption that the law firm of Castle and Castle was at his beck and call. Over the years, he had pulled off some staggering legal maneuverings that would not only have landed him in prison, but would have been the envy of his peers—had they but known.

Still, one lawyer, even one as talented as he was, could only do so much when the US government was involved. He sighed. "Edward, I already told you that Castle and Castle has formally filed charges against Wallace for using Sioux script to purchase the Oreornogo mine…it's in litigation as we speak! What more can I do?"

Branson snorted with disgust and then farted. Ignoring the noisome gust, he turned to Farnsworth. "And what have you been doing lately?"

Timothy blushed. "I sent my men into the Wallace area. So far they've cleared out almost a half a dozen claims…"

Branson blew a raspberry and frowned at the younger man. "That's not enough, goddammit! Until we can purchase the whole kit and caboodle, we need to get our hands on every single acre of land surrounding that mine. Then it will be easy peasy to move in—once that bastard Wallace is gone."

Trying to diffuse the situation somewhat, Stephen asked, "How long have your men been there, Timmy?"

Looking relieved at the change of topic, Timothy replied, "Over six months now. I was going to say, it's probably time to rotate them out of there before the local law starts putting faces to the deeds."

Branson glared but couldn't think of a retort. They had decided, long ago, to keep their operation as clandestine as possible—and that meant keeping their hired thugs from #1—getting arrested and #2—being recognized.

Turning to face Castle, he asked, "Whose turn is it, Stephen?"

Stephen said, "It's your turn to bring in a crew now, Edward."

Branson made a moue of disgust and contemplated the flames that flickered and hissed against errant drops of rain finding its way down the chimney.

The other men watched as he muttered under his breath. Then he said, "I...we have invested too much to give up now. I want the deeds and mineral rights on every inch of land within an eighty mile radius of Hecla. Do whatever it takes, gentlemen. Kill every person who gets in the way or refuses to move from the area... I don't care!"

Looking away from the fitful fire, he added, "I...WE will own that mine...if it's the last thing I ever do!"

## 1908

Two months had passed since the Wilcox and Son Detective Agency pulled off the successful sting operation against the Chowder brother's dirty boxing scheme. Now Matthew was sitting in his home office finishing up some paperwork. He and Chance were between jobs at the moment but he thought a couple of cases were imminent. Meanwhile, he was itching to go outside and watch Samuel and Abner put their new stallion through his paces.

Matthew's big gelding, Lincoln, was in the pen with a new two-year-old colt, and Matthew could see that the younger horse was both calmed by and interested in the older horse's movements. He saw Chance sitting on the fence rails watching the show as well. His son had healed quickly enough from the Swedish boxer's assault, but his shoulder still ached sometimes and he tired quickly when he tried to do too much with his right arm.

Matthew studied the documents on his desk one last

time, finding one uncrossed "t" and a missing comma. Then, satisfied, he gathered the papers together and put them in an envelope. He was just standing up to walk outside when he almost jumped out of his boots.

The telephone was ringing! He had finally had the modern device installed in his home office. Most of the time it lurked silently on the wall, but once in a while it shrilled out in alarm. It was loud (too loud) and Matthew noticed both horses standing still with their ears pricked toward the house. Chance was crawling down off the fence, eager to see who was on the line.

He picked up the earpiece and, feeling like a fool, said, "Hello?"

A male voice sounded in his ear. "Hello! Is this the Wilcox and Son Detective Agency?"

Matthew cleared his throat. "Yes, sir. How can I help you today?"

Suddenly, the man was weeping into Matthew's ear. "Sir, my daughter, Annie Thurston, asked me to call you. She was severely beaten last night and is in the hospital!"

Matthew's heart sank. He had gone out on a couple of dates with the beautiful lady reporter and their relationship was, just now, starting to blossom into something blessedly real and possibly permanent. She had recently asked if she could introduce him to her father and now, here was the man himself, calling with the worst news possible.

For a moment, Matthew's vision darkened with rage and fear. Why did almost everything he touch get hurt... or die...or leave him behind? His heart thudding with anxiety, he took a deep breath to calm his nerves. "Mr. Thurston, will she be alright?"

Thurston struggled to keep his words calm and Matthew could hear the man take a couple of deep breaths of his own. Then he replied, "Yes, sir. She will be fine, I think. But she has a story to share with you...you and your son. Will you come?"

Matthew answered, "Of course! Chance and I will meet you at your office in about two hours. See you then," he said and hung up the earpiece.

Matthew turned to face his boy, who had just walked in the front door. "Pack for a trip, Chance. We're heading into Spokane."

Although the weather was fairly mild for March, enough snow had fallen in the last few weeks to turn the road from Granville to Spokane into a series of icy rivulets and crevasse-sized pot holes. Accordingly, Matthew and Chance decided to hop on the train. They would arrive later than expected but, at least they would arrive—rather than be stuck in the mud.

The train pulled to a stop in Spokane at 4:35 and they were met at the station by Clyde Thurston himself. He was a short and rather rotund sixty-two year-old man. Although Matthew gathered that he was from a wealthy family, Thurston had an open, almost child-like face with round blue eyes and a guileless expression.

As the train screeched to a stop, Matthew saw the older gentleman standing by himself next to a beautiful black automobile. As soon as he and Chance stepped down to the platform, Thurston ran up to them with his right hand extended in welcome. "Hello! I'm so happy you came. Please...follow me and, if you don't mind, we'll head to the hospital directly!"

He stopped talking and gazed up at the two taller men in consternation. He blushed and shook his head as though he was just now remembering his manners. "Excuse me...you must be weary! I booked two rooms for you at the Davenport Hotel...it's quite grand! Perhaps you would like to rest first and go to the hospital to talk to my Annie in the morning?"

Matthew shook his head, touched by the old man's obvious concern for his beloved daughter. "No! Please, let's get to the hospital as quickly as possible."

Thurston smiled and said, "Thank you, yes...the car is over here."

The three men piled into the fancy four-seater and they took off with a lurch. During the seven mile trip to Deaconess Hospital, Thurston filled them in on the case Annie had been working on.

He said, "A prostitute named Chloe Brazil came to the office about three months ago. According to Annie, this woman looked and acted like no other prostitute she had ever talked to or written about. She was rather old, for one thing—probably in her mid-thirties. She was educated too, and dressed like a proper lady."

He cleared his throat, and glanced over at Matthew. "Pardon me, but my daughter and I are rather progressive...I hope you don't disapprove of prostitutes, overmuch?"

Matthew smiled. "No sir. One of my oldest and

dearest friends was once a Lady of the Night. She still runs a halfway house for young women."

Thurston grinned. "Now I understand why my Annie likes you so much. She says you are a fair-minded man, who won't hold our idiosyncrasies against us."

Matthew squirmed slightly, wondering just how much Annie had told her father about a certain Matthew Wilcox. Feeling at a distinct disadvantage, he murmured, "Please, tell us what happened."

Sobering, Thurston continued. "Anyway, Mrs. Brazil told Annie that she was forced into prostitution when claim-jumpers murdered her husband Ben, and her only son, Billy, last summer. The Brazils had scrimped and saved and finally purchased a twenty-five acre parcel of land just north of the Hecla mine in Wallace, Idaho last spring.

At first they were a little worried. There was very little pasture land for crops or livestock… just a lot of granite outcroppings and plenty of small streams. They knew this going in, though, and had purchased the land for the mineral rights. Still, Ben saw no sign of gold or silver until about June—when he panned up a few good-sized gold pebbles."

Thurston shook his head. "As you can imagine, he was thrilled. He took the gold into Wallace and came away with enough cash to order in the parts for two large sluices and all the equipment he needed to start a small mining operation. He even put up help-wanted posters around town. He was looking for two experienced miners to help out in his new claim."

"A couple of weeks later, three men came on to the

property asking for Ben. Unfortunately, Chloe thought they were potential new hires and sent them down to the creek to meet with her husband. It wasn't until almost four hours had passed that she started to fear something was amiss."

Suddenly the name Chloe rang a bell in Matthew's mind. He and Annie had gone out to luncheon once and he distinctly recalled a tall, blonde woman stopping by their table with a sheath of papers in her hand. She seemed genuinely embarrassed by her intrusion into their privacy, but Annie was having none of it.

She had grasped Chloe's hand in hers and introduced her to Matthew as her good friend, Chloe Brazil. He had smiled at the woman's blush of pleasure and taken her hand in friendship. Now he said, "Sir, I think I might have met the lady, but I certainly didn't think she was a prostitute!"

Thurston shook his head, "No, you wouldn't have thought so, for sure."

The old man drove silently for a few moments and then he continued. "Chloe told Annie that Ben and Billy had gone to the creek to fish and should have been back by now, especially since it was past suppertime and she had seen the visitors leave a couple of hours earlier. So she grabbed her coat and headed down to the riverbank to fetch her tardy husband and son home... only to find their slaughtered bodies floating in shallow water."

Thurston sighed. "The poor woman's memories were a bit muddled after that, understandably, but she did remember one thing very clearly..."

They were approaching Deaconess Hospital, which

rose up into the murky skyline like a castle on a high hill. Driving the car into a gravel parking area, Thurston turned the engine off and said, "Apparently, Mrs. Brazil owned a beautiful, cherry-wood Highboy. It's where she and her husband kept all their cash and important papers, like deeds of sale—both for their land and their mineral rights."

"Well," Thurston's voice rose in agitation. "She believed that someone stayed behind and hid after they killed her husband and son. She also thought that the minute she walked down to the river, that same person snuck in, destroyed the chest of drawers and stole all the paperwork proclaiming her as sole owner of the property!"

Turning to face Matthew and Chance, Annie Thurston's father said, "Here is where it pertains, I think, to the attack on my daughter. When Mrs. Brazil told Annie what had happened, she also confided that she and her husband had been hearing rumors for months, all up and down the Clark Fork, of folks either being killed or run off their legal claims!"

The fat little man shook his balding head. "Well, we hired Mrs. Brazil as a secretary, and a harder, more conscientious worker you will never find. She was helping Annie interview people in the area, taking copious notes and taking turns driving the car."

He stared into space for a moment, and then he added, "The one thing I failed to mention in my earlier phone call was that Chloe, bless her heart, was with Annie when she was attacked. While, barring the worst, Annie will survive the attack, Chloe was bludgeoned to death!"

The car rang with silence as the three men contemplated the savage actions taken against two helpless women and then Thurston said, "Let's head in before the staff closes the doors to visitors, shall we?"

Matthew and Chance climbed out of the fancy conveyance and followed Clyde Thurston up a long series of wooden steps into the hospital foyer. While the old man checked in, Matthew turned to his son.

"This sounds big, son. Maybe too big for us to tackle alone. What do you think?"

Chance stared into his father's eyes. "It sounds pretty bad for sure, Pa. We might have to get a bigger team and go undercover, for sure, but we don't want a bunch of claim jumpers getting away with murder, do we?"

Matthew closed his eyes for a moment and then he said, "Of course not. I want to talk to Annie first, but I feel sure we'll take the case."

## 2

# ANNIE

Annie Thurston lay in her hospital bed and dreamed. Although she was heavily sedated, the laudanum extract in her medicine made her dreams bright and colorful... almost lucid. A slight smile crossed her bruised face as she and her friend Chloe walked down a snowy boulevard. They were laughing at a joke they had heard at the newspaper office earlier that morning and preparing to climb into the car when they saw four men approaching.

They were well-dressed and Annie could smell an expensive cologne wafting toward her on the sharp breeze. Preparing to smile and call out a friendly greeting, she paused when she saw the expressions on their faces.

Each and every one of them were staring at her companion with fierce, avid eyes. Their faces were filled with ill-intent and as Annie watched, they surrounded Chloe, who stood by the passenger door of her car. Before her eyes could even register what was happening, she saw one of them hit her friend over the head with a sap.

Hearing a dreadful cracking sound, Annie cried out and ran around the front of the car. Risking a quick glance up the street, she saw that there were no people anywhere and hardly even any windows through which these men's activities could be observed. Not knowing what else to do, Annie screamed as loudly as she knew how. "HELP! Somebody help us, PLEASE!"

Heart pounding in dread, she stood by the hood of the car, staring down at Chloe's head leaking blood onto the dirty snow and knew that, although the men were taking turns kicking her in the head and torso, she was already dead. Her shy hazel eyes were fixed and staring, all spark of life fled. Annie screamed again, this time not in an attempt to cry out for help, but in horror of what these thugs had done to her friend.

One of the men, the one who had first struck Chloe with the club, looked up at where she stood, frozen, by the car's hood. "Stop, the job is done." He barked and spat on the snow by Chloe's head, adding, "Better grab that witness, though, before she blabs…"

Annie spun on her heels and started running up the street. Her thin leather soles were too slick, however, and she slid on the ice with a squeal of fright before falling in a heap. Almost instantly, she felt herself being lifted up by the elbows. She howled in fear and was dealt a devastating punch to the jaw.

For a moment, her whole face was numb but then the pain of the blow registered. Her mouth filled with blood and she could tell her nose was broken. Suddenly, she could hardly breathe and she writhed within the ruffian's grasp. She tried to scream again, but her wails were nothing more than muffled squeaks.

Her right eye was swelling and she could hardly see through the fear and pain, but she realized the men were dragging her toward a car parked behind her own automobile. She dug her heels into the snow and tried hurling herself backwards out of their grasp, but a heavy punch to her back sent her reeling to the ground.

She knelt on her hands and knees and vomited. She had heard a sharp crack and knew that one or more of her ribs were broken. She reeled in shock and pain and stared as blood from her nose and mouth stained the snow red.

The man with the sap walked up and Annie stared at him with angry eyes. "You will pay for this!" she muttered and saw the man grin.

"Mebbe so, ma'am," he drawled. "But, you won't be around to notice." He lifted the weapon high, and Annie closed her eyes against her own impending demise.

Then she heard a shout. "Hey! What's going on there? Get away from that woman!"

Annie wept with relief, sinking to the ground as the men surrounding her ran away. Then, police whistles and the clang of ambulance bells filled the air around her.

She awoke to the sound of her father's voice. She also became aware of the pain which seemed to encompass every square inch of her body. Her jaw had been dislocated during the altercation, and her nose and two ribs were broken. Her right eye was swollen shut and her lips were bruised and cut. The doctor had told her she was lucky, but as she squirmed against the pain, she figured the man's words were nothing more than platitudes. There was nothing "lucky" about what had happened to her and Chloe.

Remembering the empty look in the woman's eyes, her own filled with tears. She lifted her right hand to wipe the moisture away and gasped at the overwhelming pain the slight movement caused. Suddenly, her hand was seized in a warm, exceedingly gentle grasp.

"Annie!" a deep, masculine voice spoke close to her ear. "How are you feeling?"

On one hand, her heart filled with joy that Matthew had come to visit her in the hospital. On the other—he was seeing her at her absolute worst! "Oh Matthew, they killed Chloe!" she choked through the tears clogging her already painful sinuses.

"I know," he said, "and I'm so sorry this happened to you, both," Matthew whispered, gazing down at Annie's face in shock and anger.

Her golden brown hair was in wild disarray on the pillow which, somehow, seemed to throw her wounds into stark relief. The right side of Annie's face was black, blue and green with bruises. There was a wide bandage across her nose disguising most of the damage, but Matthew could tell that the whole area was discolored with abrasions and contusions.

Her right eye was puffy and swollen shut and her pretty lips were split as well. She gazed up at him with her one good eye and whispered, "Did my father talk to you about the story I've been working on?" She licked her bottom lip, wincing at the pain.

He nodded, "Yes, he did." Pausing for a moment, he

tried to frame his questions so she didn't have to do too much talking.

"Annie, I'm going to ask you a few questions. Hopefully, you can either nod or shake your head yes or no, okay?"

Annie smiled and nodded her head. Grinning at her little joke, he sat on the edge of the bed. He thought for a moment, then asked, "Do you think these men are connected to the claim-jumping ring your father spoke of?"

Annie nodded her head. "I'm sure of it," she murmured softly.

Matthew smiled. "Okay, that's a start," he said. "Did you recognize them?"

Annie shook her head, and a frustrated tear escaped from her swollen eye. "No, I can't…"

"Shhh!" Matthew crooned. "That's okay! I'm beginning to think that this is a pretty big ring—a criminal enterprise with a lot of moving parts. I don't know much yet, but if what your father told me is accurate, it would take a lot of resources… and a LOT of cash to pay men to grab land-claims all up and down the Clark Fork!"

"It's true, Matthew!" she gazed up at him, and he could see the pain of her injuries mirrored in her brilliant blue eye.

Deciding to make his exit so she could rest, he said, "Listen, I'm going to investigate this to the best of my ability. I will be bringing the law into it as well…eventually. First, Chance and I need some solid evidence of wrong-doing, okay?" He clasped her hand again, applying a little more pressure.

"It might take time to find proof so, in the meanwhile, I want you..." he turned toward Clyde Thurston, "and you to stay safely at home." He was not surprised when Annie and her father frowned in surprise.

Clyde sputtered, "But, sir...I have a paper to run!"

Matthew sighed. "Mr. Thurston, I understand that this might be an inconvenience, but I believe you are both at risk now. You need to assume that Annie—and by extension, you, are witnesses to murder, at the very least!"

Thurston's face turned red with frustration but he nodded, finally, in agreement. "Yes...you are probably right, Mr. Wilcox. Besides, much of my work can be done at home, and Annie needs time to recover her health."

Matthew smiled. "I would like to arrange for police protection, sir...at least until we know who and what we're dealing with. Is that alright with you?"

Clyde rolled his eyes, but shrugged in surrender.

Looking down at Annie's wan face, he saw that her eye was drooping with pain and fatigue. She startled awake when he leaned over and kissed her lightly on the forehead. "Don't worry, Annie. Chance and I will figure out who did this to you and your friend. Then, we...all of us, will make them pay for their crimes!"

She smiled up at him and then fell into a dreamless slumber.

Matthew stood up and glanced over at Annie's father who had perched on the opposite side of her hospital cot. He was muttering to himself about how he was to blame...for putting his daughter in an untenable position...and how, from now on, she should just stick to the news desk, rather than put herself in harm's way.

Clearing his throat, Matthew said, "My son and I will take the case, Sir. Like I said before, please stay by Annie's side and when she is free to go home—stay there with her. I hope this won't take long, but I will be sending someone by your house to help keep you and your daughter safe."

The older man looked stunned and defeated, but he nodded in agreement. "I will, Mr. Wilcox. Here..." he fumbled in his vest pocket, finally handing Matthew a gold-embossed business card. "My address and phone number—plus, the phone number for the newspaper. Please, keep in touch, won't you?"

Matthew nodded. "You will be hearing from us very soon, sir. I intend to bring these criminals down!"

## 3

## THE LINDSAYS

Seventeen miles due east of Wallace, Idaho, a man by the name of Jacob Lindsay, his wife and his two youngest children milled around in back of their small cabin. It was the end of March and frost rimmed every surface of their property, painting the evergreens silver and filling the air with frozen, rainbow crystals. The small family broke ice away from the water troughs, threw piles of hay toward their horse and two mules and fed their milk cow.

There was additional work for Jacob to do this morning, as his two older sons were down on the river panning for gold and silver. The family had learned over the last year to hide their enterprise from prying eyes, so he and his boys took turns panning in a hidden glade on the river three hundred feet below the house.

So far, their ruse had worked. Although lean-tos, cabins and shacks all up and down the river stood empty, the Lindsay's were still in operation... at least so far. The claim-jumpers were becoming bolder, though, and Jacob was losing heart.

Nothing in the wide world mattered to him more than his family, but their circumstances were starting to take a toll. Really, the only reason they were still here, slowly accumulating tiny pebbles of gold, was that they had started out poor to begin with. He could not yet afford the equipment needed to really succeed, and that alone had saved their bacon.

It seemed to him that it was the more successful enterprises up and down this valley that kept getting hit by the shadowy, claim-jumping thieves that descended like locusts every few weeks. Just five months earlier, their neighbors to the west had been hit—and hard. The Brazils were hard-working and exceedingly kind people, but perhaps a little too talkative and boastful about the riches on their property.

Hubris had killed Ben Brazil and his son, Billy, and fate had blown Mrs. Brazil to the far winds, much to the dismay of Jacob's wife, Marta, who felt, for the first time since moving to this wild and far-flung country from their German homeland, that she had finally found a friend.

Well, Jacob thought, leaning his pitchfork against the rapidly diminishing haystack by the stable, I'll be damned if my loose tongue costs me my family and my life savings!

"Go ahead and milk that cow while she's eating, Frannie," he called over to his seven-year-old daughter who stood a good distance away from the long-horned heifer.

"But she kicks, Papa!" Frannie whined.

"I'll do it! Gilda likes me, Papa! Frannie pulls too hard!" his son Peter exclaimed with a snort of disgust.

Jacob started to scold his daughter when he heard a slow clop of hooves approaching from the west. Turning to his children, he barked, "You go to the house with your Mama!"

His wife and children wasted no time in high-tailing it to their small, but sturdy home. He heard the plugs fall away and knew that Marta and Peter were in the process of resting firearms (a shotgun and a rifle) on the bolt hole's lower casings, while Frannie scrambled into the cellar through the trap door.

Jacob unsnapped his holster and rested his hand on his pistol, watching as two men turned off the road and walked their horses slowly toward the house. His heart thudded with dread but he could hardly keep his lips from twitching with mirth when he spied the lead rider's horse. *What a peculiar looking animal,* he thought.

Jacob had been around horses his entire life and never seen anything like the big gelding that approached. Its creamy-white coat was covered entirely with tiny, red spots but its head was roan-colored. The horse's mane stood straight up in red and white spikes and the beasts measly tail was nearly naked but for a colorful plume of red and white on the tip.

A handsome, middle-aged man rode the speckled roan, and an equally handsome, but much younger man rode behind him on a showy gray mare. They were nicely dressed but had ridden a while, if the mud and slush on their boots, pants and long coats was the judge of such things.

"Hello the house!" the lead rider called out, stopping his horse. "May we approach?"

Although Jacob had every reason in the world to be cautious, frightened even—something about the man's appearance...and his comical-looking horse, put him at ease. He tipped his chin, gesturing them forward.

The two men smiled and walked their horses up the drive. Stopping about ten feet away from where Jacob stood, the older man climbed down from his saddle. He stretched with a groan, and then, noticing how Jacob stared in fascination at his mount, he grinned and said, "Lincoln—say hello!"

Instantly, the big gelding lifted his velvety lips in a toothy grin and stuck his right front hoof in the air. Then he lowered his head in a bow.

Flabbergasted, Jacob burst out laughing. The horse's antics and his owner's smug grin of fatherly pride tickled Jacob's funny bone to no end, and he continued to wheeze and snort with gales of glee, the like of which he had not felt in years.

Finally, the man stuck out his hand and said, "My name is Matthew Wilcox and this is my son, Chance." The three men shook hands and, after handing over a business card, Matthew said, "Can we have a few minutes of your time? We represent the Wilcox and Son Detective Agency and we would like to talk to you about what's been happening the last year or so, to the land claims in this valley."

Jacob's mood darkened. *So, these strangers have heard about the claim jumps...I wonder if they know about the murders, too.* The middle-aged man studied their faces for a moment and said, "Yes, I would like to speak of that as well. Tie your horses up at the rail and then come over here...we'll sit and talk."

While Chance and Matthew led their horses to a hitch-rail in front of the stable, Jacob stepped up onto the front porch. Sticking his head in the door, he said, "Go ahead and close the bolt holes, but keep the weapons handy." Looking at his wife of twenty years, he added, "Marta, I think these are good men, but keep a close eye on them, yes? Meanwhile, please bring coffee and maybe, some of your nice cake."

She nodded and put some grounds on to boil, while her youngest son yammered on about the trick the big, spotty roan had performed and asked if he could go outside to pet the animal. Marta had also grinned with amusement when she saw the horse's funny greeting, but she also knew with the certainty of age and experience that the devil sometimes wore a clown suit. She snapped, "Never mind that horse! You stay here until your Papa tells you it is okay to step outside!"

Whining, but obedient, Peter opened the trap-door under the rug and let his little sister out. She instantly ran to the window to see who had come calling. She had missed Lincoln's trick but visitors were rare and she really wanted to lay eyes on the new and interesting faces. She stared at the two men and at her papa for a second before Marta said, "Frannie, come and cut the streusel...quick!"

Mathew and Chance stepped up onto the porch and joined Jacob at the far end. Matthew couldn't help but notice that the far end of the porch, where they sat in finely-crafted cane chairs, was hidden from the road, although whoever resided there could easily see who approached.

Matthew admired Mr. Lindsay's caution. The man had set his home up with a clever eye for self-protection. What Matthew and Chance needed right now was a regular citizen to help them pull off their scheme, and he hoped that Jacob would be the man who helped them.

The three men sat and talked for a couple of hours. At one point Jacob's wife, Marta, came out with coffee and cake. She was accompanied by her two children—a boy and a girl. The girl stared into their faces with curiosity, but the boy was more interested in Matthew's horse.

"Would you like to pet him?" Matthew asked. "If it's alright with your father, Lincoln loves children."

Jacob shrugged and said, "Just for a moment, Peter. Give those animals a bite to eat. Then, I want you to go down to the river and fetch your brothers."

Matthew and Chance exchanged glances. They were both amazed, having had no clue that there were more members in Jacob's family. It was another sleight of hand ploy that spoke to Jacob's intelligent but cautious nature.

Peter picked up two bundles of hay and threw them in front of the visiting horses. Then he crowed with laughter as Lincoln promptly threw the hay back in Peter's face. Horse and boy played for a few minutes until Peter put his hat on his head and took off running around the house and down to the riverbed below.

Matthew and Jacob had already exchanged intelligence about the claim-jumpers but now Matthew talked about what had happened to his friend Annie Thurston and her unfortunate companion, Chloe Brazil, stopping in surprise when he heard a crash come from inside the house.

Jacob held up his hands and said, "Excuse me, please. My wife and Mrs. Brazil were friends. We did not know what had become of her...please! I'll be right back!"

He stood up and went inside. Matthew heard Marta weeping and he cursed himself. He and Chance had studied the plats of land that had sold up and down this river and he should have known that Marta and Chloe were probably acquainted—they were neighbors, after all!

Feeling like a heel, he sat back in his chair with a sigh of disgust. Chance studied his father's face for a moment and said, "They were going to find out eventually, Pa. Better coming from us than a stranger, right?"

Matthew murmured, "As far as this family is concerned, we are strangers, son."

Chance shook his head. "You're right, but if things go like we hope, we are the strangers who will get revenge on the crooks who did this."

Jacob walked back outside and sat next to them again. He took a sip of cold coffee and said, "I understand that you and your son are going to try and stop these claim-jumpers and I am glad for that. I have invested everything I own into this property."

Putting the cup down on the floorboards at his feet, he stared into their faces. "But, tell me—why did you come to my home?"

Matthew smiled. "We would like to take up residence here—for a while, at least. It's a good spot to reconnoiter...not too close to Wallace but not too far, either. This way we can get the lay of the land and eyes on the people who are coming and going in these parts. I think that, eventually, we will find out just who is responsible for these claim-thefts."

He took a sip of his own coffee and continued, "In return, you and your family will go to my home in Granville, Washington. It's a big house...a ranch, actually, and if you didn't mind, you could help my son Samuel care for the place, as he will be left alone during this investigation. It's not far from here—maybe a three hour train ride."

Taking the last sip from his cup, Matthew added, "We are prepared to pay you for the inconvenience..." He saw the shock and speculation in Jacob's eyes as he turned the offer over in his mind.

Clearing his throat, Jacob said, "You and your son want to stay here, in my home, and trap the thieves when, and if, they come?"

Matthew nodded. "Yes, exactly...along with a few of our own men. This way, Chance and I can stay hidden in plain sight, if you get my meaning. Your home and land claim will be safe and your family will be out of danger, while we do our best to bring this thievery...and murder...to an end."

Jacob stared into the distance for a few moments, and then he turned to face Matthew again. "We will do it, but I stay with you here, along with my oldest son, Hans."

## 4

# THE THURSTON'S AND THE DEPUTIES

Three days later, Jacob and his family were met at the train station in Granville, Washington by Matthew's step-son Samuel, and his farm hand, Abner. Sam was a tall, rather long-faced man of thirty-three years who sported a lop-sided grin and Abner was one of the largest men the Lindsay's had ever seen.

He was wearing a threadbare wool suit and sported a deputy's star on his lapel. According to Mr. Wilcox, Abner had once been a lawman (before handing in his star and going to work for Samuel on the Imes' ranch) and had agreed to help Matthew and Chance in their investigation.

As Jacob understood it, Abner and another man by the name of Dick McNulty would accompany Matthew, Chance and himself back to Spokane tomorrow. Deputy McNulty would be in charge of guard-duty at the Thurston's home, while Abner traveled on with Matthew, Chance, Jacob and Hans to the Lindsay property in Idaho.

After shaking Sam's hand and observing his

respectable demeanor, Jacob couldn't help but feel a little guilty. He knew that Matthew and his son were in a hurry to get their investigation underway, and his insistence on seeing (with his own two eyes) where he would be installing his family in the meanwhile was costing the detective time.

Still, he mused, his wife and children were far too precious for him to take a stranger's word that they would be safe! For all he knew, the Imes' ranch was a den of iniquity! Considering the deferential nods, and respectful greetings of Granville's citizens toward Sam and Abner, however, Jacob was starting to think his suspicions were entirely unfounded.

Sam and Abner had arrived with a handsome carriage and a large freight wagon. Although the back of the wagon was loaded with sacks of grain, there was enough room left for the Lindsay's luggage and their two youngest children. Jacob, Marta and the older boys climbed into the luxurious carriage. "Sorry for the inconvenience, folks," Samuel said, apologetically. "We have an automobile, too, but Pa is using it right now. This buggy is pretty comfortable, though, and it's only about five miles to the ranch."

Jacob had never ridden in anything as fancy as this before, and he could see his wife and sons studying the brass-tacked leather seats and glass windows in awe. "He smiled, and said, "Don't worry, young man. This is very nice...thank you."

Samuel grinned in return and jumped up onto the driver's bench. They rode down a well-tended road for a few miles and then onto a long, tree-lined drive toward a beautiful house, surrounded by two separate barns and numerous out-buildings. There were fenced pastures stretching as far as the eye could see, filled with cattle, horses, sheep and goats.

It was a snowy landscape, but Jacob knew that when the thaws came this ranch would nestle like a diamond on folds of verdant, green velvet. Why, he wondered, would a man of such wealth and means become a private investigator?

Taking his wife's hand, he murmured, "You will never want to leave this house."

She grinned. "It is a beautiful place, husband, but unless you were here with me, I would never want to stay."

The carriage pulled up in front of the house and stopped. Jacob saw a handsome woman with three children standing on the front stoop. She was obviously an Indian and, for a moment, Jacob felt a thrill of alarm. Then, he saw a brilliant smile cross her face as Abner jumped off the freight wagon and ran up to her and the kids with a loud whoop of joy.

The door to the carriage opened and Sam said, "Welcome to the Imes' ranch!"

Jacob and his family climbed down out of the conveyance and walked towards the big white house. The dark-haired lady approached with her hands outstretched in welcome. "Hello, my name is Sarah Smalley...Abner's wife, and these are our children, Adam, Noble and little Iris."

The three children smiled politely, staring at Frannie and Peter with fascination.

Sarah said, "Would you children like to feed a carrot to Lincoln, and Sam's new stallion?"

"Yes, Mama!" Iris, Abner and Sarah's tiny four-year-old daughter shouted.

Sarah reached into her apron pocket and pulled out a few carrots, handing one to each of the children. "Now, stay on this side of the fence, do you hear me?"

"Yes, Mama!" they cried and ran toward a paddock close to the front yard.

Sam said, "I'll keep an eye on them, Sarah," and started after the children.

Turning to the older Lindsays, Sarah gestured. "Please...come inside. Mr. Wilcox has installed indoor plumbing, and I have lunch ready for you. You can rest up a little bit, before Matthew and Chance get home."

They filed into the house, and Jacob heard his wife gasp. The wooden floors were polished to a high gleam and the glass in the windows was hardly rippled at all. The furnishings were a beautiful mix of Regency cherry wood, oak, wicker and Native Indian art, all of which somehow seemed to merge together into a new, better style.

The living room was to their right, a small office to the left and the kitchen area in back of the house was painted bright yellow with large, mullioned windows peeking out at snowy mountains in the distance. A small, feminine-looking writing desk sat in front of one of those windows, and Marta couldn't help but wonder what had become of the Mrs. ...had she left her hearth and home behind, or had she passed on?

"The washroom is back here...but the gentlemen can

use the outhouse if necessary." Sarah walked toward the back of the house, taking Marta's hand in hers. "My husband will be going back to your home with the rest of the men, but you and I will have fun here while we wait, okay?"

Marta felt of thrill of happiness pierce the worry in her heart. She knew that her husband and Matthew's men were going to try and save their home and livelihood. It was a grand scheme but also a dangerous game—played against evil men—and she couldn't help but fear for Jacob and Han's lives.

Still, it had been so long since she'd sat in a fine parlor or cooked in a wonderful, modern kitchen. The thought of relaxing, for once, and trading gossip with another woman, was starting to make this trip seem like a holiday. Feeling suddenly guilty, Marta stared into the kitchen with blind eyes.

Sarah saw fear reflected in the woman's face and smiled. "Please, go into the washroom and freshen up. When you're done, perhaps you'll help me make coffee?"

Marta nodded, and whispered, "Thank you!" before scurrying into the fancy washroom.


Matthew, Chance and Deputy Dick McNulty showed up about an hour later. They all sat down to dinner, and Jacob listened as the young deputy spoke about the population explosion happening around the Granville area and some of the latest news about town.

"Are you sure Roy doesn't mind your leaving for a while?" Matthew asked.

Dick shook his head. "Nah, he really doesn't. I have

some leave coming to me anyway, and the Spokane police force is using this opportunity to train some of their newer deputies here under Roy's tutelage."

Matthew grinned. "I bet he's just loving that…"

Dick rolled his eyes and smiled in return.

Listening to their banter, Jacob realized that these men had known each other a long time and were the best of friends. He and his family were fairly new to the area, and he found himself longing to be amongst friends like these, safe in their camaraderie.

He also realized how extremely lucky he was to have met Mr. Wilcox and his network of friends. Men like these would go to the ends of the Earth to watch each other's backs. Knowing that their umbrella of protection extended to him and his family—at least for now—made Jacob feel a sense of hope that maybe…just maybe, he would find success in North Idaho.

Chance had been wolfing down Sarah's fine venison stew and flaky biscuits, but as he listened to his Pa and Dicky talk, he studied the young man who would be traveling back to Idaho with them. Wondering how old the boy was (and secretly worried that the kid was too frail to be much use in a fight) he wiped his mouth and said, "So, Hans, do you help your pa out a lot on the claim?"

Chance's words fell into the middle of a natural silence, and he saw the boy turn red with embarrassment. Wondering at the smirk on Hans's younger brother Timothy's face and what he had said wrong, Chance added, "I just meant, you seem kind of small, that's all…"

The boy studied his bowl of soup in silence, and Chance looked to his pa for help, only to be met with a slight frown. Not quite sure how he had stepped into a social gaffe, he sighed. "I only meant to say, good job helping your pa out like that."

Jacob cleared his throat. "Chance, Hans doesn't speak...at least, not very often. He is very shy, but he's a good, strong worker and can shoot as well as any man."

Chance was as red as a beet himself by now and he murmured, "I didn't know...um, I'm sure he's just great. Pa, may I be excused, please? I still have some packing to do..."

Matthew, feeling a little sorry for his son, said, "Sure you don't want some of Sarah's pie?"

The pie maker spoke up. "I'll save you a slice, Chance."

Chance stood up, said, "Thanks, Sarah!" and fled the room.

A few hours later, Chance came back downstairs. He looked around and, to his relief, saw that the women and children, including young Hans, had gone to their rooms for the night.

Helping himself to some lukewarm coffee and a slice of Sarah's apple pie, he wandered out onto the front porch where the men sat drinking brandy and smoking.

"Chance," his father's voice rose out of the dim, "Come and join us. We're making some final plans." And so, Chance joined the men and over the next few hours he learned what was expected of him in the upcoming investigation.

## 5

# THE TRINITY AND DEPUTY MCNULTY

Edward Branson glared at his henchman and spat into a brass spittoon on the table next to where he sat. "What do you mean, there was a witness? Another one?"

Frank Ludlow stared at the toes of his boots. Then he looked his boss in the eye and replied, "It took a long time to find the Brazil woman. Once we finally spotted her, in Spokane, she was with another gal. We knocked the Brazil woman off, but before we could finish the job some citizens showed up and called the coppers. We had to run for it."

"What do you mean finish the job—was she wounded?" Edward snarled.

"Yes - badly," Frank said.

"Do you know who this woman is?" Branson asked.

Frank wished he could float away… far away from the wrath he knew was about to descend upon his head. Still, there was no help for it. The boss was going to find out, eventually, anyway. Clearing his throat, Frank said, "Yes, sir. Her name is Annie Thurston—a reporter and, I think, part owner of the *Spokane Journal*."

The old man sat straight up in his chair. "What? Are you kidding me?" he roared.

Frank bowed his head. "Sir, we didn't know! Our orders were to put the Brazil woman down—which we did. No one said anything about making sure she was all alone! It wasn't until afterwards that I found out who her companion was."

Branson calmed, somewhat, staring into the fireplace with a scowl on his face. "Well, do you know what happened to Miss Thurston? Did she survive?"

Frank nodded. "Yes, I'm afraid so. A few days after we left her in the street, I sent two men out to the big hospital in town—Deaconess. They asked around and found out that Miss Thurston had been released and was recovering at home."

Branson looked up, studying Frank's face with cold, flat eyes. "Tell me you know where Miss Thurston's house is."

Ludlow grinned. "Yes sir. I sure do."

The old man smiled as well, and said, "Well, I suggest you finish the job you started. Get that witness and anyone else she might have talked to, while you're at it. If she really is a reporter, she might have notes about us... find them too! In fact..." Branson lapsed into a thoughtful silence.

Frank stared at the back of his boss' head for a moment. Then he said, "Sir?"

"What kind of neighborhood does she live in? Is it crowded with houses?"

Frank nodded, "Well, it's a fine and fancy sort of place, close to the downtown area. All the houses are big, like mansions, and each house is sitting on its own large lot. Why?"

Branson nodded, "Perfect! I want you to set the house on fire. That ought to get rid of the evidence and the witnesses! Then, when you're done with that, go to the newspaper office and set it on fire, as well!"

Dicky McNulty stared morosely at a hedgerow and plucked the petals of a daffodil off one by one. He was both frustrated and offended. His frustration stemmed from the fact that he was stuck in Spokane, cooling his heels, while Matthew, Chance and Abner were in the thick of things in North Idaho; solving crimes, chasing down bad guys and...and having FUN!

He felt offended by the two young deputies who were assigned to him by the Spokane police department. Curtis Downy and Hank Rogers treated him like he was a stupid kid (although he was older than both of them by at least eight years!). They were openly bored and in no hurry to take either instruction or advice—at least from the likes of HIM!

It was the same old problem...his diminutive size. He stood only five foot four, and his body, though strong and lean, was hardly bigger than a child's. He had grown used to his boss and his friends, who treated him as a man— and a formidable man to boot!

These two young deputies had no reason to respect him, and weren't afraid to show their scorn. Although he had warned them that the people in the house were at risk, he had caught Curtis snoozing in the shade—twice! He'd also searched high and low for Hank yesterday, only to find him strolling up the street with a bag of pastries in one hand and a warm cross bun in the other.

Although it seemed like a childish thing to do, he had wagged his finger under the kid's nose and threatened to tell the boy's boss, but Hank just grinned. "Forgot to pack a lunch, Dick. Why don't you relax a little?"

Today was no better. Curtis had shown up with a pack of cards and the two deputies sat on the front porch of the house, playing poker. Dicky knew that his boss, Roy Smithers, would have sent these sprouts packing, but what was HE supposed to do?

He grabbed another innocent daffodil and stood up to walk the fence line again. He had to admit...this was deadly dull duty, for sure. The three of them had been stationed here at the Thurston home for over two weeks now, and there'd been no sign of foul play. Each day came and went without mishap, the only thing to show for his diligence—the slowly melting snow and the appearance of spring bulbs—crocuses, daffodils and tightly folded tulips, which he was demolishing in his fit of pique.

Also, he acknowledged, the returning health of the nice lady inside the house. Rumor had it that his oldest, dearest friend, Matthew, was sweet on the journalist, and it was easy to see why. When Dicky had first met Annie Thurston, he took one look at her home and expected a high society snob to snap orders at him and make sure he only used the "back entrance."

Instead, he found her to be warm, gracious and down-to-earth...despite her awful injuries. Her father, Clyde

Thurston, was a little more brisk but Dicky thought it was worry and frustration at being stuck at home—under police protection—rather than the snobbishness of great wealth.

Still, Dicky thought as he waked toward the alleyway behind the home's large backyard, maybe it's time to either head on in to North Idaho to help Matthew in his investigation or head back home to Granville.

He stopped and stared at two horses that were tied up to the neighbor's back fence. He had walked the perimeter about an hour ago and the horses were not there then… where had they come from? he wondered. The only thing he had ever seen in this alleyway was the milk wagon and the coal truck, both of which came as regularly as clockwork every Tuesday and Thursday.

Feeling a sudden chill, Dick looked around and started jogging toward the house. He called out, "Hank—Curtis, better look sharp. We might have visitors…"

He was close enough to the back porch the men should have heard his shout, but there was no response. Picking up the pace and pulling his pistol from his holster, Dick ran along the side of the house. Clearing the front, he stopped as he saw the two deputies lying sprawled out and still on the front porch.

Gulping, he crouched down and studied the front yard, the heavy shrubbery by the porch, and the numerous trees lining the walkway. Seeing nothing, he climbed the steps and walked to the front door. He turned the knob and realized the door was still locked.

Shaking his head, he stared down at the two young boys gazing at nothing from cold, dead eyes. Whoever had done the deed favored knives, Dicky thought, seeing the red bibs of blood leaking from the slits in their throats, coating their gray blouses and covering the tin stars on their shirt pockets.

Feeling a tingle of fear, Dicky stared in the front window. There were lace curtains on two of the big windows and if he looked closely, he could see Mr. Thurston's profile as he bent over his desk.

Hoping against hope, he peered around the sill, and saw Clyde talking on the telephone. He seemed to be just fine, for now. Seizing the opportunity, Dick knocked sharply on the glass.

He saw the old man jump and glare at him from his desk. Gesturing, Dicky shouted, "Mr. Thurston! Come here...QUICKLY!"

Seeing the look on the deputy's face, Clyde said something to the person on the other end of the line and hung up, scurrying over to the window. Unlocking an interior latch, Thurston opened the window and asked, "Deputy! What on Earth is the matter?"

Dicky stepped aside so Thurston could see the carnage on his front porch. Gasping in shock, Clyde glanced upstairs.

"Go and get your daughter, right now! I'll be waiting for you...HURRY!"

Clyde bolted up the staircase, while Dicky crouched behind an outdoor chaise lounge with his gun cocked and ready. Then, he heard two things simultaneously: the tattoo of feet flying down the staircase and the sound of breaking glass from the back of the house.

Jumping up, Dicky saw Thurston stick his head out the window. "Is it safe?"

Dicky shook his head. "I don't know, but we have no choice—they're in the house! Come on—we have to make a run for it!"

Annie and Clyde stepped out the low sill onto the porch and Dicky hustled them both down the front walk toward their car, which was parked on the street.

All three of them felt is if there were targets on their backs but they made it to the vehicle unharmed. Climbing inside, Thurston yelled, "Someone has to turn the crank!"

Dicky looked back and saw smoke coming around the back of the house and the red flicker of flames through the front window. He also saw some of Thurston's neighbors looking their way, and running toward them from the safety of their own lawns.

Running to the front of the car, Dicky seized the crank and gave it a mighty heave. The automobile rumbled to life and he yelled at an approaching man, "Harvey, get back! It's not safe here! Go home and call the fire department!"

Suddenly, shots rang out. Harvey Campbell fell to his knees with a yelp of fear and scrambled back towards the safety of his own home. He ran inside and telephoned the police and the fire department, watching through his front windows as the Thurston's shiny new automobile became pocked with bullet holes and gunfire filled the air.

The deputy sheriff who turned the crank on Clyde's car had somehow made it inside the car, but then Harvey saw blood splatter the interior windshield. He gaped in dismay but the car managed to limp down the road, despite the damage to its exterior.

Just then, there was a huge roar and the Thurston's beautiful gray mansion spouted smoke from every window, as glass blew outward and flames blossomed, stretching into the sky overhead.

## 6

## MATTHEW AND CHANCE

Two weeks had passed since Chance and his companions arrived at Jacob's home in North Idaho. He and his father had made a few trips into the town of Wallace and, except for general knowledge that some of the claims in the area had been raided, no one had a clue as to who the mysterious claim-jumpers might be.

"Just look around you…" one of the barkeeps in town stated. "Hundreds a people a week come and go through these parts, and every one of 'em wants a piece of the action."

Indeed, the actual population of Wallace was far more than Chance had originally thought—almost four thousand souls. Scores of men, women and children roamed the streets, cavorted in the saloons and went about their business, even as the bartender dismissed his query with a snort of contempt.

Chance asked, "Do you think the claim jumpers might be affiliated with the mine?"

Studying the high, barbed wire fence that separated

the town from the actual mine, he saw timber-covered hills stretching around the town as far as the eye could see. Up close though, the ground had been scraped bare to the bedrock and a number of large, wooden buildings, flumes, walkways and trestles had taken the place of nature's cedar scented, swampy splendor.

Just past the architecture, numerous port holes were drilled into the side of a large hill. Tracks led into and out of the shafts and small wooden railcars, filled to the brim with ore, trundled back and forth.

There were numerous waterways winding through the property as well. Some were natural, Chance figured, but some had been made by man. A couple of railcars made their way out of a shaft to a particularly large mill pond and dumped their loads at the edge. Shouting, mud-covered men converged on the ore and heaved the bigger boulders, by hand, into the water.

Even as he watched, the water boiled and churned, turning its glassy surface a ghastly, greenish-gray color. As the pond's overflow, a sickly iridescent sludge, trickled down a steep embankment into a creek that ran through the middle of town, Chance stepped back, vowing not to drink from the town's water supply again.

"I dunno..." the bartender continued, "most of our troubles begin and end with the labor unions..." He held his hands up in a surrender gesture. "Mind you, I ain't for, nor against the union. It's just that, if you know anything about this town, you know that men have lost their lives pursuing that particular argument. I gotta keep my eyes peeled—all the time—as to who is frequenting my establishment. I don't got no time to worry 'bout what's happening upstream of here."

Chance saw his father making his way down a busy thoroughfare. Waving in his direction, he heard the old man add, "Word to the wise, though…"

Turning back to face the bartender, Chance said, "What's that?"

"Well, I ain't got the fanciest place in town, but I do know that when men want a stiff one and a quiet place to talk, Bernie's Brewery is where they go. I've seen some of the richest men in the world sittin' in the back of my place talking 'bout stuff that should never be spoke of outside a boardroom." He took his slouch hat off and scratched at his balding scalp.

"If'n you had some time, you and yer Pa could prob'ly learn quite a bit, just sittin' in my bar and listenin' to what the customers have to say…just so long as you don't tell none of 'em what I told you. Spies for the mine aren't looked on kindly in these parts, ya know."

Chance started to tell the bartender that he and his father were not spies, but Matthew stepped up and said hello. As his pa and the old man shot the breeze, Chance realized that was exactly what he and Matthew were doing—spying… not for the Hecla, Sunshine or Phoenix mines—or their union counterparts—but they were trying to sniff out just who was responsible for the criminal enterprises going on all over the Silver Valley area.

Matthew finished his conversation with the old barkeep and turned to Chance. "Well, I say we grab a bite to eat before heading back to Jacob's house. What do you think?"

"Sounds good, Pa. You heard nothing on your end, either?"

Matthew shook his head. "Nah…it's like trying to find a needle in a haystack. Frankly, I didn't realize this town was so big."

Nodding, Chance agreed. "Guess we better just head back to Jacob's and wait for the claim-jumpers to show up."

"I guess." Looking up the street, Matthew said, "Let's go there, they have good coffee." They stepped up on the boardwalk in front of a modest café. Suddenly, they heard a shout. It seemed so unlikely to hear his name called out in a town full of strangers, Matthew spun around in bewilderment, scanning the crowd on the street and touching the grip on his firearm.

Peering through the random strangers, Chance exclaimed, "its Dicky, Pa! What's he doing here, I wonder?"

Pondering the same thing and feeling a prickle of alarm, Matthew murmured, "I wonder too, Chance."

They stepped down off the boardwalk and walked toward Dicky's small form. Studying the deputy's face, Matthew knew that something was definitely amiss… whenever Dicky was scared or worried about something, his numerous freckles stood out on his pale, Scottish complexion like specks of paint.

They met up and Dicky said, "I'm so glad to find you two here. I was thinking I was going to have to rent a mount and travel up to Jacob's place!"

Matthew said, "What's going on, Dick? Why are you here?"

Dicky took off his hat and wiped sweat from his brow. "You were right Matthew...whoever is doing wrong up here has decided that your friend Annie, and any other witnesses to Mrs. Brazil's murder, are on their "Hit" list. Yesterday, they set fire to the Thurston's home!"

Matthew blanched. "... And? Is Annie okay?"

Dicky nodded. "Yes, sir. I managed to get both Annie and her father out in time. You should know, though, that Clyde was grazed in the arm when we were trying to make our getaway. He'll be alright—apparently Annie has some medical training—but he's stubborn, Matthew! I tried to take him to the hospital, but he refused to go. Instead, he had me drive both of them to the newspaper office downtown."

Matthew nodded. "I'm not surprised, Dick." Gazing into the far distance for a few moments he added, "Did you happen to clap eyes on the perpetrators?"

Dicky shook his head. "No, sir. But they're a bad bunch. They murdered those two young deputies assigned to me. Slit their throats while I was patrolling the backyard!" For the first time, the young deputy let his feelings of horror and anger show. His bright brown eyes turned red and he sniffed tears away. "Goddammit, Matthew! They weren't much, but they were just kids, really. They didn't deserve to go out like that!"

Chance touched his friend's shoulder and Matthew said, "I'm sorry that happened to you, Dick. Honestly, I didn't think the skunks we're up against would be that bold."

Dick spat on the ground. "Yeah, they are bold as brass —whoever they are. My worry is if they knew where

Annie and her father lived, they probably know that Clyde owns the newspaper. What's to stop them from firing that place next?"

Matthew had been thinking the exact same thing. Skin crawling with worry and trying to remember if the newspaper office was built with wood or brick, he heard the afternoon train whistle sing. Glancing at his pocket watch, he realized that the outgoing train to Spokane would be leaving in the next twenty minutes.

Making up his mind (and not knowing if it was the right course of action or not) he said, "Change of plans. Dicky, I want you to go back to Jacob's house with Chance, okay? I think that I'd better go to the newspaper office. I'll either try to talk Clyde and Annie out of there and into police custody...or, I'll stay there with them and make sure they're safe, in case the perpetrators make a go at them again."

Dicky nodded in agreement. "Yes, sir, will do. Listen, are you going to talk to the Spokane County sheriff?"

Matthew answered. "Yes, definitely. I want to see if they'll release more officers to help us out."

Dicky said, "Well, tell him, please, how sorry I am about his two new hires, okay?"

"I will, I promise," Matthew answered. "We'd better get a move on if I'm going to make that outbound."

The three men walked quickly down the muddy road to the train station. Dick told Matthew everything he knew—specifically, that the fire had engulfed two houses, and that Clyde had suffered a painful but non-life-threatening graze on the upper arm. In turn, Matthew filled Dick in on what they'd been doing the last couple of weeks…specifically, mining for silver and gold in the icy waters below Jacob's home, and waiting for some rough customers to make an appearance.

"Yeah," Chance concurred with a snort. "I'm learning WAY more about river mining than I ever wanted to know!"

"That's okay, Chance." Matthew admonished, gently. "Just be glad you don't need to take that route to make a living. I heard, just a few minutes ago, that maybe one in a thousand of the men who work in these mines are even remotely successful."

He sighed, stepping up onto the train platform. "Mainly, the workers in these mines end up owing most of their wages to the company-run stores. That's why there is so much civil unrest in these parts. The workers want to unionize, but the mine owners will do just about anything to make a profit, including fighting the union tooth and nail."

Turning to face Chance and Dicky, Matthew said, "I'll try to get this mess in Spokane sorted out as soon as possible, alright? Meanwhile, keep your heads down and be on the lookout. Jacob and his son Hans are game hands but…Jacob is a little too ornery, I reckon. I don't want him to get his head shot off if those punks do show up while I'm away."

The departing whistle sounded, and he stepped up inside the train. Hanging on to the door frame, Matthew called out, "Don't come back here until I return!"

Chance and Dicky nodded and watched as the train left the station, taking Matthew with it.

## 7

## MATTHEW

MATTHEW STEPPED OFF THE TRAIN IN SPOKANE AND STOOD staring at a crowd of people gathered in the street. A woman was standing on a wooden box shouting about worker's rights and the crowd who listened, mainly men, roared their approval, shouting, "Wobblies want to work!"

Matthew saw that the city police were in attendance. They seemed content, for the moment, to stand guard passively...mainly keeping the boisterous crowd away from the trains and the businesses situated across the street. There was also, he noticed, a fire engine parked on the corner and he heard a firefighter sporadically ringing the alarm bell.

It was there for two reasons, Matthew knew. One, rioters were well known for starting fires, literally—if they felt they were not being taken seriously enough and two, sometimes the firefighters turned their hoses on an out-of-control crowd. It seemed that cold, stinging water cooled tempers better than billy clubs did, and at far less cost than broken noggins.

Matthew had heard the allegations...apparently, crooked agents who worked for employment agencies in Spokane had hired whole work crews (for a fee) for some of the logging companies and mining outfits in the region, only to fire them at will, for no reason other than to collect fees—twice—for whole new work crews needed by the same employers.

Shaking his head, he stepped off the platform, skirted the growing crowd and hailed an approaching cab. A small buggy pulled up and the young driver grinned. "Get in quick before the coppers shut the place down!"

Matthew climbed in back and said, "Take me to the sheriff's department, please."

The driver nodded, snapping the reins over his elderly horse's rump. They took off with a lurch and headed down the muddy street. Matthew asked, "How long as this been going on?"

The driver shrugged. "I've seen it happen a couple of times the last few weeks, but this is the first time Lizzy Flynn has showed up. She really brings in the crowds but if she's not careful, the cops will shut the rallies down for "soapboxing.""

Matthew knew about the civil unrest...it was happening all across the area. Not only were the employment agencies double dipping, mine owners throughout the Coeur d'Alene area were well-known for fleecing their employees. For years now, there had been constant and often deadly confrontations between union party members and industry owners.

In fact, unfair labor practices were so prevalent in the Northwest, laws (like the afore-mentioned "Anti Soap-

Boxing" Act) were being passed on an almost daily basis by the state legislature and the National Guard had been called in more than once.

The sheriff's department wasn't far from the train station and, within a few minutes, the cabbie pulled to a stop in front of the busy Police House. Handing the driver three bits, Matthew said, "Here you go, thank you...and son—stay out of trouble, okay?"

He had seen the fervor in the young man's eyes as he spoke about the labor rally and its members. He knew that scores of young men had been seriously wounded, even killed during those protests. He also realized however, that sometimes it took brave young men (and women) to rectify injustice in all its many forms.

Matthew sighed as the kid winked, thanked Matthew for the generous tip and took a U-turn in the street, heading straight back to the train station and the crowds surrounding it.

Turning his back, he walked into the sheriff's department and asked to speak to the man himself. He waited in the lobby for a few minutes and then, when summoned, walked back to the sheriff's office. Frank Lobey was hollering at someone behind closed doors as Matthew waited on an uncomfortable wooden chair. Then, the door to his office flew open and three disgruntled-looking deputies scurried out.

Frank glared at Matthew for a second and then he sighed, gesturing him inside his personal lair. As Matthew took a seat across from Frank's desk, the sheriff growled, "Matthew, Goddammit! What the hell happened?"

Matthew knew that the man was referring to the death

of his two young deputies, who had been loaned to Wilcox and Son Detective Agency as a courtesy, and were now lying dead in the city morgue.

Matthew said, "I am sorry, Frank. As I said before, though, I truly believe that I...we are up against some bad hombres here...so bad, they are not a bit afraid of spilling a cop's blood or firing half a city block to shut someone up!"

The sheriff nodded. "As you can probably tell, I have had my hands full lately. There are labor riots almost every day, and those folks ain't afraid to spill blood neither. Plus, someone bombed a railcar just last week, killing three men in the caboose. And now, this!" His voice had risen to a hoarse shout and Matthew shifted in his chair.

His temper was starting to heat up as well. *It's not like I lied!* he thought, resentfully. I TOLD him that we are up against some savage killers. Now, that the truth of my words have come home to roost, Frank wants to blame me?"

Frank studied Matthew's green eyes...orbs that had grown colder and colder over the last few minutes, and realized that he was hounding the wrong man. Matthew had warned him, weeks earlier, they were dealing with powerful criminals, and had objected to the fact that Frank wanted to send a couple of green chicks to serve guard duty with Dick McNulty, instead of two veteran police officers.

Instead, because of the civil unrest in town, he had taken the easy route. And now he, Frank Lobey, had to pay the piper. He had already informed those young deputies' grieving parents, and had been forced to raid the sheriff department's purse to pay death restitution.

Holding his palms in the air, Frank muttered, "I am the one who is sorry, Matthew. I was the one who made a bad judgment call concerning guard duty at the Thurston house...and it's my fault those two sprouts are dead."

Matthew studied Frank's face. Lobey was an old man now...probably too old to be acting sheriff for such a large city, and the toll of his job was starting to show in the heavy lines etched in his face and his bowed shoulders.

Matthew sighed. "It's not your fault, Frank. You didn't kill those boys, but...someone did. The same people who shut an innocent woman up for good, and who are now hunting my friend Annie Thurston and her father Clyde!"

Frank nodded in agreement. "So, why did you come in today, Matthew?"

Matthew cleared his throat. "I don't know if you have been informed of this latest news, Frank, but Clyde Thurston insisted on holing up at the newspaper office after the attack on his house. Now, he, Annie and the rest of the staff are at the *Spokane Journal* and I have reason to believe that's the perpetrator's next target."

Frank couldn't help but roll his eyes - not at Matthew's concerns, but at the thought that truly, "When it rains, it pours!" Staring at Matthew's face he grumbled, "What do you need?"

Matthew knew he was asking too much, but he ploughed ahead anyway. "Three good... mature police officers to help me watch the newspaper office" Matthew replied.

"Three!" the sheriff blurted.

Matthew nodded. "Yes sir. I'm sorry, but that's a minimum! That's only one man to guard each street on that particular block!"

He paused for a moment, adding, "Did you know that the *Spokane Journal* resides in the middle of one of the last standing wooden store-front blocks in the downtown area? Honestly, if the crooks we (Matthew put particular emphasis on the word "we") are fighting actually manage to fire that block, at least seven businesses will go up in smoke, including a Chinese laundry, a restaurant, a bakery and one of the best and oldest confectioners in the city!"

Lobey grimaced. He had attended his fill of city council meetings and knew that last vestige of wooden buildings in the downtown area had long been slated for improvement. It really was a threat to the city center as a whole and if it went up in flames, so would his career, if the towns-fathers found out that he refused to help Matthew Wilcox!

Making up his mind, Sheriff Lobey growled. "Okay, okay! I'll get you some help." Standing up, he walked to his office door, stuck his head out and barked, "Myrtle! Go and fetch Patrick Spears for me…and bring me a fresh cup of coffee!"

An hour later, Matthew and three veteran police officers, who also happened to be good shots, headed ten blocks away to the *Spokane Journal* newspaper office.

8

CHANCE

Chance followed Hans up a steep incline and turned left on a deer path that wound through tall cedars, spongy moss-covered boulders and damp evergreen needles. It looked like a church, with leafy arched ceilings overhead and the sun streaming through green and golden stained glass windows.

The boy was moving swiftly down the path, intent, Chance presumed, on looking for a better place to dig for silver and gold ore than the place his father had chosen. Although the kid didn't talk much, Chance had heard him tell Jacob more than once over the last couple of weeks that "there's not enough black sand" in their current location to house a good show of minerals.

He wasn't sure why he had decided to follow Hans today. Boredom probably...a trait his father had chided him for more times than he could count. Still, Matthew had been gone for three days now, and for the time being, Jacob's mining operation was suspended.

Chance had overheard the youngster ask his pa if he

could go down to the river a little earlier while Jacob, Dicky, Abner and another deputy out of Spokane by the name of Bill Nash, sat around back of the house, cleaning their guns and keeping a weather eye on the road for trespassers.

Jacob knew Han's was looking for a better place to mine and frowned in annoyance at his offspring's temerity, but he couldn't think of a good reason to say no. Nodding curtly, he said, "Don't go too far, and if you hear gunfire, go and hide in the place we set up, okay?"

Hans mumbled, "Yessir," and darted around the house to the path that led down to the water below. On a whim, Chance stood up a few minutes later and followed him. At one point, although the kid was as fleet as a deer and seemed to float down the trail ahead of him like a will-o-the-wisp, Chance saw him stop and pick up a small bundle from behind a stand of gooseberry bushes.

Since he had come to Jacob's high mountain home, Chance had become fascinated by his young companion. There seemed to be something...off about the kid. Not in a bad way, really, but Chance could tell that Hans was hiding something.

For one thing, he was just too...young-looking. After some persistent questioning, Jacob allowed that Hans was just turned fourteen, which explained the boy's fine features and hairless chin. It didn't explain the aloof maturity in the kid's eyes though, or the superior training such a young sprout had demonstrated in target shooting.

Chance considered himself a fine shot—indeed, he had received quite a few medals in military school for his prowess with firearms. But just last night, as he and his comrades took turns at target practice, Hans had stood in front of the man-shaped targets and put every one of the older men in the group, including the legendary Dick McNulty, to shame.

After staring in shock at the tattered paper target, Chance had walked over to the boy and offered to shake hands. Looking up at him, briefly, with wide blue eyes and silky black lashes, the kid hesitated for a moment and then stuck his hand out to shake.

Chance almost dropped the kid's hand like a hot potato—it was so frail and...and soft. Staring, he studied Hans pale, creamy complexion and his beautiful, delicate lips. The boy noticed Chance's confusion and tore his hand away in embarrassment. Then he ducked his head and walked away. Chance stared after him in bewilderment.

"Like I said," Joseph spoke softly, "My son is real shy around folks he don't know. Pay him no mind, okay?"

Chance nodded, but every instinct in his body was on high-alert. Which was why he was picking his way through this living, green cathedral now. He paused, watching, as Hans cut to the left and headed back down a steep incline to another point on the river. There wasn't a lot of underbrush on this side of the water and no way to hide himself, so Chance sat down in the weeds at the top of the incline to watch the kid's activities from his present perch.

Hidden by a large clump of wild roses, he watched in fascination as the boy walked across a fallen log to the other side of the river. The water was shallow here, most of it rushing through and under a pile of gigantic boulders, leaving its higher tides in shallow pools that glittered in the open sunlight.

Chance watched as Hans reached the other side. Bending over, he studied the sand beneath his feet, took a small, sharp hammer from his trouser pocket and started tapping away at the sheer rock face of a cliff rising from the ground.

Looking away for a moment, Chance felt the sunshine warming the top of his head and heard the drowsy hum of bees making their way through the new growth of tightly wound rosebuds he crouched in. Sunlight banged off the still pools of water below and, for a second, Chance allowed his eyes to drink in the first signs of spring.

Gazing at the boy again, who stood still now, inspecting a piece of quartz in his hand, Chance saw a bright flash of silver glitter off the face of it. Then Hans put the shiny shard in his front pocket with a grin.

Then, to his astonishment, he saw the kid step sideways, and vanish into the rock wall. Gaping, he stood up and studied the cliff but the higher the sun rose from the tree line, the darker the rock face became. Shaking his head, Chance crept out onto the deer path and made his way to where he thought Hans had headed downhill toward the felled log.

His scramble down the steep hill was far less graceful than the boys had been, but soon enough he stood by the same uprooted tree Hans had skipped across. When he stepped up onto the log, he almost fell over the other side. Though he'd seen the kid prance across the log like a ballerina, he hadn't realized, until now, that it was soaking wet and slick with moss.

He took a deep breath, climbed up and minced his way across the shallow water. Expecting at any moment to pitch headfirst into the river, Chance managed to reach the other side with nothing more than a few strained muscles. Finally, he jumped onto some moist river rocks and made his way to the cliff face.

He walked up close to the cliff and finally found the place he thought Hans had squirmed into. Pressing his ear close to a cut in the rock walls he heard the sound of fast, furious water on the other side. Studying the narrow crevasse between two slabs of rock, he took off his vest and gun and placed them on the ground by his feet.

Then, he commenced to squeezing his body through the stony outcropping to the other side. He got a couple of scraped knuckles in the attempt and for one horrifying moment thought that his hips were truly stuck, forever, between two large boulders. He finally found himself on a narrow ledge of flattened boulders, staring down at a waterfall and the pool below it.

Seeing the creature that bathed in the sparkling waters with soap and a washcloth, Chance at last understood what had been bothering him about the kid known as Hans...for that was no boy that washed in the blue, sparkling pool, but one of the most beautiful women he had ever clapped eyes on.

Her hair was very long...she must have been rolling it tightly to the top of her head and hiding it under her ever-present hat. Chance gulped as he saw it now in the light of the sun...it was as black and shiny as a raven's wing. Although her breasts were small they were perfectly formed and her slender body curved enticingly in all the right places. Her skin was as white as alabaster and seemed to glow in the sunlight like the creamiest of pearls. Feeling himself growing hard with desire, Chance ducked as Hans looked up.

He'd been so mesmerized by the beautiful vision standing thigh-deep in the water below, he didn't hear the grizzly bear that approached from up top and behind him. He saw, rather than heard, Hans shout at him and point, but his own guilt at being caught spying on her clouded his judgment.

Chance turned hastily around to make his way back out of the cleft in the cliff wall and came face to face with the bear. He shouted in shock and the bear stood up on its hind feet. Even though the waterfall was so loud it was nearly deafening, Chance heard the bear roar, felt its hot, rank breath wash over him and saw the animal's saliva streaming from fangs as long as daggers.

Chance took a step backward, cursing himself for leaving his pistol on the other side of the stone wall. The beast advanced a step and took a swipe at him, missing his face by inches. It roared again and dipped its giant head, lunging at him. Then it fell back down on four paws as a piece of its left shoulder blew away in a cloud of bloody red mist.

Chance saw the enraged beast cringe and bite at the bloody wound, but then it focused on him again and stumbled in his direction. Glancing down at the pool below, he figured he was about thirty-five feet up. Heart pounding hard in his chest, Chance backed away until there was no more ledge to stand on and then, knowing there was no place to go but down, he took a deep breath and jumped.

Praying to God above that there was enough water in the pond to cushion his fall, Chance yelled at the top of his lungs as he fell. Seeing the look of shock on Hans face and smoke still drifting from the pistol in her hand, he hit the water with a mighty splash.

## 9

## HANNAH

CHANCE CAME RIGHT BACK UP AGAIN WITH A GARGLED YELP of pain. Hannah Lindsay saw the beautiful young man with his slanted green eyes and strawberry blonde hair—the same young man whose attentions she had been trying to elude for the last three weeks—back up three steps and then glance at the water below with mortal fear on his face before he jumped.

He had no choice, really. Although she was a good shot, the bear was simply too close to Chance for her pistol to stop its advance. Still, the pool was shallow, too shallow for a full-grown man to plumb its depths.

Glancing up at the angry bear, she saw it pace back and forth on the stone ledge, roaring its displeasure. For one terrifying moment, she thought the wounded animal was going to leap into the water after its quarry, but it finally turned around and disappeared back from whence it came.

Chance, meanwhile, was thrashing around and hollering with pain. She saw him go under for a moment and knew that, despite her state of undress, she had no choice but to swim over to him and haul him to safety—unless she wanted to watch him drown.

Gritting her teeth, Hannah tossed her pistol onto the shore, dove into the pool and swam about twenty-five feet in his direction. Nearing her target, she yelled, "Chance! Grab my hand!"

Chance was facing away from her when she shouted his name, but managed to turn around and reach out. She grabbed his fingers and started swimming backwards toward the shoreline. She only needed to tow him about twelve feet before both of them could touch the bottom with their feet, so she stopped after a few moments and let him go.

The young man's eyes grew wide with fear and Hannah's heart pinched a little with sympathy. He was afraid of deep water, and worried that she was fixing to let him drown. "Don't worry, you can touch the bottom here!" she yelled over the roar of the waterfall behind them.

He seemed to calm down a bit and she saw him stare through the waves at the ground beneath his feet. Then he screamed in pain. "Dammit! I think my ankle's busted!"

Hannah's heart sank. No wonder the boy's face was so white and he seemed so...shaky. Making up her mind, she shouted back, "Can you stand on your other foot and keep yourself afloat for a minute or two?"

He tried it out and nodded. "Yeah, I think so," he answered.

"Okay, I'll be right back," she said and turned around to slog her way to shore. She heaved up out of the water and quickly put her clothes on. Glancing behind her, she noticed Chance watching with wide eyes. She gave him her best dirty look, and saw him hop around on his good foot so he faced the other way.

Finishing quickly, she ran to where she had stockpiled a few supplies. She was absolutely sure, by now, that she had found a wonderfully profitable place to her family to dig for ore. The sand around this pool was as black as night and almost every rock she touched was veined with silver and gold. It had taken her a while, though, to search out this hidden cache and she had brought a number of supplies to help in her search...including a long length of rope.

Grabbing it, she ran back to the shoreline and hollered, "Chance! Grab on to this rope!"

He turned around and, looking dubious, nodded in agreement. Hannah tossed the rope and it hit his chest, dead center, with its coils. He wrapped it around his belly and tied it off so she could pull him to shore.

He gave her a thumb's up and felt the rope tighten. Then, he was hauled into the shallow depths. He was being as careful as possible not to put weight on his left foot, but at the last minute, he misjudged and felt a surge of nausea coil in his guts as his boot scraped along the bottom.

He tried to act manly, but couldn't help the groan of agony that issued from his lips. Then, he felt Hannah seize him under his armpits and pull him onto the beach. She didn't look at his face, but knelt at his feet studying his leg. After tugging his sodden pant leg up to his knee, she sat back on her heels with a sigh.

"Well," she declared. "This is a pickle."

"Probably just sprained," he muttered.

She stared at his boot—specifically at the leg above his boot which was already huge and turning an alarming shade of purple. Not sure what else she could do, and afraid of causing further damage, she carefully eased the boot off his foot. Chance cried out with pain and Hannah turned to face him.

"I'm pretty sure that your ankle is either badly sprained or broken, Chance." She studied the look of alarm on his face and added, "Listen, there is a cave back behind that waterfall. There are a few supplies in there, like blankets, a little bit of food and some water. I want to get you inside, build a fire in the fire pit, and then go fetch the men to help get you up that path to the other side, okay?"

The pain radiating from the bottom of his leg was nauseating and for a moment, Chance saw stars and heard a high-pitched buzzing in his ears. He murmured, "Okay...whatever you want, Hans. Say," he asked, "what's your real name and when did you turn into a girl?" Then, he fell in a swoon onto the black sand.

"Shoot!" Hannah exclaimed with a sigh. Looking from Chance to the cave entrance, she shook her head. Chance was a big man and she didn't relish having to drag him fifty feet to safety, but it looked like she had no choice. She reached down and started to pull his body toward the hidey-hole she had found a few months earlier. She hauled him about ten feet and had to stop. Staring down at his chalk-white face, she said, "You, sir, weigh a ton!"

She was teasing, but suddenly she felt bad about it.

Blue circles were starting to show under his beautiful green eyes and even as she gazed down at him, she saw his whole body shudder. He's going into shock! She thought, in alarm.

Galvanized, she reached down again and pulled him toward the cave. Although her lower back groaned and her arms trembled, Hannah kept going. She knew that shock could be a killer, if the patient wasn't tended to properly. Knowing there was sugar, water and blankets in the little cavern, she heaved with all her might.

Finally, she reached the mouth of the cave and pulled Chance inside. Letting his arms drop, she grabbed two moldy blankets from the back wall and tucked them around his shivering body. Then, she flew over to a small tin canister and found the little bit of sugar stashed inside.

She poured the sugar into a canteen of tepid water and knelt by Chance's side. Slapping his cheek lightly, she murmured, "Chance...wake up! I need you to drink this. Come on, open your eyes!"

Staring at his face, Hannah saw Chance awaken, and struggle to open his eyelids. Even though the young man was in serious trouble, she couldn't help but admire his pretty features. His reddish eyelashes were as long as a girl's, his lips were soft and wide and his cheekbones were high and finely chiseled.

The fiction she and her family had concocted—that she was a boy rather than a twenty-year-old daughter, had kept her safe, so far, from undue and unwelcome attention in this wild new land. Still, this young man had awoken in her breast a longing that she never even knew was there, and a passion that had caused her more than one sleepless night.

Finally, his eyes opened and he stared up at her. "I didn't mean to spy on you, Hans," he murmured.

She shrugged. "My real name is Hannah and...it was bound to happen, sooner or later. My pa was just trying to keep me safe—at least until my family was more secure here in Idaho." Holding the canteen up so he could see, she added, "I need you to drink this down, okay? It's sugar water and should help with the shock."

Chance frowned, "I'm not in shock!" he argued.

Hannah rolled her eyes and snapped, "Drink!"

Chance sighed and then lifted his head to drink from the canteen she held to his lips. Gagging a little as the sweetness hit the back of his throat, he took a few long pulls and then laid his head back down on the ground. "Sheesh, it really smarts!" he growled.

"Yeah, I'm sure it does," she agreed. She was watching him closely, and was pleased to see some color leaking back into his pale cheeks. "Listen, I'm going to build a fire and then go and get help, okay?"

His eyes opened and for a second, he looked as frightened as a small boy. Then, he nodded. "Yeah, I don't think I can make it on my own. If nothing else, Abner can carry me outta here."

"That's what I was thinking, too," she said. Pulling the blankets up around his chest and shoulders and making sure there was enough water left in the canteen to slake his thirst, she gazed down at his wan face for a moment.

He stared back at her and gave a small grin. "Run

quick, Hannah, okay? I know you can do it..." Then he closed his eyes with a groan of pain.

Hannah grabbed her gun and her jacket, and stepped out onto the sandy beach again. The fire pit was piled high with dry driftwood and she poured a little bit of kerosene on it before lighting a match. Watching as the wood caught fire, she nodded in satisfaction. That ought to keep him warm until we get back, she thought.

It wasn't too far to the house—maybe a couple of miles was all, but she was worried. Chance didn't look too good. Although she knew that she could bring help, she hated to leave him alone for the hour or so it might take to do so.

Knowing that worrying about the problem wouldn't solve anything, she took off up the deer path that wound down from the cliff above. She skirted around the waterfall and was just starting up the steep incline when the same, bloody-shouldered grizzly bear that had terrorized Chance earlier came around a pile of boulders...this time with two cubs in its wake.

Hannah's blood ran cold. No wonder it had attacked! Grizzlies were antagonistic by nature, but get a couple of young ones in the mix and any human in its path was considered a threat. But, why in hell-fire was it bringing its two cubs back to the scene of the crime?

Shuddering, and knowing there was no help for it, she back-tracked down the narrow path. The only reason she could fathom that the she-bear had decided to return was because her cubs were hungry, and the bear figured the two young humans might make a pretty good meal.

This time, instead of going in front of the waterfall, she ducked under the swiftly falling torrent of water. She hoped that the bear might lose her scent—at least for a few precious seconds. Emerging, soaking wet, about five feet away from the cave's entrance, Hannah ducked inside and shouted, "The bear is back! Chance, you need to help me out now…"

Chance woke up with a start, took one look at the girl's panicked face and, despite the pain in his foot, helped her pile more driftwood onto the fire.

## 10

## MATTHEW

SHOTS RANG OUT IN THE NIGHT. MATTHEW, LYING sleepless in an upstairs storage room of the newspaper office, slid quickly off his cot and moved in a crouch toward the window. He'd been wondering whether his concern for the Thurston's welfare was warranted, as nothing significant had happened in the three days since he had arrived.

Besides that, he couldn't get his mind off of his son. Matthew knew Chance could take care of himself but, for some reason, his heart was telling him that something was amiss. He knew it was just a matter of time before the mysterious claim-jumpers made an appearance. Had it happened already? Had Chance been injured or killed in the altercation? Or, was his restlessness just a loving father's unfounded worry?

Thinking back on the last few days, Matthew remembered how horrified he'd been at Thurston's determination to keep the newspaper in operation. When he first stepped into the *Spokane Journal*'s office, it had seemed like just another workday. The giant, noisy presses were wheezing and clanking and a number of busy men and women scurried around the large room and sat at desks lining the room's interior walls.

There were two telephones, both in use. A young man who sat close to the front door jumped up from his chair with a smile. "Hello! Can I help you?" he shouted.

Matthew asked, "Are the Thurston's here?"

The kid pointed to a staircase and said, "Yes, they're upstairs, but...due to unforeseen circumstances, I must announce your presence first and make sure you are on their list of callers."

Matthew nodded. "That's good. Will you tell them that Matthew Wilcox is here?"

The youngster smiled and said, "I'll be right back...you can sit there while you wait, okay?"

Matthew saw a long, wooden bench by the front door and took a seat as the teenager ran upstairs. He was fuming...although he had cautioned Clyde that his newspaper might be the next target it was still running full-steam ahead! Knowing, though, that three policemen and a fire engine would be arriving shortly made Matthew breathe a little easier.

A few minutes passed before the young man returned and gestured for Matthew to follow him upstairs. When Matthew arrived at Clyde's door, he stepped inside and barked, "I thought I told you two to make yourselves scarce!"

Annie looked somewhat guilty, but Clyde said, "Now listen here, young man! I have a business to run and I'm not about to let a bunch of hooligans run me away from my livelihood!"

"Sir," Matthew sighed with frustration. "With all due respect, look at yourself...look at your daughter! These are serious men who have no qualms about killing anyone who might implicate them in their crimes! Is your newspaper so important to you that you are willing to risk innocent lives—like your daughter's and all of those people downstairs—to hold on to your pride?"

Clyde looked, for a moment, as though he would argue but then his shoulders drooped. Sitting in a chair, he winced a little as his wounded arm bumped up against the upholstery. He stared at Annie for a moment, noting her fading bruises and knowing, for a fact, that her ribs still ached horribly. Looking up at Matthew, he murmured, "I am sorry, but I thought to fight fire with my own brand of fire."

The older man reached out to a side table and rang a little brass bell. Instantly, Thurston's secretary stood in the doorway. "Yes, sir...what can I do for you?" she asked.

Clyde said, "Mrs. Williams, could you round us up a pot of coffee and maybe some pastries, if there are any left?" Clyde hesitated for a second and added, "Also, have Mr. Fulbright come up to see me as soon as possible."

"Of course, sir...right away," she replied and disappeared.

Turning to face Matthew again, Clyde said, "I have learned over the years that nothing rouses vermin better than light. Rats, maggots...even outlaws scurry away from bright lights that shine upon their activities. I thought that if my paper were to make what has happened to Chloe,

Annie and now, to me...public knowledge, the criminals might be forced to flee!"

Looking down at the floor, his chubby cheeks turned red with hurt and humiliation. "That is just the old journalist in me, though, I suppose. I honestly didn't stop to think about all the people who might get hurt while I revealed my story." Turning to face his daughter, he murmured, "Please forgive me, my dear."

Annie smiled and started to say something, but then an older man knocked at the door. "Clyde...you wanted to see me?"

Clyde struggled to his feet, and said, "Yes, Marty. Listen, I want all of you to go home now. It's not safe here, and my daughter and I have decided to put a hold on this story until some of the more...immediate issues have been resolved."

Fulbright frowned and replied, "But Clyde! We are only an hour—two hours, at most, from publication! Please, don't pull the plug now!"

Thurston looked torn and Annie stared at Matthew a moment before saying, "My father and I know the risks, but this isn't the first time we've published under duress! We have been threatened by the Labor party, and by political thugs. High society patrons have tried, in the past, to buy us off and more than one rich farmer has threatened to shut us down. In this case, a friend of mine was murdered—right in front of me!"

Her voice had risen to a shout and she took a deep, calming breath. In a slightly calmer tone, she added, "Not to mention the fact they tried to finish the job by burning my father's home—with us inside—to the ground."

She stood up and walked slowly to where Matthew stood. Taking his hand, she said, "I agree, it's probably time to send our employees home. But if my father and I pitch in to help, we could print this story in less than an hour. The minute the job is done, each and every employee can head home to safety."

"I'm not going anywhere!" Marty exclaimed. "You will need help in distribution—you know you will. I'm staying!"

Matthew stared at the folks he had sworn to protect, and knew that they were willing to risk everything in order for their story to be heard. Knowing a lost cause when he saw one, he said, "Okay, okay. I'll go and tell the police that the employees will be leaving within two hours' time." Thinking for a moment, he asked, "How are the papers delivered?"

"We have three young men who come by at four o'clock each day to deliver fresh ink...why?" Clyde asked.

Matthew said, "They should be safe enough but, just in case, I will try and find another couple of kids to help...at least for today. I will pay their wages."

"That is not necessary, Matthew." Reaching into his pocket, Clyde produced four silver dollars. "I'll be happy to pay for the extra help!" Turning to his right-hand man, he smiled and said, "Well, we should get started!"

As promised, the paper, with its inflammatory content, was circulating all over town by five o'clock that afternoon. Even people who did not subscribe were given free copies and by dinner time, thousands of Spokane's citizens were openly discussing the newspaper owner's troubles.

The staff, excluding the loyal but stubborn Marty Fulbright, had gone home and, for the rest of the night, Matthew patrolled the perimeter with the police force stationed outside. Nothing happened that night though, and finally, when dawn broke, the sleepy policemen were relieved of duty. As soon as he instructed the two day-time replacements what to watch for...and where, Matthew went inside the building to catch some much-needed rest.

Two days passed in this manner...no nefarious activity and no apparent threat. Matthew knew that the sheriff was losing patience with the whole affair and would soon be asking for his policemen back...which was why he was wide-awake now. He knew, in his gut, that the crooks would try to finish what they started, right here—and soon. He needed the extra police presence to keep Annie and her father safe!

Hearing another volley of shots outside in the alley below, Matthew peeked over the window sill. He had wanted to close that particular alleyway down but it was not possible. The bakery-confectioner's shop received daily deliveries of raw sugar, powdered sugar and flour every morning before dawn, and the laundry next door to the newspaper office was open all night. They needed to pull their laundry carts through the alley on their way to the area hospitals and doctor's offices.

The policemen on duty were stationed on the busy thoroughfares, and Matthew knew that they were trying to keep an eye on the alley, too. But, it was a natural blind spot—one, in retrospect, he should have been watching, rather than trying to catch some sleep.

Staring down into the darkness, Matthew thought he saw a figure lying prone on the cobbles. *Is it one of the policemen or one of the crooks?* he wondered, backing away from the window. He moved to the side of the cot, pulled his boots on and grabbed his pistols from the top of a ream of newsprint paper.

He was just stepping out into the hall when he saw Annie standing in the shadows with a lantern in one hand. "Matthew, did you hear the gunshots?"

"Yes. Listen, I need you to go find Marty. Then, you two go to your father's room and stay hidden out of sight. Also, if I say run, you need to be ready, okay?"

Annie whispered, "Yes, all right." Then she stepped toward him, grabbed his upper arms and pressed her lips to his. As he wrapped her in his arms, returning her kiss, he could smell the sweetness of her hair and the soft warmth of her body. He felt a sudden, almost unbearable need for this beautiful woman, but he also felt tremors of fear running like electricity through her skin. She was scared to death and with her injuries, terribly vulnerable.

Matthew bit back his surge of desire and put her at arm's length. He knew that Annie had felt the brunt of her enemy's hatred, administered with all the cold calculation of a butcher at a meat shop. Although he understood that she was a brave woman, she was petrified right now, and he needed to keep her safe. He gave her shoulders a slight shake and said, "Go!"

Annie turned and fled down the hallway to another room. Matthew watched her for a moment, then he turned around and headed downstairs. Reaching the front door, he heard the clang of the fire engine bell and a number of high-pitched screams echoing down the street.

Opening the door a crack, Matthew peered outside, his body pressed flat against the jamb. He saw smoke rolling up the street and smelled ashes rising on the chill, early morning air. He also spied a number of darkened silhouettes bending over a still form on the ground by the foot of the alley. "Fire! The building is on fire!" someone shouted.

Growling with wrath, Matthew stepped outside to see who the fallen man was, where the fire was...and if there was a still a crook in the vicinity he could finally take his frustrations out on.

## 11

## MATTHEW AND THE TRINITY

MATTHEW RAN DOWN THE ALLEYWAY AND STOPPED IN front of the fallen man and those who attended him. Both of the young deputies seemed unharmed, but the man on the ground was groaning and clutching at his belly. Matthew could see blood streaming steadily through his fingers.

Gut-shot, he thought, and spoke to one of the young lawmen. "I take it one of you stopped this fella from firing the building?"

"Yes, sir, I did," a tough-looking deputy said. "He was the one who set that fire, down on the corner. I told him to drop the torch but he pulled iron on me. I had no choice!"

Although the kid looked like he could take care of himself in a pinch, his voice was unnaturally high with nerves and he kept wiping shaky hands on his dungarees. He stared at Matthew with wide eyes, expecting apparently to be dressed down for his troubles.

Matthew smiled though, and said, "Good job, deputy. This man, and the men he works for, wouldn't have hesitated to shoot you dead." He paused for a moment, wondering whether it was worth the time and effort or not, and said, "One of you make sure the ambulance comes this way, okay? And then, go ahead and head over to that blaze. Sounds like the fire brigade has it under control, but we don't want the whole block going up in flames."

"Yes, sir!" both young men said in unison and started running toward the street, where the fire engine and a number of concerned citizens were putting water to the inside of a small milliner's shop.

The sky was beginning to lighten with the sun's first rays, and Matthew could see that the fallen man was fading almost as fast as darkness was giving way to the light of day. He was young, probably no older than thirty, and his bony but rather handsome face seemed to glow in the shadows.

Matthew heard him panting for air and knew he was starting to fight for the last few minutes that remained of his mortal life. Kneeling by his side, Matthew murmured, "Don't worry, it'll be over soon."

The stricken man turned his head and studied Matthew's face. "Am I gut-shot?" he gasped.

Matthew nodded, and the man looked away. "The ambulance is on its way," he said, "but I don't think you're going to make it...anything you want to get off your chest before you go under?"

Matthew had experienced, over the years, that dying men often found comfort in confession. Sometimes they wasted precious minutes assigning blame for the series of misdeeds their lives had become, and sometimes they whispered the whereabouts of hidden fortunes in order to ensure their loved ones' security.

Often enough, it happened that wounded and dying men liked to know they were not heading into death's clammy embrace all by their lonesome. They had gambled against the odds —and lost. In the end, they needed to know that their gambling partners would not get off Scott-free.

The young man gulped for air and Matthew held his head up for a moment so he wouldn't strangle on his own spit. He stared up at Matthew's face and said, "My bosses want all the land around that mine…the Phoenix, I think it is, in Idaho."

Coughing and groaning in agony as more blood welled up from the wound in his intestines, the man continued. "They got teams of men assigned to roust the land-owners outta there. I ain't been in on that, but me and my friends was told to do whatever it took to shut that Brazil woman up about what she saw."

He gagged as blood rose up in his throat, spilling from his mouth. "I hated to do that, you know, but orders is orders…" His eyes closed and a great shudder wracked his bones.

Matthew gently shook the man's shoulders and leaning close to his ear whispered, "Son… wake up! Come on, tell me who your bosses are!"

The young man, whose face glowed now with an eerie inner-light like a jack-o' lantern, opened his eyes and murmured, "I never met them...but they are called the Trin...the Trinity."

"The Trinity...okay. Who is your head honcho, can you give me that?" Matthew urged.

The dying man took a long, shuddering breath and whispered. "My boss' name is Delray Adams—he is a prick, too. Likes beating up on girls before he kills 'em.

His glassy gray eyes looked up past Matthew's anxious face and he smiled at a small flock of chattering sparrows that had settled on an electrical wire overhead. "He sent me and Lester down here to torch the newspaper office..." He coughed again and then, as Matthew watched, his eyes grew dim and he died in a pool of his own blood.

Matthew looked up at the sound of fast-approaching hoof beats. The ambulance had arrived and two attendants jumped down from the wagon. As soon as they saw the dead man, however, they slowed down and took their time loading the body on a wheeled gurney.

Matthew was just about to head on down the alley and help the fire brigade when he spied the two young boys he had hired three days earlier to help distribute the *Journal*'s last edition. The two street urchins were standing close to the front door of the newspaper office and one of them gestured for him to come closer.

The kids couldn't have been less alike had they tried, but for some reason, they acted like brothers. One of the boys, whose name was Tommy O'Rourke, was short and stout with curly ginger hair and impish, green eyes. His friend's name was Chen Li, a thin, frail-looking Chinese boy with slanted black eyes and a wide, sunny smile.

When Matthew walked up, Tommy said, "There were three men, but the other two took off before you got here."

Matthew smiled. "You didn't happen to see where they went, did you?"

Chen Li grinned. "Sure did, Mr. Matthew...they headed down to the tracks. We followed them, quiet-like, and saw them head into one of the closed-up warehouses —it's the Wenatchee Orchard warehouse, and it won't open up again until later on this spring!"

Matthew pulled a few bills out of his pocket and handed each boy two dollars. "Thanks for your help, boys."

The kids grinned and tucked the bills into their shabby coats. They looked like they were about to flee and Matthew asked, "Say, where are your parents, anyway?"

Tommy's eyes got big in panic and he stared at his friend, whose gaze grew cold as he studied Matthew's face. "They are dead, Mr. Matthew, but we are okay, right? Don't tell the authorities—they will stick us in jail or put us in an orphanage!"

Matthew sighed. Unfortunately, Chen Li was probably right...orphaned children were often treated likes dregs of society...scorned, abused and subject to the most vile treatment. If he were to alert the authorities, chances were these two boys would end up in worse circumstances than they were already in.

Making a snap decision (and wondering if he had finally lost his wits, entirely), Matthew said, "How would you kids like to work for the Wilcox and Son Detective Agency?"

Both boys stared at him in bewilderment, and Matthew added, "That's my name...Matthew Wilcox. My son and I are in the middle of an investigation right now and we could use a couple of good hands."

Suddenly, the youngster's faces were wreathed in smiles. "You mean it really, sir?" young Tommy whispered. "Chen and I...well, we need the work and we'll do our best for you—honest!"

Matthew grinned in return, "Yes, I mean it. How does two bits a day, to start with, plus room and board suit you?"

Their eyes sparkled and both of them nodded in agreement. Chen spoke up, "What do you want us to do, Mr. Matthew?"

"Right now, I want you to come inside with me so you can get washed up a bit, grab a bite to eat and maybe catch a little rest. Then, you can watch over the Thurston's while the police and I go out to look at that warehouse. Agreed?"

Both boys seemed almost speechless with joy as they followed him inside the building. In the daylight, Matthew could see how thin, dirty and starved-looking they both were and he felt good knowing that, at least with him and his son, they stood a chance against a harsh and sometimes brutal world.

The Thurstons, along with their friend Marty Fulbright, were dressed now and standing together in a group at the back of the office when Matthew and his two new hires stepped inside.

There was a flurry of questions and he answered their concerns to the best of his ability. When he introduced his new employees, Annie took one look and whisked them away to the back rooms. Matthew knew there was a washroom and a small kitchen in back where she could give them a good scrub and put food in their bellies.

Turning to Clyde, Matthew said, "I've got a lead to look into. Now that there has finally been a move made against you, I'm sure the sheriff will authorize more men to stand guard. They should be arriving shortly." Staring into Clyde's face, he added, "Are you sure you don't want to pack it up and move into the sheriff's office...at least until we catch these perpetrators?"

The old man shook his head. "Thank you—but no... I'm convinced that with both the Spokane police force and you helping us, we'll be safe enough. And don't forget, the people in this fair city know—now—that there is a rat, so to speak, in their midst! They may, or may not, care for my daughter and me personally, but they will not tolerate rodents ruining their feed corn...."

His eyes twinkled and he added, "Remember what I said to you earlier, Matthew? Vermin like these don't like a bright light shining on their activities!"

Matthew wasn't so sure, but he also thought that, for the time-being, the Thurstons were safe enough. Tipping his hat, he said, "Still, lock the doors and stay away from the windows until I get back, okay?"

Marty Fulbright answered, "I'll make sure of it, Mr. Wilcox. Clyde and I need to do some work on the presses in back, and I think your new employees will be keeping Miss Annie busy—at least until your return."

Matthew smiled and said, "I'll be back soon...hopefully

with some information on who is trying so hard to kill you!"

Then he walked to the front door and stepped outside to find...and root out...a few rats hidden away in an abandoned warehouse.

## FANG OR FLAME!

CHANCE DID NOT KNOW WHICH WOULD HAPPEN FIRST... that he and Hannah would both end up as bear food or, they would perish from smoke inhalation. Coughing—gagging really—Chance threw another stick on the smoldering fire and dodged backwards with a strangled shout as he saw the bear run towards him again, swiping at him with sooty claws.

He and Hannah had been fighting the bear's approach for about twenty minutes and Chance was starting to despair. Most animals would have been long gone by now! The flames should have been deterrent enough, and he was sure that Hannah had hit the bear at least twice with her pistol.

He had watched it jerk back and roar with pain, but minutes later the bear was still intent on reaching its prey. To make matters worse, smoke from the fire had shifted and filled the tiny cavern now with noxious fumes and fiery embers.

Under normal circumstances, the fire would have been

a good idea, but there was something wrong with the maddened beast that kept it coming toward them again and again, despite its injuries. And who could have guessed that the gentle spring breeze would turn sharp and shift in their direction?

Stumbling and almost blind he called out, "Hannah! Hannah...we have to make a run for it!"

Bending over, Chance tried to find the young woman in the thick smoke. Finally, he almost tripped over the top of her. Peering down, he saw that the tears pouring from her eyes had turned into sooty rivulets on her face. She had an old shirt pressed against her mouth, but it looked like she had lost consciousness.

He picked up her gun and checked the chamber. *Only one bullet left...*he thought, and stumbled through the smoky air to the back of the cavern where Hannah kept some extra supplies. Pain shot up his leg and his foot was numb, but Chance knew that was the least of his worries right now.

Knowing that they would both die from asphyxiation, and soon, if they didn't leave the cavern, Chance rifled through the contents and found a small wooden box that thumped with a metallic rattle. Opening the lid, he grinned in relief and loaded the pistol with extra bullets. He hobbled over to Hannah's still form and heaved her up over one shoulder with a grunt of pain.

Chance stood still for a second, gathering his courage and then, holding Hannah in place with his left hand, he lifted the pistol and crept toward the daylight. The fire was dying again. (That had been the problem all along... the wood had started quickly enough with the addition of kerosene but most of the wood was waterlogged—thus the smoke).

He could see the enraged bear pacing back and forth on the other side of the diminishing flames. As Chance eyed the open ground, he felt his heart pound in dread. There was simply no place to go! The small pond was ringed around with high, stone walls and the only beach he could see was at least a hundred feet away from the cave entrance.

The only place to go was either around the waterfall or under it and both routes were blocked by the bear and her cubs. Eyes watering fiercely, Chance stared through the smoke at the cubs standing behind the sow. He saw that they were wet from the waterfall's mist and seemed confused as to what was going on.

Knowing there was no other way to go but through, Chance let out a holler and ran, screaming, toward the grizzly bear. For a moment, the beast paused as if in awe of the strange-looking beast running its way. Then, it started to stand in challenge.

He fired the pistol but Chance knew immediately that he had missed. Cursing the tears that continued to flow from his stinging eyes, he cocked the hammer again and pulled the trigger. This time, he saw the bear drop to the ground with a growl of pain.

He didn't know where the creature was hit, but there was no time to stand and assess the damage. With a defiant shout, Chance ran past the bear toward the waterfall.

Instantly, though, he saw the bear take chase. Heart drumming hard in his chest, Chance ignored his throbbing ankle and picked up speed, praying that he could make it to the tumbling waters before the bear took both him and Hannah down.

He could actually feel the bear's pounding gait through the soles of his feet and hear its labored breathing when another sharp report filled the air. The bear fell away and Chance took a second to peer over his right shoulder. The animal was on the ground now, and he could see that her eyes were wide open with shock and pain.

Panting, Chance watched as the bear jerked once and died. Not quite believing his good fortune, he stared about and saw Deputy Dick McNulty scamper down the pathway from the cleft in the cliff wall high overhead. He had a rifle in one hand and his pistol in the other.

He also saw Hannah's father, Jacob, half in and half out of the stony cleft he himself had navigated earlier. Wiping sweat from his face, he studied the sow's two offspring as they paced in panic at the shoreline. Thankfully, they appeared to be last season's cubs...probably yearlings, weighing in at around two hundred pounds each. He hoped they were mature enough to go on alone without their mother.

He placed Hannah on the ground and waved his arms threateningly at the two young bears. Startled, they turned left and then right. Finally, seeing the deputy disappear under the waterfall, they took the route in front of it. Both of them had to get wet and swim part of the way but they ended up on the path from whence they came.

As the humans watched, the two young bears ran up the stony path and around the pile of boulders at the top of the hill. Still shaking with nerves and a fierce renewal of pain from his swollen ankle, Chance sat on the ground next to Hannah, who was just now waking up and gasping for fresh air.

Dick emerged from under the waterfall, and walked up to where Chance and Hannah sat on the rocky shore. He stared at their sooty faces and at the young man's swollen ankle. "Well," he said, "looks like you two got yourselves into a fix."

Chance nodded. "Yeah, that she-bear was a handful…" Turning around to face the beast, he added, "Thanks, Dicky."

Dick nodded. "No problem…sorry it took so long to get here. We heard the first shot about a half hour ago, but it took a while to find this place. For a minute there, I wasn't sure if we would find you at all."

Hearing a panicked shout, they all looked up to see that Jacob had made his way through the cleft in the cliff wall and was moving toward them down the stony path. They waved at him and heard him shout, "I'll be there in a minute, Hans!"

Gazing at the young woman, who was soaking wet and still trying to clear the ash and smoke from her throat and mouth, Dick said, "Luckily, Jacob had a pretty good idea about where young Hans here was headed."

Hannah looked up at the deputy and wiped her mouth with the back of her arm. "I'm guessing, by now, you know I'm a girl?"

Dicky grinned. "I knew that a couple of weeks ago, but I tried to play along with the notion you were posing as a boy."

Hannah sighed and shook her head, while Chance stared up at his oldest friend. "Why didn't you tell me, Dicky?"

Dick shrugged. "I figured that Jacob and..." he raised his eyebrows at the young woman.

She said, "My real name is Hannah, sir."

Dick continued, "I figured that Hannah and her father had their reasons for keeping mum about her being a girl. It's not the first time I've heard of it, and in these wild parts, it's not a bad idea, either."

Jacob emerged from under the waterfall's rushing waters. He shook himself like an old dog and ran the remaining steps to where his daughter sat on the ground. "Hans! Are you alright?"

Hannah grinned. "I'm okay, papa, and...you can call me Hannah from now on—at least with these fellas."

Jacob straightened up and said, "I'm sorry about that, but we really didn't know you men, at first. The family decided to keep my daughter's...persuasion a secret.

"Good idea, Jacob," Dick said. "And a secret I think we should keep, at least until this sorry business is over and done with." Turning to face Chance and Hannah, Dick said, "We need to get back to the cabin. Chance, we'll help you back up and through the wall. Then, I want to send Hannah and her father back to fetch Abner. He can carry you back. Sound good?"

Chance nodded in agreement. "Much as I'd like to say I can get there on my own, I'm not so sure."

Dicky eyed the boy's ankle and said, "Nope. I think that ankle is broke." Turning around, he said, "Jacob, can you give me a hand? This boy weighs a ton!"

Jacob moved in to help and Hannah said, "Listen...I can run—fast! Why don't I go on ahead? I could be halfway home by the time you get Chance up that hill!"

Dick nodded and looked to the girl's father. Jacob grinned and said, "Yeah, go on. Don't forget to take your pistol!"

Hannah bent over, grabbed the gun, and stared at Chance for a moment before turning around and taking off up the path.

They watched her go for a moment and then they pulled the young man to his feet. Chance winced in pain as his foot touched the ground, but knowing there was no other choice, he gritted his teeth and, with Dick's and Jacob's help, made his way slowly up the path toward the Lindsay home.

## 13

# MATTHEW

MATTHEW HELPED WITH AS MUCH CLEAN-UP FROM THE small fire as possible. Once the day-shift replacements showed up, he asked the tough young deputy, Will Riley, if he would care to give him a hand in following, and possibly apprehending the perpetrators.

Will said sure, and seemed ready to go that very minute. Matthew held up a hand, laughing a little at the kid's enthusiasm. "First," he said, "I need to clear it with your boss. If he gives the go-ahead, you need to go home and get a little sleep, eat something, and then meet me back here in about five hours' time."

Staring into the young man's face, he added, "You realize that these men are stone-cold killers?"

Will nodded. "Yes sir, I do, but I'm handy with a gun. Bad outlaws just like these killed my ma and pa about five years ago. That's why I joined the sheriff's department."

"Okay, that's good. Go on home and meet me back here at...one o'clock," Matthew said.

"Yes, sir!" Will replied and walked swiftly down the alleyway, disappearing around the corner.

Matthew studied his watch. It was almost seven-thirty in the morning, and he figured Sheriff Lobey was in his office by now. He needed to go in and visit with the man…ask to borrow young Will and beg for a few more days of police presence around the newspaper office.

He knew that the old man was frustrated and feeling besieged but there was no help for it. Lobey knew, as well as he did, that crooks did not honor a convenient timetable and often the phrase "It never rains but it pours" seemed to apply, specifically, to trouble.

Seeing the two relief deputies show up on the street, Matthew ran to catch a ride on the carriage, back to the sheriff's office. A few minutes later, Matthew was standing in front of Lobey's desk.

As usual, Frank seemed to be in a foul mood, but he acquiesced quickly enough when Matthew asked to borrow Will Riley for the afternoon. "He's new and pretty far down on the roster list," Lobey replied, "but, he needs to show up for work, as scheduled…" peering up at a calendar on the wall behind his desk, he added, "Um…the day after tomorrow."

"Thank you, Sheriff," Matthew said.

Lobey stared up at him from under gray, beetled brows. "How long do I have to send half my man-power your way, Matthew?"

Matthew sighed. "I don't have an answer for you, Frank. I'm hoping that, with Will's help, I can round these crooks up this afternoon. That would take care of the immediate threat, I think." He sighed with frustration. "I am still working on getting the Thurston's out of town but, so far, Clyde is refusing to budge."

"Well," Frank grunted. "I will offer protection for just so long, you know. This is a big city, and if some fool wants to put a bull's-eye on his own back, so be it!"

Matthew studied Frank's cantankerous face and knew he was operating on borrowed time. He couldn't blame the sheriff, really. Each and every sheriff's department had a limited budget and, so far, Lobey had been generous with his meager resources. Too much more, though, and he would pull the plug.

Matthew stuck his hand out and said, "Understood, Frank, and...thank you!"

Lobey studied Matthew's hand for a moment and then stood up with a ghost of a smile on his craggy face. "I ain't pulling my men out quite yet, Matthew. Just...let's get this over with, okay?"

"Today, I hope," Matthew said and took his leave. Hopping a cab ride, he made his way back to the newspaper office, ate a little breakfast and checked in on Tommy and Chen, who were sleeping like puppies by the wood stove in the kitchen. As predicted, they were both scrubbed clean and it looked as though there were two sets of new clothes draped over the kitchen table.

He could hear Annie, Marty and Clyde talking, softly, in the print room and suddenly, he felt an overwhelming surge of fatigue. He walked into the little store room where he had set up his cot and, within seconds, he was snoring into his pillow.

Five hours later, a soft hand shook him awake. "Matthew, wake up." Annie said.

Matthew snorted and sat up with a start. "What time is it?"

"It's a little past two o'clock. The boys are up and dressed and your deputy, Will, and another young man are in the kitchen drinking coffee. Will told me you wanted to check things out at a warehouse this afternoon?"

Matthew rubbed his hands over his face and shook his head to clear the cobwebs from his mind. *Frank sent two deputies to help out?* he wondered in confusion. Finally, after a mighty yawn, he said, "Yes. I wanted to leave at noon, though."

Annie nodded. "I know, Matthew and I'm sorry, but I thought you needed a little extra sleep."

Matthew shook his bleary head and mumbled, "It's all right, Annie. Thanks for waking me."

Standing up from the side of the bed, Annie said, "I'll let you have your privacy, but when you're dressed, come out and have a little lunch before you go, okay?"

Matthew gazed up at her for a moment and knew, in that moment, he would ask her to marry him. He had no way of knowing whether she would say yes or no, but he knew he wanted a second chance at love.

Seeing the quizzical expression on his face, Annie said, "What?"

Matthew just grinned. "Oh, it's nothing, Annie. You just look very beautiful this morning, that's all."

Pleased, she said, "Thank you, Matthew. I'm flattered. Now, hurry up and come out to the kitchen before the soup gets cold."

An hour later, Matthew, Will, a Spokane County deputy named Tory Young, and Tommy crept between the high walls of warehouses that were lined up by the railroad tracks. Will was telling Matthew that the reason Sheriff Lobey had sent two deputies his way was to legitimize any arrests—or killings—that might take place today.

Some of the warehouses were quite busy. One was a fish house, judging by the smell of the place, and others were filled with grain and heavy pieces of machinery. Trains chugged, whistles blew, freight wagons and fast-moving carriages zipped here and there, adding to the clamor of the busy industrial district.

Matthew figured that his mug was recognizable, so he wore his hat down low and a neckerchief pulled up high over his mouth and mustache. The others in his group, though, could (he hoped) be anyone and his prayer was that if the crooks were on the look-out, the (starless) deputies would be able to blend into the hustle and bustle of the busy work-a-day crowd without raising any alarms.

Tommy came to a stop and said, "We should stop here and hide. That's the place me and Chen saw those men go into."

Matthew gestured to his companions and they slipped between two large buildings, where they were out of sight but could still see most of the crooks' hide-away. The day had grown cold and moist. Dark, heavy clouds were settling over the city like a great, gray goose over her brood. Staring though a light mist that had begun to fill the air, Matthew spied a thin stream of smoke coming up through the roof of the warehouse.

He sighed with relief. There was a good possibility the crooks had made a hasty exit while he and his men slept, but there was simply no help for it. No man could be expected to go for days on end without rest. That was a good way to get dead and Matthew did not want anyone to come to harm—much less Sheriff Lobey's borrowed deputies.

Turning around to face Tommy, Matthew said, "I want you to go back to the newspaper office now and help Chen watch over the Thurstons and Mr. Fulbright."

For a second it looked as if Tommy wanted to argue, but thinking better of it, he tipped his new tam and said, "Yes Sir!" Then he ran swiftly down the rubble-strewn corridor between the two warehouses and out of sight.

Will and Tory were studying the Wenatchee Orchard warehouse and discussing the best way to approach without being seen. *There's no doubt the front door is padlocked*, Matthew thought, staring at the side of the long structure and at the numerous windows dotting the high, wooden walls.

He noticed that one window was broken. An attempt had been made to seal it shut...either wood or some sort of heavy canvas was stretched across the shattered pane. It was a little too close to where the smoke emanated from the chimney pipe, though.

Deciding that a window closer to the front of the building would make a good entry point, Matthew spoke softly to his two companions. Pulling his hat low over his brow and tugging his kerchief up over his mouth, Matthew walked back out onto the street with the two Spokane County deputies in tow.

They strolled along until they were on the opposite side of the warehouse. Then they ducked out of sight again and studied the warehouse's windows. None of them were broken, but Matthew figured he could rectify that quickly enough, and with all the noise on the busy street, without drawing undue attention.

Drawing a deep breath, Matthew told his companions to be ready, and then he ran in a crouch to the second window from the road. Checking to be sure no one was watching, he used his pistol to shatter the glass. Reaching inside, and hoping his hand wouldn't be blown off by the crooks hiding inside, he felt around and found the window latch.

One by one, Matthew and the two deputies clambered inside the building to find and arrest some thieving, murdering, fire-starting, woman-beating sons-a-bitches.

## 14

# THE TAKE-DOWN

Matthew, Will and Tory crept as quietly as possible through the warehouse toward the back. The huge building was filled with large wooden bins, a mechanized belt assembly that wound overhead, mountains of wooden slats and spools of metal bands, used, presumably, to bind crates shut.

The place reeked of apples gone sour. The high, vinegar odor filled nostrils and brought tears to the eyes. Matthew couldn't help but wonder if the owners of this outfit didn't make either sour mash or apple vinegar as a sideline to their fresh apple sales.

The closer the men crept toward the back of the building, the more they could smell wood smoke. Matthew heard a low, popping noise and gestured toward the two deputies to get down! Then he realized the sound was merely wood settling in the stove. He also heard men's voices.

Matthew grinned. He and the deputies had gotten the

drop on the crooks. He felt pretty sure there was a back door to the building—probably for access to the business office. He figured if they could get close enough without being spotted, the men they sought wouldn't have a chance to pop out the back door and make their escape. Unless, of course, he thought, there are a bunch of them.

He was operating under the assumption there were four or five men—at most. If he was wrong, and there were twenty outlaws hanging around in the back room, he and his young helpers would be outnumbered. Matthew knew that he, at least, could take out quite a few before he was shot down but he didn't know if the deputies were good enough gun hands, or not.

It seemed to him that more and more these days, young men were hanging up their pistols. That was fine by him…the less guns there were, the less chance there was of someone getting shot down. But, he thought grimly, what did that mean in the long run? Only the crooks had guns? Matthew shuddered at the thought of it.

Matthew saw a shadow pass by the entrance to the back room. Signaling to the deputies, he knelt behind an empty apple bin and watched the two younger men crouch down as well. They were about twelve feet away from the door and the men's words could be heard clearly now.

Matthew quietly ordered the deputies to stay where they were. Then he ran five feet or so, ducked behind a bank of dusty file cabinets and peeked carefully around them to get a glimpse at the room beyond.

At first, he couldn't see much, but as his eyes adjusted, he saw two sets of denim-clad legs stretched toward the woodstove, a small pile of kindling and a brown jug of hooch sitting by one of the men's socked feet. Peering around the doorjamb, he also saw the front of a large desk, and two sleeved forearms perched on the desk's blotter. A hand clutched a shot glass.

"Well," a voice growled, "You gotta know that Mr. Farnsworth ain't gonna be happy about it."

Another voice answered, "I know, Delray, but what were we supposed to do? Let ourselves get shot down…or arrested? I'm telling ya, the place is crawling with lawmen!"

For a moment, silence filled the air and Matthew strained to hear more. Then, he stepped back when he saw the figure behind the desk stiffen. A moment later, the man's shot glass streaked through the air to land with a thud and a muffled curse.

"God dammit, Delray! What did you do that for!" One of the men by the woodstove stood up and walked past the open doorway toward the desk. Matthew saw a stout, well-dressed man rubbing the back of his balding head, as he placed the shot glass back on the desk, then turned around and headed back to his chair by the stove.

"I did that because you men seem to think that your failure…no, FAILURES, in killing the Thurstons are going to be tolerated! Well, they're not. Our bonus depends on success and, so far, not only have you failed in your mission, but half the law-dogs in Spokane County are gunning for us!"

Matthew changed positions and saw that the balding man was still rubbing the back of his head. He sat with another man who, so far, had decided to keep his mouth shut. Try as he might, Matthew could see no others in the room. Knowing that three on three were the best odds he could have hoped for, he turned around to gesture the two deputies forward.

He caught Will in the act of already creeping towards him on his own, with Tory in hot pursuit. Glaring briefly at the two youngsters, Matthew rolled his eyes and motioned for them to proceed quickly.

Within moments they stood by his side.

"What are we gonna do, Mr. Wilcox?" Will whispered. The young man's voice seemed to echo throughout the warehouse, and Matthew frowned in alarm.

Will, hearing his own volume, cringed and clapped his hands over his mouth. Matthew shook his head and peered carefully around the end of the file cabinets to see if they'd been heard. He relaxed, though, as none of the men had stirred and he realized that the crackle and pop of the wood fire were filling the ears of the men inside the office.

Turning back around, Matthew placed his fingers over his lips until he saw the deputy's shame-faced agreement. He pointed to the three of them—holding up three fingers. He saw Will and Tory watching his every move, nodding in understanding. Then he then held up three fingers again and pointed toward the office.

Smiling now, the young men watched as Matthew pointed two fingers to the left of the room and one to the right. Then he gestured for them to cover his left flank while he took the man on the right.

Leaning forward, Matthew pulled Will's shaggy black mane toward him and whispered in his ear, "It would be best to take these men in alive for questioning, but if anything goes wrong—at all—you shoot. And, I mean, shoot to kill! Now, tell Tory what I just told you and be quiet about it!"

Will grinned and gave Tory the message as Matthew watched. Once Tory gave a thumbs up, all three of them pulled their pistols. Then Matthew held one finger in the air and mouthed the word, "ONE!"

He moved a step forward and could feel the deputies dogging his footsteps. Listening, he heard the man at the desk say, "I'm going to go and make a phone call. I'm damned sure I'll get an earful when Farnsworth hears about what happened, but I need to find out what he wants to do now. It's almost time to rotate on outta here, anyway. Hopefully, once we get back to Seattle we'll still have a job!" The man's voice rose a notch in anger. "That is, if we make it back at all! You know how old man Branson is…he might just arrange to have us all killed!"

Matthew filed the names in his head, praying that he wouldn't forget. Farnsworth, Branson…Seattle. Could these men be a part of the so-called "Trinity"? he wondered. He had no way of knowing, but it was a clue. Swearing that, from now on, he would always carry a paper notebook on his person so he could never possibly forget a clue, Matthew held up two fingers and whispered, "TWO!"

The young deputies watched like hawks as Matthew took a deep, steadying breath and then shouted, "THREE!"

Instantly, Matthew and the two deputies crowded into the office yelling at the top of their lungs, with their pistols held high. Matthew knew immediately that they were in luck. His guess that there were only three men present was accurate and moments later, all three of the miscreants were spread-eagled on the dusty floor.

The two men by the woodstove were in various stages of undress, and neither wore their guns. The man behind the desk did have his gun belt on, which Matthew quickly removed. Then, knowing the old trick by heart (especially since he did the same thing), Matthew found a small 22 cal. pistol tucked into the man's right boot.

Plucking it away, Matthew nodded to Will, who said, "You men are under arrest for suspicion of murder! Stand up now, and put your hands behind your back!" The men struggled and swore a bit but, all in all, it was a smooth arrest.

Pulling the men to their feet, and clapping handcuffs on all three, Matthew and the deputies marched their prisoners outside. After Matthew opened the door and peered up and down the narrow alleyway, he told the deputies to don their stars. Then, he gestured for them to follow with the prisoners. The small procession moved slowly toward the street in the dusk of early evening.

Matthew was beginning to feel a great gust of relief. They had finally managed to stop these bandits! Not only that, but he and Chance had more clues to go on. It was possible, now that the immediate threat was neutralized, that he and his son could head into Seattle and put a stop to the Trinity and their minions for good!

The deputies were in a fine mood, as well. This was their first collar, and they hoped that Sheriff Lobey would put in a good word on their files. Both of them were grinning as they kept their prisoners at gunpoint.

People on the street stopped to stare, and a few onlookers whistled tauntingly. "Go back to your own business, folks," Matthew said. "This is a police matter..." He was smiling as he called out, both with the neatness of the whole take down and, to keep the crowds gathering around them calm.

Suddenly, a sharp crack filled the air. The sound seemed to bounce off the bottoms of the thick clouds overhead and echo throughout the maze of industrial buildings.

Looking up in alarm, the deputies ducked and searched the rooftops for the shooter but, seeing nothing, looked back down at where Matthew lay bleeding on the street.

## 15

## MOVING ON

Will and Tory gaped at Matthew for a moment and then, while Tory held the prisoners at gunpoint, Will ran to where the private investigator lay unconscious in a pool of his own blood. Kneeling, Will stared down at Matthew's pale face and placed his fingers on the man's neck to see if there was still a pulse.

Matthew's hat lay a few feet away in a mud puddle, a wisp of smoke still rising from the bullet that had passed through it. Will concentrated and thought he could feel blood coursing through Matthew's veins, even though he had been knocked unconscious. Blood ran down his face in a slow but steady stream. Touching Matthew's scalp, Will could see that the bullet had deflected along the hat's crown and scraped a long but mostly shallow graze on the man's hairline.

Sighing with relief, Will saw Matthew open his eyes and squint up at him. "Owww," he mumbled.

Turning around, Will hollered, "Someone go and fetch an ambulance!"

"Alright!" someone hollered back. Will felt his hands start to shake in a delayed reaction to the attack. Looking up at Tory, he asked, "Did you see who did the shooting?"

Tory shook his head, "No. He must have shot at Mr. Wilcox and skedaddled."

"Well, we need to get a few more deputies down here to take these prisoners in!" Will replied.

The three men in custody were clearly excited, and one of them sneered, "Better hurry up, before our pard finishes all of you off!"

One of the spectators, an enormous blonde-haired man, suddenly ran up from behind, and clobbered the prisoner over the head with two fists. Delray sank to his knees with a groan. "You better show these lawmen some respect... Pard!"

Tory and Will stared at the huge man and Will muttered, "Thanks! We could use a few more like you at the sheriff's department!"

"Nah," the man muttered. "I'm doing okay here. I just don't like crooks."

Tory agreed, "Me neither!"

Turning back to Matthew, Will asked, "How do you feel, Mr. Wilcox? Good enough to let us move you under cover so that shooter ain't tempted to give it another try?"

Matthew sat up, slowly, and fresh blood oozed out of the long scrape on his head. "Yeah, I'll be fine." Staring askance at his smoking hat, he added, "Damn...I really liked that hat."

Will smiled. "You should give it a little kiss, sir. I think it just saved your life!"

Matthew grinned back and said, "Give me a hand up."

Just as Will started to pull Matthew to his feet, the sound of whistles filled the air. The police had already arrived and along with them, an ambulance. Matthew watched as Tommy approached first, a shame-faced yet proud expression written clearly on his freckled face.

"I saw you get shot, Mr. Wilcox. I was the one what ran and got the cops." Tommy took his hat off his head and stared at his own boots, knowing that his disobedience might cost him and his best friend in the whole world their newfound jobs.

Matthew stared down at the boy for a moment. Tommy knew he had gone against orders but, right now, Matthew was glad. From the way blood kept leaking from the wound on his scalp, he figured he might need to be stitched up...plus he really wanted to take a powder. He was lucky, and grateful to be alive, but the wound hurt like hell.

"We'll talk about it later, Tommy. But, right now, I just want to say thanks..." Matthew stuck his hand out. Tommy stared up at him for a second and then he grinned and gave his boss's hand a shake.

Then ambulance attendants and deputies swarmed into the area. Within minutes, the three prisoners were tucked into a paddy-wagon and Matthew was on his way to the hospital.

A couple of hours later, Matthew was lying in a hospital bed, taking notes. The doctor had put six stitches in his head and given him a shot of morphine, instead of an aspirin powder. For the moment, Matthew was content to let the more powerful drug ease the pain of his injury.

The bullet had not penetrated his skull, but its passage was deep. Also, he was slightly concussed. The doctor felt it was a minor concussion, but he had insisted on keeping Matthew overnight for observation.

Sighing, Matthew cursed himself in annoyance. There were three names he was supposed to remember; names that had great significance but, so far, he could only come up with two; Seattle, Farnsworth and, and…"Bah!" he snarled and threw his pencil across the room.

A white curtain that separated him from the other patients twitched and a nurse stood over his bed. "Are you all right, Mr. Wilcox?"

Matthew looked up and said, "Yes, I'm fine…sorry. I threw my pencil—could you fetch it for me please?"

The nurse smiled and searched for the wayward implement. Finding it, she returned it to him and said, "I was just about to say that you have a couple of visitors. Do you feel well enough for company?"

"Sure, send them in, and thanks for finding my pencil." Matthew laid his head back on the pillow and tried not to cringe at the pain. While he waited, he whispered out loud, "Seattle, Farnsworth…Seattle, Farnsworth…"

"And Branson," Clyde said.

Matthew's eyes flew open in excitement. Clyde Thurston and his beautiful daughter Annie stood by his bed, grinning down at him.

"That's it!" Matthew cried. "Hurry, write it down, will you?"

Clyde took Matthew's notebook and jotted down the name, while Annie sank down on the side of the bed, taking Matthew's hand in hers. "Oh my God!" she said. "I was so frightened when I heard what happened!"

Matthew smiled and said, "I'm going to be fine, Annie, it's just a scratch." Turning to Clyde, he said, "How did you know about the other name...Branson?"

Clyde took a chair by the foot of the bed. "Your young deputy, Will, heard the names spoken out loud back in the warehouse. He told me everything he knew about the incident. Plus, the head gun of that bad bunch you took down is singing like a canary!" The old man grinned.

"There hasn't been a formal inquiry, yet, but he gave up all the names he knew! Luckily, because of what those scoundrels did to me and Annie—not to mention sweet little Chloe, Sheriff Lobey let me listen in on the first round of questions. The formal interrogation is being held off until you are able to attend."

Matthew grinned. "Tell me what you heard."

"Well, Delray...didn't catch the man's surname, said he works for an outfit out of the Seattle area. He knows the head honchos' names, but says he's only ever seen and spoken to a man by the name of Edward Branson...one of three men who call themselves the "Trinity."

Pausing for a moment, Clyde stared off into space and sighed. "I was born into wealth, Mr. Wilcox. The kind of wealth that can turn a person's head, if you know what I mean. But my parents, God rest their souls, were free spirits. My father was an explorer and he worked most of his life for one university or another, seeking out and cataloging the world's greatest antiquities." The old man seemed lost in the past for a moment, while he remembered his youth.

Resuming his narrative, Clyde said, "For years, my mother and I followed around him around the globe. We were happy too, until I met Annie's mother. That's when I settled down and opened my newspaper." He reached out and took his daughter's hand, patting it gently.

Sighing, he continued. "Growing up, I understood that neither my father nor my mother cared for the trappings or the inherent arrogance of high society, and they taught me to feel the same way."

He shook his balding head and went on. "The fact that these men call themselves the Trinity tells me we are dealing with enormous wealth. Men like these are class-conscious snobs who think they can do whatever they like, to anybody they wish. They also feel they are above reprisal...God-like."

Staring into Matthew's eyes, Clyde added, "I would bet a thousand dollars that these men were—and perhaps still are, sorority members. I would also bet they are affiliated with the Freemasons. That would explain much of their carte blanche, and the ease with which they've seized so many legal contracts around that mine in North Idaho."

Matthew felt sick. Claim-jumpers were one thing—crooks like those, he could deal with. But high society fat cats with delusions of grandeur, power hungry moguls with enough money to implement their schemes; they were another thing, entirely. Feeling his head throb with pain, he gulped against the nausea rising up in his gullet.

Clyde was studying the expression on Matthew's face. He stared back and forth between his daughter and the man she had fallen in love with and made up his mind.

"I have made a decision, Matthew." he murmured.

Looking up at the old man, Matthew said, "What is it?"

"I think that Annie and I should go to my mansion in Seattle. I did what comes naturally to me—I exposed these crooks and their schemes to the light of public opinion. But now, I feel like we're fish in a barrel." He sighed. "Maybe, if you and your son can round up the rest of these crooks, here and in North Idaho, Annie and I can do a little research on the men who are pulling the strings in the Seattle area."

He studied Matthew's expression and said, "Just as soon as you've made progress, and feel like it's safe to do so, call me and we'll come back home."

Matthew felt relieved. If Clyde and Annie were out of harm's way, he could move on into Idaho and help Chance round up the claim-jumpers who were threatening the landowners around the mine. Then, if all went well, they would hunt down the puppet-masters behind this foul enterprise.

Smiling, Matthew said, "Just be careful, Clyde. It sounds like this…Trinity has some pretty solid resources. If you are going to snoop into their affairs, be sure you don't get caught, okay?"

Clyde's eyes twinkled. "Don't worry, Matthew. That's one of the good things about having a lot of money on hand…I have some pretty solid resources too!"

## 16

## SCOOTER AND THE TRINITY

Scott Little, better known as Scooter, boarded the east bound train from Spokane to Seattle two and a half hours after he shot and, unfortunately, missed killing one of the lawmen who had rousted his buddies from the warehouse.

He had hoped to shoot the man's head clean off, so his companions might escape, but after crouching behind the warehouse's chimney for almost fifteen minutes, he saw that the man was merely wounded. He also noticed that the crowds teeming below him on the streets were restive and looked to be in the mood for a little citizen's justice.

Choosing to fight another day, rather than be strung up by a vigilante mob, Scooter ran off and hid behind the stables by the train station as his co-workers were pitched into the paddy wagon. He went into the ticket office briefly and purchased a one-way ticket, looking over his shoulder the whole time, but once the train arrived, he walked on without a hitch.

Staring morosely out the train window, he squirmed uneasily. The last thing he wanted to do was face his boss, Mr. Branson. That job was usually reserved for his immediate supervisor. But now that Delray and the rest of the crew were cuffed up in jail, the news of their failure fell to him. Sighing, he thought, how many times has Delray told us how men who fail the Trinity usually suffer a fate worse than death?

Shaking his head and brimming with anxiety, Scooter closed his eyes and tried to sleep away the miles separating him from his fate.

Branson was in a foul mood. His gout was acting up again and now, to make matters worse, Farnsworth had just dropped an unpleasant bomb in his blanket-covered lap.

"What do you mean they're in jail? All of them?" he roared.

Timothy studied the beautiful, floral patterns on the carpet beneath his feet. He was growing mighty sick of his old friend's attitude. Edward seemed to think that, like kings of old, he could snap an imperious finger and whatever he desired could—and would—happen...instantly. Well, maybe that worked at one time, long ago.

Things were different now, though. Telephones and telegraph machines, fast moving trains, automobiles and...people! Thousands of people cluttering things up—wagging their tongues, calling the sheriffs, taking things into their own hands!

But, no matter how many times Timothy tried to set

things straight for the old man, Branson just couldn't get his head around the idea that he could no longer move his players around the board with impunity. Feeling the warmth of the overheated room, Farnsworth cleared his throat and loosened his silk necktie.

"Well, speak up!" Branson snapped, sensing fear in his friend's demeanor rather than the annoyed frustration Timothy actually felt.

"Edward, like I told you before, it seems there are other forces at work here. According to Mr. Little, an older man seems to be sniffing our back trail. Scooter doesn't know this man's name, but he thinks he has been actively protecting the Thurstons. He also seems to have the sheriff's department at his disposal. It's really too bad that Delray saw fit to kill those two deputies when he fired the Thurston's house."

The room was thick with an uncomfortable silence. All three men knew that it was Branson's team who had made the most mistakes in this endeavor. First, they had made a public spectacle out of silencing the Brazil woman. Then, to make matters worse, a whole city block was involved in the house fire that was set to silence the Thurston's. And now this...

Stephen Castle spoke, "I'll send my team in, Edward. Five men into Idaho to finish what we started there and another five to deal with Delray, Lester and...what was his name?" he asked.

Branson glared. "I'll take care of my own men, thank you very much!"

Stephen smiled and held his hands in the air with an

innocent expression. "It's just that we know you have a soft spot for your own employees, Edward...understandably. I was just trying to help." The easy grin left his face as he added, "You DO see the necessity of silencing any witnesses, right?"

Branson frowned at the sullen flames in the fireplace. Finally, he grunted, "Of course I do... it's probably too little, too late, but the sooner we can shut those three up, the better it will be for all of us. Do we have men in place who can be counted on to do the job?"

Timothy grinned. "Yes, I have two men on the payroll who work at the sheriff's office in Spokane. All it would take is one or two phone calls and any singing canaries will cease to be a problem."

Branson grunted, "I hope that your men can do it without making a scene?"

Farnsworth smirked. "Oh, certainly. My men work in the kitchen, you see, which reminds me—Edward, the other man's name, if you please?"

Branson answered, "Its Delray Stinson, Lester Knowles and Paul Delany. They should all be in one cell, for now, anyway."

Spying the telephone across the room, Farnsworth asked, "Shall I?"

Branson said, "Yes! Use that telephone there, quickly!"

Timothy got up and made a couple of phone calls. After a few minutes, he sat back down with a wide smile on his face. "You were right, Edward. All three men are in one cell. My man can't be sure, but it sounds like they haven't been formally interrogated yet. Seems that the sheriff is waiting for Mr. Wilcox to be released from the hospital.

"Wilcox? Who is that, again?" Stephen sat up in alarm.

"That is the man who has been hounding our trial, I guess." Farnsworth replied. "He was shot—in the hat, mind you—by Edward's man, Scooter. Got his gourd rattled a bit, but he's due to be released from the hospital in the morning."

"Well, let's take care of the man!" Branson shouted. "I don't know who the hell he thinks he is, but we don't need him sniffing around either!"

Stephen frowned. "Don't you think we ought to wait a little while and gather some intelligence on him before we knock him off? Honestly, if we're not careful, and a bunch of dead bodies start piling up, the Spokane County sheriffs will call in the Washington State marshals and maybe even the Pinkertons! Do we really want that?"

It was Farnsworth's turn to frown. "Edward, I agree with Stephen. Why don't you let us do a little checking first? If I know my men…and I do, our three possible songbirds will be dead, soon after dinner is served."

Grinning, he added, "This Wilcox fellow can show up at the jailhouse tomorrow, but there won't be a witness left to implicate us, right? Meanwhile, we can use the next couple of days to reconnoiter this new player…and maybe make another move on the Thurstons. They'll probably feel pretty safe, knowing that the men who have been gunning for them are all dead."

Branson stared at his two old friends and nodded. "Okay, then. Check this Wilcox out. See who he works for and what he's doing. In the meanwhile, someone, please, take care of Thurston and his daughter. So far, I think they only know about Delray and his men, but sooner or later, they might piece things together and implicate us all!"

Timothy sighed. "I'll take care of those two myself."

"Sure you can handle it, Timmy?" Castle asked.

Farnsworth stood up and, for a second, Stephen Castle was reminded of the formidable young man he had met so long ago. "You bet I can handle it, Stephen. And, if you don't start treating me with a little more respect, you will be feeling the hard end of my fists!"

"Now, now, gentlemen…" Branson murmured.

But Stephen had already stood up. "Timmy, I am truly sorry," he said. "I am behaving badly, and have offended one of my oldest and truest friends! Please, forgive me… and my sharp tongue!"

Farnsworth studied Castle's contrite expression. He no longer trusted Stephen, any more than that old lunatic, Branson, but he was in just as deeply as the other two men.

Sighing, he said, "Okay, Stephen. I forgive you." He put his hat on his head adding, "Now, if you'll excuse me, it seems I have a train to catch."

"Just one moment, Timothy," Branson growled, ringing a little bell on the table by his side.

A few moments passed, and then two of Branson's henchmen came to the parlor doors holding young Scooter in front of them at gunpoint.

Branson sneered and picked a pistol up off the little round table. "Timothy…Stephen, you make think I'm soft on my men but you're wrong...observe. He raised the gun, aimed and shot Scott Little between the eyes.

Then he put the pistol back on the side table and said, "This is what happens when our men fail in their duties. Best to remember it from now on..."

## CHANCE

Five days had passed since Chance jumped off the cliff and broke his ankle. Once he'd been carried back to the Lindsay's cabin, Dicky and Abner did a good job of binding the break. Luckily, Hannah found some aspirin powder tucked away in a kit in the kitchen, and after taking two powders and drinking a few shots of whiskey to dull the pain, he'd fallen asleep and slept for a full day.

He had jerked awake a few times dreaming, alternatively, of roaring bears and naked girls but, finally, he woke up feeling sore but rested. He was able to move about now—slowly—but too much activity caused his ankle to swell painfully.

He was bored, though, and growing prickly, so Dicky tasked him with the chore of sharpening blades, cleaning firearms and loading bullets. He sat at the table now, his hands slick with gun-oil.

Hannah and her father were often gone (another source of frustration for Chance, who wanted nothing more than to sit with the young woman and drink in the sight, sound and smell of her.) They traveled back to the mineral-filled place she had found, where the she-bear lay butchered in the weeds.

While Chance had slept, the men took turns skinning the animal and quartering the meat for eating. Now, the only thing left of the maddened beast was its skeleton. The pelt was stretched onto a drying rack in back of the house. Hannah had informed Chance that she would make him a fine bearskin coat but, right now, when he looked at it and caught the faint smell of decay wafting from its surface as it dried in the sun, he shuddered with dread.

He remembered a young draftee he had met once in military school. The boy wanted, more than anything, to be a soldier; to fight for his country, hearth and home, but he was afraid of heights. So fearful was he that even boarding a horse caused him to break out in a cold sweat. It was a condition the Army doc had called Latent Hysteria, and it was enough to get the young man mustered out of service.

Chance recalled the tears of disappointment streaking the kid's face as he left the barracks for the last time and wondered now if he, himself, had just become "hysterical" over bears! Shaking his head, he thought, better get over it quick...bears are thick as thieves —everywhere!

He could hear Dick and Bill Nash, the deputy on loan from the Spokane sheriff's office, talking outside on the front porch. They were repairing and oiling all of Jacob's leather tack, while Abner was spending his time replacing loose roofing and broken or rotting boards on the outbuildings.

"The telegraph Sheriff Lobey sent says he wants me to come back home," Nash said. "Trust me, though, I would rather stay on here. I haven't had such a restful time in a long while, but Lobey is the boss and I got to do what he says."

Dick said, "Well, I haven't heard from Matthew in a while, but I know that things seem to be okay here. If you have to go back to Spokane, I sure won't try to stop you."

Chance heard regret in Nash's voice as he replied, "Thank you, Dick. Like I said, I'd rather stay on but I can't be losing my job, what with a family to feed and all." There was a pause, then he added, "I'll leave in the morning, alright?"

Dicky answered, "That will be fine, Bill. Thanks."

The slow but steady sound of cloth and pumice being stroked over metal and leather resumed and Chance got up to make a fresh pot of coffee. His left foot dragged a little and he heard Dick call out, "Chance, do you need help in there?"

"No, I got it, thanks," Chance gritted through clenched teeth. Any time his foot met the least bit of resistance, the broken bone in his ankle sent waves of pain through his whole body. Standing still for a minute, and letting the agony fade to tolerable levels, he heard Dick mutter under his breath.

"Oh, oh...looks like we got c...company," he said,

Chance felt a chill of recognition. When he was a young boy, he had often heard Dick stutter. It was something his old friend had struggled with for many years.

Now, the only time Dick ever became tongue-tied was when he was angry, excited...or scared.

Dick let out a high, shrill whistle, both for Abner and for the Lindsay's who were a couple of miles away, but could still hear certain tones—like a whistle or a gunshot as it echoed up through the high canyon walls.

"You think that's them?" Nash asked.

"Don't know, Bill," Dick answered. "But we'd better be ready, just in case." A moment later, Chance heard Dick say, "Chance, you stay inside now, you hear? Are you close to the guns?"

"Yes Sir, I am. I'll cover you from behind, okay?"

"That'll be fine, son." Dick replied.

Chance hobbled back over to the long, plank table by the kitchen window. It was heaped with pistols, rifles and shotguns. Gun oil fumes stung his eyes as he picked up two rifles and two pistols, along with three boxes of shells. He limped to the front door, bent over and scooted the firearms out onto the front porch between Dick and Bill, who stood watching the road, and the five men on horseback that approached.

"Thank you, Chance," Dick said, "Now, get back inside and arm yourself."

Chance walked slowly to the table and sat in a chair. Heart pounding with dread, he started loading every rifle and pistol within reach, listening all the while to what was going on outside.

For a moment, all he heard was the slow clip-clop of horse hooves, then he heard a man call out, "Hello! Are you the owners of this here property?"

Dick shouted back, "We are and we ask you fellas to back up and move on!"

"Why, that's not very neighborly! My men and I just need to water our horses, that's all." The same man called out, his voice a mixture of pleading and threat.

"Nope! Sorry, but we are all dried out here! Move on down the road a spell, and you'll see the river bends up close to the road. You can water your horses there."

Dick's voice held no stutter now. In fact, Chance could just picture his friend's face, and how his faded freckles sometimes blazed to life, along with his brown eyes when he got riled up.

There was a shuffle just outside the door and Chance heard Dick whisper, "You ready, Bill?"

"Ready as I'll ever be, I reckon," Nash whispered back.

Another loud whistle pierced the air and then the shooting began. Chance thought Dick got off the first shot but, after that, it was anyone's guess. Gunfire filled the air, pistol fire mainly, with the occasional shot-gun blast announcing itself in ear-shattering glory.

Chance knelt on the floor, loading the other men's guns as they slid in the door, smoking and hot. Over the sound of gunfire, he could hear angry shouting and yelps of pain as a bullet found its mark.

Chance thought that his companions were kneeling on the porch floor, using the rails as cover but, at one point, he heard Dick exclaim, "Bill, get d...d...down!"

Almost immediately, he heard Nash cry out as a bullet buried itself in his body. There was a mighty crash as the man fell backwards, half in and half outside the front door. Chance struggled to his feet and thought he heard happy cheering as he pulled the wounded deputy inside the house.

Glancing down at the bleeding lawman, Chance saw a large patch of red staining the front of Nash's chest. He gulped and bent over to peel his shirt off. Nash was gasping for air and his face had gone the color of spoiled milk.

Wiping the blood away as much as possible, Chance knew the deputy was a goner. A large caliber bullet had entered the man's chest, close to his heart, and he could hear air whistling out from the ruin of his left lung.

For a moment, it looked as though Bill was trying to speak but then his eyes went blank…fixed on some vision only he could see. Chance trembled as he saw death steal the soul of a man he had grown to like and then he reached out and closed Bill's eyelids.

"Chance! A little help here…" Dick hollered.

Chance sprang to his feet, grimly ignoring the agony that shot from his ankle to the top of his thigh. Grabbing two pistols, he dropped down and squirmed out the front door on his knees and elbows. Glancing through the posts and rails on the front porch, he saw that two of the five men were down but the three other men had scattered into hiding behind the trees dotting the property.

There was a lull in the action as everyone seemed to take stock at once. Then Chance heard Abner's shotgun roar. There was a howl of pain from the north end of the front pasture.

Then a voice cried out, "Steve! Steve, help me out, will ya? That big bastard with the shotgun just filled me fulla buckshot! I think I'm dying!"

There was no answer and, for a second, Chance wondered if they had managed to put down all five men. Then he froze as he heard, "Put down that shooter before I plug ya in the back of the head!"

The man named Steve had stolen around the house from behind and now had the drop on them. Chance saw Dick stiffen and say, "Steady now, Mister. We're putting our weapons down…see?"

"You too, kid. Put your pistol down, NOW!" the man snarled.

Chance felt bile back up in his throat. Under normal circumstances, he thought that they could have prevailed over these bandits but, five men to four was pushing the odds, especially since he, himself, was next to useless.

Chance set his gun on the floorboards and stayed on his knees with his hands held high in the air. Dick fell to his knees as well, and said, "You go ahead and take whatever you want. We know when we're beat."

Steve grinned as his gun swayed from side to side, first pointing at Dick's face and then to the younger man. Chance's heart slammed in his chest and a wave of sorrow made tears prick his eyes. It wasn't as though he was afraid of dying, or of the pain…this close, Steve's bullet would spell an almost instant death.

Nah, it was the fact that he wouldn't be able to hug his Pa's neck and say goodbye or, take the delectable young woman named Hannah in his arms, place his lips over hers and feel the smoothness of her flesh against his. Furious, suddenly, at crooks in general and at this particular crook specifically, he glared up at the bandit named Steve and snarled in defiance, "Screw you!"

Dick's voice sped up a little, but Chance was proud to hear no sign of a stutter as he blurted, "Shush now, Chance…let me handle this!" Turning back to Steve, he added, "If you're in a killing state of mind, go ahead and do me, okay? Just leave the kid alone!"

Steve smirked and answered, "Nah, you all made too much of a mess here. Best I put all of you outta your misery. Can't be leavin' any witnesses around, can I?"

Dick opened his mouth to plead some more, but before he had a chance to utter a word, a bright red flower blossomed on Steve's chest, followed closely by the sound of a large caliber pistol.

The man's jaw sagged open as he stared down at his body and then at the two men kneeling before him in confusion. Then, he fell backwards with a sigh.

Dick and Chance exchanged their own bewildered glances and then turned around in time to see Matthew riding up on his favorite horse Lincoln, Abner trailing behind him and cradling his right arm, which was soaking red with blood.

## 18

## TAKING TIME TO CATCH A BREATH

Matthew stepped off his horse and made his way, quickly, up the porch steps to where Chance and Dick still knelt on their knees. Both men seemed uninjured but were visibly shaking with nerves. Dick stared at Matthew with stricken, remorseful eyes but Chance kept his eyes down even as his body quaked with spent fear.

Matthew stood over his son and raised Chance's chin with a gloved finger. Green eyes met, but it was the older man's eyes that filled with tears of relief. Matthew pulled Chance to his feet with a groan and wrapped his arms around the younger man's shoulders. "I'm sorry, son. I'm so sorry I didn't come sooner!"

Chance was trying hard to be brave—for his old man, Dick, Abner...but especially for himself. It took a moment for Matthew's words to penetrate the jumble of emotions in his mind, but then he stepped back and said, "No! It's my fault for breaking my ankle, and not being able to help more in this shootout! I'm the one who's sorry!"

Matthew stepped back and looked down at the young man's left foot, which he saw was wrapped in bandages, purple toes sticking out the front of the wrappings and a purple ankle peeking out from behind. "My God, Chance! What the hell happened?"

Chance blushed and started to answer for himself, when Dick spoke up. "Matthew, let's go on inside and take a minute to catch our breath, okay?"

Matthew looked at his old friend and apologized, "Yeah, I'm sorry. How are you doing, Dicky?"

McNulty grinned and said, "Besides having the piss scared outta me, I'm just fine. Looks like Abner could use a hand, though, and Chance needs to take the weight off that foot."

Abner, after making sure his friends were all right, had already stepped inside the house and sat down on a chair by the wood stove. He was peeling the shirt off his shoulder to get a gander at his gunshot wound when Matthew's hand took the fabric and peeled the cloth away from a long but shallow graze on his upper right arm. "Doesn't look too bad, Abner. Let me get some soap and water, and some medicine out of my kit. We'll have you fixed up in no time."

Abner looked up, smiling, and Matthew reached down to pat his left shoulder. His face was still pale with left-over fear, as he whispered the words, "Thank you so much, Abner...really."

Abner nodded solemnly, watching as Matthew walked to the large barrel by the front door, filled a tin pan with water and put it on the wood stove to heat. Just as he started to walk outside, young Hannah came flying up the steps with her father Jacob, red-faced and wheezing, close behind.

"What happened?" she cried. "Is everyone alright?" Her eyes sought and found Chance, who was sitting in a chair by the stove. Abner saw her start toward the young man and then pause, as if worried that Chance's father might notice the affection that had grown between them the last couple of weeks.

Matthew, for his part, had seen Hans and Jacob fly around the front of the house and mount the stairs, but it wasn't until he reached into his saddlebags for his medical kit that his mind registered the long, shiny length of jet-black hair that hung down the boy's back or how high and feminine Hans' voice seemed now.

He paused for a moment, both to let his nerves settle and to grin in understanding. He had not really had an opportunity before he left for Spokane to figure out what was so different about Jacob's oldest son, but now it made perfect sense. Rolling his eyes, he thought, "It figures that Chance would find himself a girl to woo, while I'm chasing down criminals in Spokane!"

Then, remembering just how close Chance, Dicky and Abner had come to being gunned down themselves, Matthew sobered and walked back inside to assess the damage and try to figure out, with the rest of his team, what to do from here on out.

Three hours later, Matthew and the other's sat in the twilight, discussing the bear attack, recent events in Spokane, and possible future plans. Fatigue and the after-math of fear had left some of them exhausted. Chance was lying on a pallet with his eyes closed and Abner was starting to doze off as well. He never drank alcohol, but he was succumbing to the small dose of laudanum Matthew had put in his coffee.

They had gathered all the bodies together earlier, except for Bill Nash's corpse, and filled the back of the wagon with dead criminals. The wagon sat outside on the entrance road now, covered with a tarp. Matthew planned on traveling the thirteen miles into Wallace tomorrow and dropping the dead crooks off at the sheriff's office.

Bill Nash, meanwhile, was wrapped up tight and lying in the "cold-house." Matthew wanted the Spokane sheriff's office and Bill's family to find the deputy in proper shape when they came to collect him.

Matthew could feel his jaw muscles starting to ache—he had been grinding his teeth, for hours, with rage and frustration. It felt like the whole world was filled with outlaws and no matter what he did or how hard he tried, there was no way to rid himself of them.

Before Chance and Abner dozed off, he had filled his companions in on what transpired in Spokane. They knew about the house fire, of course, but didn't know that their enemies had also tried to torch the newspaper office. They also had no idea how close Matthew had come to being shot down in the street.

It wasn't until Matthew told them what had happened that Chance jerked upright and struggled to his feet. Noticing the new, Australian style hat on his father's head and the small bandage on his hairline, he cried, "Pa! Are you okay? Sounds like you should be home resting rather than chasing bad guys around!"

Matthew, whose head was actually pounding like a kettle drum, said, "Nah, I'm fine now."

After staring at his father with concern for a moment, Chance said, "I'm going to go ahead and close my eyes for a minute. Don't worry, though, I'm listening to every word you're saying..." A few minutes later, Matthew and Dick smiled as snores filled the air.

"So," Dick said. "What do you want to do now?"

Matthew smiled. "One thing I was able to do was petition the Spokane County Commissioner's office. He assures me that Jacob's land deed is valid and binding and, in this case, possession will NOT be considered proof of ownership."

Turning to Jacob, who was hanging on every word, Matthew said, "That's very good news, sir. However, the bad news is, Sheriff Lobey has pulled the plug on extra security, both here in North Idaho and in Spokane." Pausing for a second, he added, "and, he doesn't even know about Bill yet...can't wait to have that conversation!"

He sighed. "This leaves us on our own—which would be all right if I knew that you and Hannah were safe." Noting the stubborn look in Jacob's eyes, Matthew sat up straight. "Jacob, listen to me! I know you don't want to be forced out of your own home, but things are better for you and your family now. This land will stay in your name, no matter who squats on it."

Sitting back, he rubbed the tender scape on his head. "But my men and I need to move on. I've got the crook's scent in my nose and a pretty good idea on where to go from here, but I can't spend any more time protecting your property, okay?"

Jacob, who had seemed ready to nix the very thought of leaving his claim seemed to deflate as Matthew's words sunk in. Thinking for a moment, he asked, "Do you want me and Hannah to move back to your home?"

Matthew nodded. "I had been planning on that but I've changed my mind. I talked with Clyde and Annie Thurston before they boarded a train to Seattle. Apparently, they own a huge mansion in the city. There are plenty of rooms and a wait-staff to help out. They have graciously asked you and your family to stay there with them, at least until this is all over."

As predicted, Jacob muttered, "I don't want to burden those folks or prey on their sympathies…"

"Don't you see?" Matthew exclaimed. "You are both in the same boat and being targeted by the same bunch of criminals! I know, for a fact, that Clyde was hoping you would come and help protect him and his daughter." (A small lie but one that Matthew hoped would seal the deal.)

A different expression came over Jacob's face as he considered the idea that some rich man might need his help. Grinning, he said, "Well, if they need our help, I say we go as quickly as possible!"

Matthew sighed with relief. Actually, Clyde had already hired a private security firm to watch over him and Annie during their stay in the city, but knowing that Matthew could no longer afford to split his resources, the old man had urged Matthew to bring the Lindsays to the city, at least until the matter was settled for once and for all.

"Okay, then." Matthew said, handing Jacob a few bills and a piece of paper with an address and a couple of phone numbers written on it. "Tomorrow we need to take care of business. Chance and I will deal with the dead bodies and the Wallace sheriff, while Dick, Abner and you two jump on the train back to Granville."

Seeing the consternation on Dick and Abner's faces, he added, "Jacob, once you get there, pack your family up and head to Seattle. When you arrive, call one of those numbers and Clyde will send a carriage to pick you and your family up."

Turning to face Dick and Abner, Matthew said, "You two head on back home. Roy has been patient but he needs your help, Dicky. And Abner needs to heal up from that gunshot wound."

Seeing that the younger deputy was fixing to put up a fight, Matthew smiled, "Don't worry, Dicky. The minute I need more help, you'll be the first person I call."

## 19

## BREATHING ROOM

Five days later, Matthew sat in a small café in Spokane, staring morosely out the window as cheerful citizens scurried here and there, intent on their morning errands...innocent of the dark doings and machinations of the criminal element within their midst. He wished that he, himself, was just as naive. Sighing, he shook his head.

Matthew knew that he would never be free of his deadly knowledge—that rotten fruit had been forced down his throat when he was just a boy of twelve. Indeed, he had actively sought out and hunted down criminals for as long as he could remember. Even after he retired from life as a lawman, he had itched to, once again, get his hands on crooks and now, at almost fifty years old, he was just as enmeshed in crime as he had ever been.

He had just come from an interview with Sheriff Lobey and the bitter hurt in the old man's eyes was almost more than Matthew could bear. He knew, as well as

Lobey did, that the deputy's deaths were not Matthew's fault. Still, things had been running smoothly enough during the last two years of Lobey's term as sheriff, until Matthew showed up, asking for help.

Now, the sheriff had three dead deputies on his hands, including Bill Nash, whom Lobey had thought of as a son. The sheriff's coffers were in ruins- what with the numerous fires, shootouts, ambulance calls and general mayhem—all of which seemed to coincide with Matthew Wilcox' untimely arrival.

Matthew had gone to the sheriff's building to give his condolences, say thank you, and goodbye—just as Nash's widow and children streamed, weeping from Lobey's office. The widow Nash had looked up, saw Matthew standing, hat in hand, in the foyer and stopped with a wide-eyed stare. Then, she snarled, "You! If it wasn't for you, my Billy would still be alive!

Her two kids, a boy of about ten and a little girl who was probably no more than five years old, gazed up at their mother, then at Matthew. The little girl turned away, burying her flushed cheeks in her mother's skirts but the boy balled up his little fists and charged. Matthew stood still and took the grieving child's pummeling until two deputies peeled the boy away and sent the family packing.

Matthew sympathized and was more than willing to take the boy's punishment, but when it became clear that Sheriff Lobey also, for some irrational reason, held Matthew to blame for the deputies untimely demise, he made an awkward, hasty retreat and now sat in this café, checking his watch and hoping that Chance would make an appearance sooner, rather than later.

They were slated to take the two o'clock train to Seattle this afternoon, and Chance was having his broken ankle tended to one last time before they traveled west. If Matthew had been angry at his friends Dick and Abner at all, it was over the fact that they had chosen a "home-remedy" over a doctor call for his son's injury.

He realized, though, they made the right decision. Matthew had met that drunken old sawbones named Troy Humphrey in Wallace, and he shuddered. If Dicky had taken Chance in to see that man, his son might have come back home missing a foot, or even a leg.

The only thing that seemed to bring Humphrey any pleasure was talking about the good old days during the Civil War and how the arms, legs, heads and feet of Union and Confederate soldiers, alike, seemed to rain from the skies overhead during that engagement...and how much he missed the "live" action.

Matthew checked his pocket watch again and thought about how deep the roots of corruption were in Lobey's city. He had been appalled to find out that all three men in the warehouse who were brought in for questioning were found poisoned the next morning. That sort of thing occurred, sometimes, but Lobey was aghast that it had happened in his own jail...especially since he prided himself on strict security.

The only possible culprits were the cooks in the sheriff's department kitchens, and after a thorough interview (and an even more thorough beating), two of the three kitchen workers (one was excused as she was an old woman who had worked with Lobey for over twenty years and was as innocent as the day was long) had confessed to being bought off.

Matthew had sat in on that interview and at the end of the day, he did not believe the men knew who was paying them, nor did he believe they were active players in the Trinity gang. Still, the whole thing was taking its toll on lawmen and criminals, alike, and Matthew felt it was high time to beard the dragon in its own den…meaning, it was time to go to Seattle.

Looking up and noticing that he was the only customer in the restaurant, Matthew signaled to the waiter for a coffee refill. Then he saw a tall, handsome, well-dressed man sit down at the next table. Matthew also saw and heard a number of other men pulling out chairs and sitting down at tables next to the newcomer. Feeling a sudden thrill of anxiety, he knew that he had just been surrounded.

The man at the near-by table was probably in his early sixties. He had a full-head of silver-white hair and large, gray eyes. He wore spectacles but had taken them off with a small smile and used his table napkin to clean the lenses as he turned his gaze on Matthew. "My name is Stephen Castle. I work with a group known as the Trinity and I wondered, Mr. Wilcox, if I might have a word?" The man's voice was whisper-soft.

Matthew studied the ten, or so, men occupying the chairs surrounding them. He noted that they were all fairly old, heavily-armed and seemed both calm and, at the same time, more than ready for a fight. As his hand fell, automatically, to his pistol he felt his heart thumping hard in his chest.

When the men watching him also let their hands fall to their gun-grips, Matthew knew that, for now, he was trapped as neatly as a rat in a trap. Lifting both hands and letting them rest on the table in front of him, Matthew stared toward the long counter that separated the kitchen area from the customers.

He saw the cook and his waiter gazing over at him, but then he spied two additional men step up and usher the waiter and the café owner outside to the boardwalk, taking up position beside them on the street.

Turning to face the Trinity member, Matthew said, "What can I help you with?"

Castle smiled. "Why…I am here to help you, sir."

"Hmmm…" Matthew said. "Please, tell me you want before I lose my temper."

Castle frowned, briefly, and said, "Arnie, why don't you bring Mr. Wilcox and me a pot of coffee from the kitchen? The rest of you men back up and give me and the investigator a little breathing room."

A tall, gangly-looking man with a bowler hat and a waxed, gray mustache hustled into the kitchen area, while the rest of the men got up and walked toward the front of the café. Many of them still fingered their pistols but seemed, for the moment, inclined to mind their head honcho's orders.

Arnie brought the coffee and a cup to Castle's table, then went to stand with the other men. Stephen looked into Matthew's face and said, "Do you mind if I join you? The things I want to say to you should stay between the two of us, for now."

Matthew shrugged slightly and watched as the man

got up from his chair and moved over to sit at Matthew's table. Castle poured coffee into his own cup and gestured to Matthew's cup with raised eyebrows.

Matthew said, "No, not right now. Say whatever is on your mind, Castle, and say it quick because I know you're a crook and a murderer and I don't like drinking coffee with dead men."

The older man sighed. "Really, Mr. Wilcox. Your theatrics are unseemly and quite unnecessary. I understand why you might be put-out with me and some of the men under my command, but I am here to help you."

"Help me?" Matthew snarled. "The only way you could help me is for every single one of you to turn yourselves in to the Spokane County Sheriff's Office!" His voice had risen in anger and a number of Castle's men turned around, glaring.

"Well," the older man laughed. "That's never going to happen. These men have been with me since I was just a young man, and not a one of them have had anything to do with the events here in Spokane and Idaho the last few months!"

Taking a sip of coffee, Stephen added, "I can tell you, however, who is involved, where they are, and even how to bring them all down—for good!"

## ONE MAN'S PERSPECTIVE

Castle sat back in his chair and took a sip of coffee, staring over the cup's rim at Matthew's face. He wondered again if this man could be reasoned with, or if he—and everyone Wilcox knew and cared about—would soon be singing a list of their complaints to St. Peter behind his pearly gates.

"Let me explain a few things about myself, sir, before I tell you about the Trinity and how to stop what they are doing," he said, taking another sip and setting the cup down on its saucer. "I come from a long line of attorneys...successful attorneys at law, who can trace their legal prowess clear back to the Revolutionary War."

He paused for a moment, and continued, "However, the Castle and Castle Law Firm is not always as solvent as we might like. We have a lot of social standing and plenty of referrals, but we are defense attorneys for the rich and powerful. This means, sometimes, that we work for future favors and added political power rather than cold cash."

He sighed. "This is the way things are done...at least, at a certain social level," he glanced at Matthew who sat listening with a scowl still etched on his brow. "But...I'm sure you're familiar with how these things are done, Mr. Wilcox."

Matthew sat up and snarled, "I have never bought justice, Mr. Castle!"

Stephen held his hands in the air. "I wasn't referring to how you, in particular, practice law but I am referring to the fact that you and your family are wealthy and travel in the same social circles as my partners and I. Please," he leaned forward and whispered, "Let's not play coy with one another. I am willing to help you out, but I will not suffer your scorn!"

Matthew sat back in his chair, eyes wide open. "How do you know anything about me, or my family?"

Castle smiled. "Tsk, tsk, Mr. Wilcox! I just told you that I come from a powerful firm of attorneys. Half of the men you see standing in the foyer and out on the sidewalk are private investigators, just like you. I, with their help, know just about everything there is to know about you and your family..."

Castle smiled. "I know that you and your son Chance have opened a brand new private detective agency...I know that you own a ranch in the Granville area, along with your step-son Samuel. I know all about your step-daughter Abigal as well, and her family..."

Matthew's green eyes were blazing with fury and Castle paused, "Please, don't be alarmed, sir. I just want you to know that you are not the only one who owns valuable information. Really, I quite admire you!"

Stephen continued, "I have learned a lot about your past. I know about your younger years, and how you were kidnapped by a gang as a boy. I know all about the outlaw Top Hat and the Granville Standoff. I know about your subsequent life as a sheriff and later as a U.S. Marshal. You are quite the character, sir, which is why I chose to talk to you—as equals—before my partners and I are forced to take action against you."

Matthew let the man's words sink in and willed his heart to stop trying to beat its way out of his chest. Swallowing, he decided, at least for now, to go along with Stephen Castle's plans. First, though, he had to make it through this meeting without throttling the man and getting shot for his troubles. Besides, if Castle was actually willing and able to undermine the Trinity, he needed to check his attitude and at least let the man prove his worthiness.

He nodded and said, "I am sorry for my rude behavior. Please, continue..."

Castle grinned. "Apology accepted, Mr. Wilcox. Now, where was I?" He paused for a moment and said, "Oh yes, solvency issues..." He shook his head. "I am the youngest son in the Castle and Castle family firm, you know. Both my older brother and sister are partners, but not I...not until my father passes and, maybe, not even then. So, I have had to make my own fortune."

He poured another cup of coffee, added cream and sugar and said, "I have known the other members of the Trinity since I was just a boy in college. We have made a lot of money together as a team, but mostly on the up and up. Lately though, the oldest of us, who is also the richest, has started to do things I can't—as a man of honor—allow to continue. His name is Edward Branson…"

Watching as Matthew whipped a notebook from his breast pocket and started taking notes, Castle admonished, "Mr. Wilcox, if putting words to paper helps you to remember names and places, fine, but my men and I will not allow you to carry proof of crimes committed out that door. Surely you can understand that?"

Matthew paused and looked up. *Well*, he thought, *it was worth a try, anyway*. Matthew folded the notebook closed and placed it back in his coat pocket. "I'm sorry," he murmured, "Force of habit." (A small lie, but one Matthew had every intention of making into a reality.)

Stephen smiled. "It is Edward who has turned a fairly honest, recent enterprise into an exercise of theft and murder. Edward decided, a year or so ago, that he wants to own a gold mine. He's not smart enough, or frankly, energetic enough to do it honestly, so we came up with the idea of buying out a number of land-owners around a couple of existing mines.

"We hit on the old Oreornogo gold mine in North Idaho. Once owned by a certain Colonel Wallace, there seems to be some questions about the legality of the original claim. We, the Trinity, knew that if we could get our hands on the surrounding properties we would be in a good position to eventually take over control of at least two of the mines in that area."

Stephen sat back on his chair and suddenly, to Matthew anyway, it seemed as though the man was far older than he had originally thought. "You know," Stephen murmured, "Branson has enough money to buy those mines in Wallace outright, but he would rather take what he wants than purchase it honestly…"

Shaking his white mane of hair, Castle went on, "So, we decided to offer cash-out plans to new claim owners throughout the region. For the most part, it worked. We managed to buy twenty-two out of thirty-four claims for just a little more than what the owners originally paid. It's a tough life, you know, mining for gold and silver… tougher than a lot of people realize, and most of those folks were more than happy to recoup their losses and move on."

The older man sighed, "Then, we started to meet resistance. One family after another decided to dig their heels in and stay—no matter how much incentive we offered. Unfortunately, once those same folks heard rumors that we were shelling out more money for their worthless claims, they got stubborn and started demanding outrageous prices for the properties."

"That's when things got ugly, Mr. Wilcox," Stephen said. "My partner and I tried to talk Branson out of his insane quest to own the biggest mine in the area, but he was adamant…and that's when his men started to kill the landowners who dared say no."

"Since then…well, I think you know the rest of the story," Castle stopped talking and stared into Matthew's eyes. "You know, I'm not trying to exonerate myself…or my other partner—whose name I will not mention. I just wanted you to know that neither one of us are happy with the way things are going. I am deeply sorry for the harm that befell the Brazil family, and still threatens the Thurstons."

Matthew stared intently at Castle for a moment. "You said you have a plan?"

Castle grinned. "Yes...well, I think so, anyway. It would depend on whether or not you and your son are good enough actors to play in high society for a while, and if you are willing to travel west of the Cascades, to the Seattle area as quickly as possible...preferably today."

Picking up his napkin again, Stephen Castle wiped his mouth and mustache. Then he added, "I am leaving as well, in..." he glanced at his watch, "a little over an hour."

Looking out the window, he said, "I must warn you, sir...another man—the third partner in the Trinity—is coming to Spokane today. He is coming here to permanently silence you, your son and the Thurstons. He's under orders from Edward Branson, and he'll do whatever Branson wants, but please, if you see him, just run. Do not hurt him in any way."

Seeing the look on Matthew's face, Stephen smiled. "Don't worry! Even now, as we are talking, my men are stalking the man who stalks you. They will keep him under wraps as much as possible but he is, and always has been, a fierce fighter. It would be better if you and your son were not here at all when he arrives."

Ignoring the rage in Matthew's eyes, Castle added, "Let me tell you, quickly, what I think you can do to stop Branson, and then if you agree with my plan, take the train to Seattle. By the time you arrive, this newest threat should be neutralized."

Castle paused, and in a hushed whisper he pleaded, "In many ways, although the third man in our group is the most dangerous, he is also the most vulnerable. He follows Branson blindly, having not done anything else since he was just a boy. Still, he is deadly."

Matthew watched as Castle's eyes sharpened. Following the man's gaze, he looked out the window and saw his son limping down the street toward the café. His hair shone golden-red in the early afternoon sun, and Matthew watched as more than one pretty lady paused what they were doing to follow the young man's progress with hungry eyes.

Castle smiled. "Fine boy you have there, Mr. Wilcox…"

Matthew's heart skipped a beat when Stephen said, "Just so we're clear, I care for the man who seeks you out…just as I know you care for your son. I am prepared to help you take down Edward Branson, as long as my friend and I have immunity for our previous actions."

Castle's eyes grew cold as he added, "However, you need to remember that I have men everywhere. They will do what it takes to stop my associate from hurting you and your boy, but I will know if you do anything to cause my friend…or me, harm."

Staring into Matthew's eyes, he added, "And, if I find out that you did anything to sabotage the man…or me, our deal will be off, my testimony will disappear…and I will send my men to visit all the people you hold most dear."

# HIGH SOCIETY

Two days later, Matthew and Chance sat in an opulent drawing room with Annie and Clyde Thurston. This particular room was only one of the thirty-four rooms in the palatial estate Clyde Thurston called home, in Seattle. The rest of the gray stone mansion boasted ten bedroom suites, an expansive kitchen, a dining room large enough to feed fifty guests, two large living rooms, a parlor, a game room, two offices, a library, five indoor bathrooms, servant's quarters and, like icing on an already delectable cake, an enormous, gilded ballroom.

Matthew was astounded. Although Clyde had admitted he came from a wealthy family, he'd failed to mention just how rich that family had been and, apparently, still were. It was a good thing, though, because ostentatious wealth was a much needed…no, necessary tool in bringing Edward Branson down.

Thinking back over the last few days, Matthew was relieved that the train ride from Spokane to Seattle had been uneventful...except for left-over nerves from his encounter with Stephen Castle, and the fact that a number of men had boarded the train along with he and Chance—many of whom he recognized as being part of Castle's crew.

He had wondered at the time whether Castle had set an ambush, or if the men were spies, or if the men simply lived in Seattle and were headed back home after Castle's show of force. The Trinity member himself was nowhere to be seen.

Matthew and Chance (who'd been told all that had transpired while he visited with the doctor) watched as Castle's men ignored them, and when the train reached the station, they saw most of the men board taxis and carriages without ever glancing back at the two of them.

Sighing with relief, they had smiled when Clyde drove up in a fancy black automobile. But even as they drove toward the Thurston mansion, Matthew couldn't shake the feeling of eyes drilling into the back of his head...that subliminal sensation of being "watched."

Still, two days had passed now and neither he nor Chance had seen the henchmen again, so they were finally able to recuperate and relax a bit before they carried out Castle's plans...which were becoming more complicated by the minute.

Matthew was financially well off, almost embarrassingly so—thanks to his own family fortune and that of his deceased wife. Although he had never been comfortable with the social aspects of his personal fortune, he understood many of the dynamics involved with ultra-wealthy men and their families.

One of the greatest aspirations of a wealthy man in this day and age was political office. Indeed, it followed that money (or the lack thereof) was the driving force behind most laws and legislation. Matthew, being a non-political man, had stayed as far away from those kinds of shenanigans as humanly possible since his stint as County Sheriff.

But he knew that, in many circles, political power was not only desired among the rich—but expected. Unfortunately, he was also aware that some of the biggest crooks in the state of Washington (and probably the whole United States) were politicians.

Matthew didn't believe that all politicians were crooks...but he knew the temptations for men with too much power and money were many, and that even the most honest man could be bought and therefore, corrupted.

There were many avenues men like these could travel in order to achieve success, but two were certainly most helpful—#1- a lot of cash could (and did) pave their way in bricks of gold and, #2—membership with the Freemasons.

Matthew felt a chill. Not because he was worried about the Masons themselves but because that particular fraternal organization was almost freakishly insulated against outsiders. Which, of course, meant it would be very hard to strike Edward Branson through his connections to the society of Freemasons, but that was precisely what Castle was suggesting they do.

Twice Matthew had been approached and asked if he

would consider joining the newly-built Spokane Grand Lodge. The first time he'd said thank you, but no. The second time, however, he had agreed. That was right after he'd hung up his lawyer's shingle and he'd thought that Freemason membership would help advance his budding career.

He was right. For a while, many a closed door had opened for the fledgling attorney, thanks to the Freemasons' influence. That soon came to a stop, though, when it became clear that Matthew Wilcox had no intention of advancing through the many ranks of membership. He didn't hold a grudge against the organization but advancement required a declaration of religious belief.

Too many things had happened in his life for Matthew to feel close to God—any God. He'd seen too much unadulterated evil, and had participated in acts as a lawman that, if he understood the words of the Bible correctly, had already condemned him to the gates of Hell.

He had also never really forgiven God for the losses in his life. Matthew knew that God was not to blame for the death of his Uncle Jon, his wolf Bandit or most recently, the death of his beloved wife Iris. Nor was He the architect of the evil deeds of the outlaws he had run into throughout his life as a lawman. Still, he couldn't help but feel resentment that the Almighty had not done more to protect the loves in his life.

He did, on occasion, attend Temple parties and once in a while, the Presbyterian Church; usually on demand from his daughter Abby for a baptism or Christmas services. But to stand in front of a group of Freemasons and swear his fealty to God was something Matthew knew he was unable to do with complete honesty.

There was another reason Matthew did not advance further into the order...the Freemason's habit of greasing each other's palms. There was nothing technically wrong, or illegal, with this age-old ritual. For centuries, if you were sworn in as a Mason, you were blessed with a large discount through life's every day commerce from other sworn brothers. Ten percent, twenty, thirty...the rumors were rampant and, as with most rumors, sometimes wildly exaggerated.

By the same token, sworn brothers were also expected to donate large portions of their income to charity. Again, rumors abounded, but Matthew himself had seen one Master Mason donate a staggering $5,000 to the tithe basket one Christmas Eve at the local Presbyterian Church.

Knowing that Edward Branson was an exalted Mason Master who had used his Freemason connections not only to swindle hundreds of people out of their life savings, but to rob and murder his way into being one of the world's richest men was a tasty bit of knowledge for an ex-lawman, but an almost impossible hurdle to climb as a private investigator, because of the fraternity's strict adherence to insulation and privacy.

Nevertheless, Matthew knew that criminal behavior was not tolerated amongst the ranks of Freemasonry brothers, and this was what Stephen counted on. All three members of the Trinity were lifelong brothers and Castle knew, to the minute, when Branson's actions had cast the group from being respectable Masons into being outlaws.

Stephen knew Branson prided himself on being an exalted Master...his enormous ego required and relished in it. Being asked by the Freemasons to vacate his position would be tantamount to Edward's ultimate social and personal disgrace.

Sighing, Matthew sat back in his chair and listened as Annie discussed the ball she was preparing to host in two weeks' time. There were a number of moving parts in what was turning out to be an elaborate plan to take Branson down...the grand ball, hopefully, being the culminating event.

First, Clyde was penning a series of candid articles about theft, murder and corruption to run, consecutively, in both the Seattle Times and the Post Intelligencer newspapers. It was a gamble, Matthew knew, but even he was impressed by the small army of security that surrounded the Thurstons and their household.

Clyde knew better than to name any one man in particular as the perpetrator of the crimes in North Idaho and Spokane but he had enough knowledge, certainly, to name the deeds, times and places the foul crimes had been committed, and to point a vague but persistent finger in Branson's direction.

Matthew couldn't help but grin at the thought of how many eyebrows were about to rise in shock when the exposes were finally published...and he couldn't help but wonder how many of society's finest might suddenly decide to decamp to other climes when their complicity in these crimes were exposed.

Secondly, it was Matthew and Chance's job to sow seeds of doubt amongst the movers and shakers in Seattle's high society circles. Bankers and lawyers...judges, political big wigs and, most importantly, Freemasons. These people were the targets and since Matthew was a Freemason member (albeit, a minor one), he was best suited to farm that fertile soil.

Finally, if things went according to plan, the Thurstons would host the season's most sublime ball. Everyone who was anyone would be invited...and that is where Matthew and Chance had decided to spring their trap.

If anyone of them survived that long, that is...

## 22

## THE ELITE

It took three days and an engraved invitation, but Matthew entered the high wrought-iron gates of the Hunter's Club (the most exclusive club in the city) at precisely two o'clock the next Saturday. The odor of high society...fine leather, expensive horseflesh, perfume and aged liquor hit his nostrils almost immediately...carried on the warm afternoon breeze.

A long, sea shell drive wound through park-like grounds. Tall conifers and a colorful assortment of deciduous trees, pale green oaks, trembling aspens and fiery Japanese maples swayed in the salty air...a scenic backdrop to the hundred or so guests attending Judge Ashworth McKinley's annual fencing match and target shoot. A large, gaily-striped tent in the near distance bustled with people and uniformed servants. Matthew smelled meat roasting and heard soft laughter and the tinkling of fluted crystal glasses.

Matthew saw a splendid white Colonial-style clubhouse to his right and the club's stables to his left. A tennis court with its bright green slate peeked through the flowering shrubbery and he could hear the steady thwack, thwack of a tennis ball being lobbed back and forth. A red barn and attending stable were on the left-hand side of the driveway. A small, hand-painted sign reading "TARGET SHOOT" pointed toward the back of the stables.

Matthew looked up, squinting against the sun's glare, and realized that the hazy blue-gray mass in the distance was actually Puget Sound. He heard hounds baying from a hidden kennel and, "Watch out, sir! Coming through..." Matthew watched as a young groom led three beautiful geldings across the drive toward the stable and realized he was holding up traffic.

"Carry on, young man!" a grizzled oldster with a grimy monocle and smelling of urine muttered grumpily in Matthew's ear as he hobbled by, almost tripping over Matthew's scabbard, followed by a very fat woman and two rather plain young girls Matthew guessed were her daughters.

Matthew stepped aside, murmuring an apology and tried to keep his distaste from showing. This was one of the many things he despised about the elite echelons of high society. Having money was a nice thing in itself, he acknowledged. It offered freedom of choice and movement in life, unavailable to those who did not possess it. He considered himself lucky in that he was able to provide a certain level of comfort and security to his loved ones.

However, many folks who did not have ready cash

often hated those who did, which caused a social divide and constant worry for the rich and their progeny. In addition, the wealthy lived in fear of losing their money and the privileges that came with it…social standing, political power and influence. This caused inbreeding, arrogance and a willful disdain of anyone less fortunate than they…which, of course, perpetuated the cycle of the "haves" vs. the "have-nots."

Matthew had no doubt that the corpulent Mamma who had sniffed at him as she and her brood swept by was, even now, trying to secure her family's fortune by finding rich husbands for her less than attractive female offspring. Shaking his head in amusement, he picked up his gun case and made his way around the stables to where the target shoot and fencing match was about to begin.

He walked down a wide pathway spongy with pine needles to a large clearing where he saw a number of men and women standing behind a long ribbon separating the contestants from the targets and seated on a set of grand-stand bleachers. A small bar had been set up near the grandstands and champagne, whiskey and hors d'oeuvres were being served to both participants and spectators. Matthew availed himself of a small glass of whiskey as he studied his competition.

He noticed Judge McKinley right away. Surrounded by a number of aides and hangers-on, the middle-aged man sported an elegant gray suit and matching chin-whiskers. McKinley was known as a staunch Catholic, a stern judge of criminals in his courtroom and, more importantly, (according to Annie's research) held the title of Grand

Master for the largest Masonic temple in Seattle. It was Matthew's duty to woo the judge today...enough so that he and, hopefully, Clyde Thurston as well, could secure a private meeting with the man.

Matthew had his doubts. From what he understood, a Grand Master never admitted to who or what he was unless he or his temple were under duress. Also, Matthew didn't know if he was a good enough shooter anymore to turn McKinley's head. He intended to try, though... if he failed to engage the man's interest, he knew their elaborate plans were for naught and they would have to start all over again with a different (and, unfortunately, less influential) Mason.

Bending over, Matthew picked up his gun case and set it atop a small table provided for each of the contestants. This particular table had his name on it. He extracted his Uncle Jon's matched Buffalo Brass-Framed .44 caliber pistols. Once, long ago, Matthew had been able to hit the "Bull's Eye" each and every time with these guns, but years had passed since he learned how to shoot. Plucking a soft cloth from the case, he ran it over the grips and the barrels of each gun before placing them back onto the velvet keepers.

Then he pulled his swept-hilt rapier sword from its scabbard. Noticing, from the corner of his eye, that many of the spectators had turned to watch, he held the beautiful but deadly antique in the air with a small smile as an errant sunbeam caught the blade's fine edge.

"A fine set of pistols, sir, as I'm sure you know..." a cultured voice spoke from behind Matthew's left shoulder.

Putting the sword carefully in the scabbard again and placing it on the table next to his pistols, Matthew turned around and saw McKinley standing close by. The man was quite handsome, viewed up close, with strong white teeth and sharp, brown eyes. Those dark orbs were shining brightly now as the judge studied the matched pistols. "Pre-Civil War, I presume?" McKinley asked with interest.

"Yes, Sir," Matthew replied. "They were my uncle's guns and he used them gallantly." He knew that mentioning the war was a gamble, but Clyde had checked and found out that McKinley's people had come from Georgia.

The judge studied Matthew's face for a moment, and asked, "North, may I ask, or South?"

Matthew smiled. "He commanded one of the largest battalions in the West Virginia Cavalry, sir."

McKinley's face flushed with pleasure, and he winked. "Not a question one asks lightly these days, is it?"

Matthew returned the man's mischievous grin and said, "No sir, I guess not. Still, in the long run, I thought you should know who had entered your contest today."

The judge stuck his hand out to shake and said, "Ashworth McKinley, sir, at your service."

Gambling again, Matthew met the judge's hand with his own and gave the man a "secret Masonic" handshake. He saw McKinley's eyes widen for a moment and then the he stepped back with a smile as Matthew replied, "Matthew Wilcox. Pleased to meet you."

The judge studied Matthew's face for a moment and

said, "Ah, yes. You were a last-minute contestant entered by the Thurston estate, am I right?"

"Yes," Matthew answered. "My friend Clyde and I wanted a chance to meet with you, privately, Sir, over a matter that we thought you would find interesting...more than interesting, actually. More like urgent..."

McKinley's eyebrows rose in skepticism. "Mr. Wilcox. Often, over the years, men and women who are in trouble with the law have tried to approach me...to sway me, if you will, when I am outside the confines of my court-room. They seem to think that I can either be bought off or moved to judge their actions more...leniently, if I first become friends with them."

McKinley's brown eyes seemed to bore into Matthew's face as he added, "I truly hope that you are not one of those misguided souls?"

Matthew shook his head. "No, sir...this matter has nothing to do with me, except for the fact that I am currently working as a private investigator for the Thurston family. The reason Clyde and I are seeking an audience with you, is that the criminals we are after are directly related to you..."

McKinley looked flabbergasted. Stepping forward to inquire further, he was interrupted by the sound of the starting whistle. Frowning distractedly, he said, "Mr. Wilcox, frankly, I don't know whether to be alarmed or offended. Still, I am intrigued. Good luck with the compe-tition and please, after you are finished, meet me in the clubhouse...I will make sure you are on the guest list."

Matthew nodded, and watched Judge McKinley make his way to the grandstand area. A foppish young man stepped up to a lectern and started yelling instructions to the ten contestants. This was a fairly common, timed elimination match, and Matthew listened with half an ear, thinking, *Well, this is going according to Hoyle!*

Realizing that he had just used one of his son's favorite sayings, Matthew loaded his pistols and readied himself for the contest. He had worried that he would need to excel in this target shoot and later, in the fencing match to gain McKinley's attention. He had once been an outstanding swordsman and he knew that, even at the age of forty-nine, he would perform well.

Shooting was another matter entirely. Although he had always come out on top of the numerous gun fights in his life, he knew it was the hidden demon that lived in his soul that took control of his guns during those moments. To stand in front of a passive target now, however, and try to hit the 10-mark was something he wasn't sure he could do with any accuracy...especially while being timed.

Sighing with relief, Matthew put wads of cotton in his ears and watched as paper targets were pinned to the target posts. Now that McKinley had agreed to meet with him despite his scores in this contest, Matthew relaxed and waited for the whistle to blow. A few seconds later, his pistol fire joined that of nine other shootists, as the first volley of gunfire rang out in the warm afternoon air.

## 23

## THE MEETING

Four and a half hours later, Matthew met Judge McKinley in a small upstairs office in the clubhouse. He was sore and tired but pleased with the results of both contests. He had acquitted himself well, and received hearty handshakes and numerous invitations to enter future matches being held throughout the Seattle area over the next few months.

Even knowing he had no intention of accepting the invitations, and that as soon as he and Chance neutralized the threat to the Thurstons and brought the perpetrators to justice they'd be heading back to Granville, it didn't diminish the pride he felt at besting men half his age during the sporting events.

He was given permission to use the men's bathhouse after the match, where an elderly restroom attendant handed him a warm towel and a bar of scented soap with a small bow. Matthew shook his head at the pretentious show of wealth, but his attitude did not diminish the pleasure of washing the sweat and grime from his tired carcass.

After showering and dressing in a clean set of clothes, he went to the Clubhouse bar for a quick shot of whiskey. Matthew noticed a few patrons glancing his way in a friendly manner and was wondering if he'd need to field more invitations when he was approached by a man in his early thirties. He was a slight fellow with round spectacles and thinning hair.

His shy smile was genuine as he presented a card. "Hello, my name is Ian Revell. I have been sent to escort you to the judge…"

Matthew took the card and gave the younger man a friendly grin. "Thank you…just let me finish my drink." He upended the whiskey glass, set the empty tumbler on the counter, and put a bill on the bar to pay for the drink. Then, he turned and followed the young man up a set of stairs to one of the many rooms set aside for private meetings.

Ian knocked on a fine oak door and opened it when he heard, "Come!" from inside the room. Matthew followed him and saw McKinley sitting in one of two chairs facing mullioned windows overlooking the ninth hole of a golf course. There was a desk to the right and a small bar on the left. Couches, side tables, and a chaise lounge took up the rest of the space.

The room itself glowed amber as the late afternoon sun caressed the wall's polished wood paneling and Matthew paused for a moment, debating whether or not he should take his boots off before stepping onto the beautiful Turkish rugs on the floor.

He heard the judge chuckle. "I'm sure the bathroom attendant cleaned and polished your boots, sir, while you were showering. Please, come and sit by me. We are having a particularly fine sunset tonight."

Blushing slightly at being read so easily by the man, Matthew walked across the room and sat down. The view was, indeed, quite beautiful. Looking past the golf links into the far distance Matthew saw Puget Sound's waters stained pink and lavender from the sun's last rays, reflecting its luminous pallet onto the fog banks sitting high above the turbulent depths.

The golfers below were mere shadows and Matthew saw many of them picking up their bags and clubs to hasten inside where it was warm and dry. Judge McKinley murmured, "I, for one, sometimes feel ashamed to be a part of this embarrassment of riches, especially since I so often see the effect poverty has on the men and women who pass through my courtroom. Still... on nights like this, I feel God's blessings and rejoice."

Matthew nodded in agreement, starting slightly when Ian asked, "Mr. Wilcox, may I bring you a whiskey, or perhaps a cup of coffee?"

Matthew replied, "Coffee...black please, Ian. Thank you."

Ian brought Matthew a cup and stood back by the far wall as Judge McKinley said, "Well, I must say, your words have set my head to spinning, Mr. Wilcox. Pray, tell me what your investigation has turned up and how these events pertain to me."

Matthew had been thinking of nothing else most of the afternoon, but now that the time to buzz in the judge's ear was at hand, he wasn't sure how to proceed. Should he start at the very beginning? Or, cut to the chase and inform the Grand Master that one of the other masters in his fraternal organization was as dirty as a shipyard rat?

And what about the young man standing back in the shadows...was he allowed to hear temple business? Matthew glanced over his shoulder to where Ian stood and then stared at McKinley with the question in his eyes.

The judge sighed. "Okay, first, you should know that Ian is my nephew by law. He is also a trusted confidant and a fine lawyer. More importantly, he is an esteemed lodge member who, even now, is aspiring to heights within the Freemasons you could not hope to attain." Matthew gazed at McKinley in surprise.

The judge grinned, adding, "Surely you didn't think I would grant you an invitation without doing my home-work first! While you were still participating in the contests, I had Ian call a number of sources. We know who you are and what you and your son do for a living. I know that you are a good and honorable man. I also know that you are a first level Freemason who showed a lot of nerve by using a third level handshake!"

Matthew squirmed in embarrassment. "I am sorry, Sir. It's just that Clyde and I felt that we needed to do some-thing—and fast—to stop a series of events perpetrated by another Freemason in this city. We felt that you, more than anyone else, could help put an end to this devilry... Were we wrong?"

McKinley frowned. "No, you were right. That's why I want to hear everything you have to say. Know before you start, that neither I nor Mr. Revell will speak to Temple business but we are all ears, and if I can help, I will." Turning to the younger man, McKinley said, "Ian, please bring that bottle of brandy over here, along with two glasses. I have the feeling we might need it."

Finally, McKinley said to Matthew, "Start at the beginning, Mr. Wilcox, so I can make a solid determination. We'll break for dinner in an hour."

So, starting at the very beginning, Matthew told the Grand Master of the Seattle Freemasons everything he knew about Edward Branson and the so-called Trinity.

Three days earlier, Timothy Farnsworth stepped out of Branson's dining room onto the flagstones of an elaborate patio and statuary. The old man sat in his wheelchair by a glass-topped table, studying a large notebook. A number of Branson's henchmen stood amongst the white marble statues of Greek gods. They looked both comically incongruous and oddly ominous in their matching black suits.

Walking up to the table, Farnsworth asked, "Where is Stephen?"

Not bothering to look up from his notebook, Branson replied, "He's not coming. Sit down, Timothy. We need to talk."

Feeling a chill settle over him, despite the warm afternoon sunshine, Farnsworth sat in one of the chairs surrounding the table. "May I?" he asked, making a move toward a pitcher of iced tea sweating on the tabletop.

Branson glanced at over at him, finally. For a moment, judging by the look on the old man's face, Farnsworth thought his request for refreshment would be denied. The chill settled further into his bones as he studied Branson's icy gray eyes.

Finally, Branson shrugged. "Go ahead, I don't care."

Farnsworth sat back in his chair without touching the pitcher. "What's going on, Edward? Why are you so angry...and why isn't Stephen here today? We have never met without all members present." Timothy's eyes were wide with equal parts fear, worry and anger.

Branson closed the large notebook with a sigh. Then he refilled his glass and poured a glass of tea for his partner. Sitting back in his chair, Branson said, "We have been betrayed, Timmy. By none other than our old friend, Stephen Castle."

Farnsworth almost choked on his drink. "What?" he grabbed a napkin and groped at the moisture on his chin and lips in shock.

Branson smiled. "You saw no sign of Wilcox or his son when you traveled to Spokane, did you?"

Farnsworth gaped. "I was just about to make a full report, Edward, but apparently there is no need. What, are you spying on me now?"

Branson shrugged. "No, not really. I actually set my spies on Castle." Noting the look on Farnsworth's face, he added, "The way he has been acting lately...his disapproval of my actions —his constant doubts—have made me re-think his commitment to the Trinity. So, after he left...the last time we met, I activated two of my spies within his ranks.

Timothy squirmed. "You actually have spies following us?" He felt like a fool after the words left his mouth. Of course Branson spied on them...he knew it and had always known it, although the knowledge rankled. Still, knowing that Stephen had been betrayed by one of his own men made his heart pound with dread.

Branson gazed at him with lizard-like eyes, not bothering to answer Timothy's question.

Farnsworth decided to let the moment pass, while he collected his thoughts. "Well," he ventured, "what, exactly, has Stephen done to betray us?"

Branson took a sip of tea and said, "My spies tell me that Stephen met with Matthew Wilcox—at the same time you were en route to Spokane. According to them, Stephen spilled the beans about our activities in North Idaho and the Spokane area. He has also enlisted Wilcox in some sort of scheme to bring the Trinity down in flames..." The old man's lips twisted bitterly. "They were unable to ascertain what this scheme entails, but I know that we must act—now!"

Farnsworth felt the blood leave his face and gasped slightly as an old, familiar pain ran up and down his left arm. Rubbing at the offended limb, he thought, Could it be true? I know Stephen is growing tired of the ever-climbing death count in our latest endeavor, and he is sick of Branson's constant bullying, but would he really betray me?

Knowing Stephen's strict code of honor, though, and understanding that his oldest, dearest friend would not allow himself to be pushed beyond a certain point of conduct, Timothy realized that he had just answered his own questions.

Sighing in sorrow, he asked, "What do you want to do about it, Edward?"

Branson glared. "I want you to finish what you started, Timothy! Kill Wilcox and his son... finish off the Thurston's and..." the old man paused for a moment, staring past his men and the splendid garden statuary. "Then you need to kill Stephen Castle, his family and everyone who works for him."

## 24

## CHANCE AT HIGH TEA

"I don't like it," Matthew growled.

Chance sighed. "Pa, we'll have three security guards with us when we go. Plus, if anything goes wrong, you know I can protect Annie and Hannah…"

Matthew, who had awoken the next morning and heard of Annie's scheme, stopped short of his reply when Hannah said, "…and you know I can shoot the eye out of a running rabbit, right?"

Both he and Chance spun around and saw an angelic vision in the doorway of the parlor. Chance's mouth dropped open as he saw the girl he was falling in love with, (despite her penchant for over-large men's shirts and sturdy leather britches) dressed in a black and lavender silk dress. Her dark, glossy hair was piled high on her head and smoky ringlets framed her blue eyes and exotic cheekbones.

She was truly beautiful and Matthew grinned in appreciation as his son blushed and stuttered in confusion. Hannah bowed her head in acknowledgment of the young man's admiration and then turned to face Annie Thurston, who had come up behind her in the hallway. "Annie," she said, "Mr. Wilcox doesn't want us to go!"

Annie was a sight to behold as well. Her dress was a rich peach chiffon, her lush brown hair twisted into braids and wound at the back of her neck in an intricate knot. The pearl earrings and necklace she wore gleamed as she swept into the room and glared, briefly, at Matthew before taking a chair.

"Honestly, Matthew," she said. "You must know that there is a time-honored way of introducing a young girl into 'society.' I can't just announce that there is going to be a coming-out ball and expect anyone to show up unless I go through the proper channels, first! Besides," she added, "calling on Fanny Castle will serve two purposes… not only is she an old family friend, and the premier social hostess in the Seattle area, we can put a bug in her ear about what her husband is doing."

She sat back in her chair with a small smile. "Stephen and Fanny seem like an estranged couple, but they're not. From what I have gathered over the years, they are very close. If I can convince Mrs. Castle that her husband's life is in danger and that he is trying to bring Edward Branson down, with our help, I am sure she will be only too happy to lend a hand in our plans."

Annie stared up at Matthew with wide eyes. "Matthew, I realize that you are used to going it alone, but this time, you are going to need all the help you can get. Let Hannah and I, along with your son, open doors that, right now, are closed to you."

Matthew studied the faces that surrounded him and knew Annie was right. He had no clue how to orchestrate a high-society ball or, for that matter, how to act like he even belonged to the more elevated peerage needed to pull off their sting operation.

Shoulders drooping, he murmured, "Okay, I know when I'm beat. Still…" he turned to his son. "You have made arrangements for the best guards to accompany you, right?"

His son nodded. "Yes, Pa. They are good men. We'll go straight to Mrs. Castle's house, have tea, talk a little while and then, come straight back here."

"When are you leaving?" Matthew asked.

Annie said, "Our meeting takes place in a little over an hour. It will take about a half hour to get there, so we should be heading out soon." She walked up and put a gloved hand on Matthew's sleeve. "Thank you, Matthew, for trusting us. We'll be back before you know it." Turning to Chance, she said, "There is a change of clothes laid out on your bed, Chance. Hurry now, so we're not late!"

Matthew watched as Chance scurried off to change clothes and wished there was something he could do, or say, to change today's events but he knew that his fears were probably groundless. Too much had happened to the ones he loved, though, to ever sit easy when it came to criminals and their doings.

He walked over to the room's large buffet table and helped himself to eggs, bacon and bread as the rest of his friends and family scurried about in preparation. Finally, Chance stepped into the room and his father couldn't help but stare. "Well, you dandy up real nice, son..." Matthew said with a grin.

Chance pulled at the dark green silk bowtie at his neck and grimaced. "There's a good reason I hate dressing up in monkey suits, Pa!" Although the young man clearly felt uncomfortable in his new duds, he looked as though he had been born to it—which, of course, he had, although Matthew had never forced him to participate in high-society events.

Dove gray pants and a matching suit jacket fit him like a glove and a snowy white shirt seemed to illuminate his red hair, which Chance had tied back in a neat queue. Annie had also picked out a vest in shades of blue, green, gray and rust. The garment spoke of wealth and plenty—an affectation necessary if they hoped to blend in to the rarified circles of Seattle's higher echelon.

Matthew stood up and extended his hand. "Good luck, son. Be on your guard at all times. I know that, even as we speak, forces are moving against us!"

"Chance shook his father's hand. "I know it, too, Pa. We'll be careful, I promise!"

Two hours later, Chance, Annie, Hannah and Fanny sat in a lovely, feminine tea room in the Castle House. Tea and small crust-less cucumber, fish paste and egg sandwiches had already been served and the dishes cleared away for the arrival of sweet cakes and cookies.

Fanny Castle sat in pensive silence, staring at the tips of her velvet house shoes as she processed the information Annie Thurston had just given her. At first, she had been somewhat irritated that Annie was clearly trying to introduce a low-born woman into high-society circles. Fanny did not consider herself a snob, but after taking one look at the young woman, she had known that the girl was no debutante.

Oh, she was lovely and her clothes were impeccable, of course, (thanks to Miss Thurston) but once Hannah's snowy white gloves came off, the girl's rough palms and broken fingernails were tell-tale enough to inform the older woman that the girl was a poseur.

In addition, proper young ladies were taught to never look their betters (or an oldster) in the eye, and this little miss stared back at her as fearlessly as a cat at a mouse!

Still, Hannah seemed sweet enough and so did her companion, a handsome young man named Chance Wilcox. He did seem to belong, somehow, to the upper-class but he acted as if that knowledge brought him no joy and the clothes he wore...no comfort. Still, Fanny believed in bearding the goat.

Once the tea was brought in from the kitchen and her servants left the room, she had turned to Annie and said, "No offense to you, my dear, or your guests but...you are proposing that I introduce a 'nobody' to society?"

Hannah looked down at her lap, blushing bright red in humiliation. Annie put her hand on the girl's sleeve in comfort, glancing over at Chance who acted like he wanted to give the old woman a piece of his mind.

Smiling, she said to Fanny, "It's a ruse, of course, as I'm sure you know. Now, if you will allow me to explain?" Twenty minutes later, Fanny sat in silence...both horrified and, unfortunately, not in the least bit surprised.

Fanny and Stephen Castle had been married when she

was only a teenager, a silly and romantic sixteen-year-old. She (and her concerned parents) carried a secret...one that caused her great shame. Fanny's lower spine was as bent as a willow switch...the result of a brief but terrifying bout with polio. The condition was not life-threatening but it did cause a great deal of pain and made sexual intercourse almost impossible to endure.

Once her wealthy father had announced the match, Fanny was both overjoyed at being wed to the handsome young attorney and terrified that he would reject her and her body in disgust. To her great relief, Stephen did not seem to mind in the least. The money in Fanny's family was enticement enough, of course, but the young man honestly seemed to like her.

They had been married for over thirty years now and although Fanny knew Stephen had entertained a number of mistresses over the many decades of their union he was a loyal, gentle and loving husband and, more importantly, her best friend. There had only, ever, been one fly in the ointment and that was Stephen's lack of money.

She couldn't have cared less. Francis (Fanny) Blyght had been extremely wealthy as a young woman, and now that her parents were dead and buried she was one of the wealthiest women in America. She had always made her fortune available to her husband, and gladly, but Stephen was embarrassed—almost resentful of his "secondhand" wealth and had always done everything he could think of "to be his own man."

Fanny sighed in regret. Time and again, whenever she met with her accountant, she was given reports on her husband's endeavors. Sometimes Stephen did very well, indeed. Despite his small salary (which he faithfully deposited into Fanny's bank account every month), he had turned a profit on a number of business ventures. His excited joy and pride were evident and served to diminish the fact that many of his schemes failed, miserably.

Although Fanny had always paid off his debts, Stephen's financial solvency was one topic they never discussed, at least if she wanted the pleasure of his company at all. Shaking her head, Fanny now realized that Stephen's recent absences lately, must stem from his relationship to that scoundrel, Edward Branson.

She had always hated Edward, both for the sway he held over her beloved husband and the way Branson sometimes stared at her when he thought she wasn't looking. Suppressing a chill, Fanny knew that the man judged her and found her...wanting in every way...and completely disposable.

Turning to Annie Thurston, Fanny said, "First, you need to elaborate on what Stephen has gotten himself into and then..." the old woman stared at Hannah for a moment, "we shall plan a coming-out ball for your young friend."

## 25

# AN UNFORTUNATE TURN OF EVENTS

Chance wandered about the small parlor and made his way into a library as the women made plans for the upcoming ball. He was bored and wondered how long the preliminary preparations would take...knowing his Pa, Chance had no doubt that if too much time passed, Matthew would be sending out the Cavalry to fetch them back to the Thurston house.

He plucked a book of poetry from the floor to ceiling shelves and made his way to an arm chair by the fireplace to wile the time, but paused by a window to catch a glimpse of the outside gardens before he sat down to read.

He pulled a long, velvet panel aside and peered out at the front lawn, the high wrought iron fence surrounding the property and the two big, security gates standing guard at the street. One of the gates was shut but the other was open, slightly, and seemed to be hanging askew of its supporting pole.

Frowning in alarm, Chance looked closely at the vast

grounds of Castle's estate. Nothing seemed out of place but long, dark shadows stretched across the grass-like fingers grasping for purchase toward the house proper. Not knowing how he knew, Chance realized, suddenly, that their security had been breached.

At that precise moment, the window in front of which he stood shattered, sprinkling his vest and pants in a hundred tiny shards of broken glass. Chance felt a sting on his right wrist, saw blood and lunged quickly to the left, to stand behind brick and lath rather than in an assassin's sights.

"Ladies, we are under attack!" he shouted. "Please arm yourselves and hide!"

He heard a small squeal of alarm from the adjoining room and then Hannah hollered, "We're okay, Chance. Be careful..." Chance heard a door closing and hoped it was the sound of the women finding their way to safety.

Chance stared out the open doorway of the library into the hallway and wondered where the three guards were...had they been overcome or were they on the prowl, looking for the unwelcome intruders? He reached into his shoulder holster, grabbed his .38 revolver and groped, also, for the .22 in his right boot.

He moved swiftly to the hallway and peered right and left toward the formal parlor. Immediately, he saw the still form of a man lying on the polished plank floor by the front doors. It was too dark in the house to make out who the man was, but Chance's heart sank in his chest. He, himself, had assigned one of the guards to that precise spot, while the other two guards were stationed on the front porch.

Biting his lower lip, Chance limped gingerly to where the man lay in the shadows. Cursing the pain that accompanied his movements, he stared at the guard's body and saw the red gash on his neck that stretched from one ear to the other. Knowing that the man was dead, Chance tiptoed past a puddle of blood and peered through lace curtains by the front window.

Looking to his left, he could see the toes of someone's boots pointing skyward and he cursed under his breath. Whoever had breached the property was, apparently, a master at knife work and knew how to operate in complete silence. Feeling the flesh on the back of his neck crawl, Chance knew that his duty lie in protecting the women in his care.

Holding his gun high, he lurched down the hallway again and entered the tea room. Looking right and left, actually feeling (if only in his imagination) the bite of honed steel on the soft flesh under his chin, Chance moved toward the back of the room. He figured there was some sort of bolt hole hidden there—otherwise, he would have seen the ladies leaving the tea room earlier.

Chance had taken about eight steps when something registered in his peripheral vision. He stopped short and stared at a man who now sat in Fanny Castle's recently vacated chair. He was an older man—probably in his middle sixties. His dark, thinning hair was oiled to a glossy sheen, and his fine, black day suit bulged at the shoulders and upper arms—a testament to the man's size and strength, despite his advanced years.

He was wiping blood and gore from the blade of a long machete-style knife and staring at Chance with wide, almost friendly eyes. "Who are you?" the man asked.

Chance was trying to keep from trembling, and wondering whether he had enough time to point and fire his pistol before that sharp, gleaming weapon impaled him like a butterfly on a display board.

The man frowned and picked up the large caliber pistol that sat next to him on the arm of the chair. Pointing it at Chance's nose, he said, "Who are you and what are you doing in Stephen's house?"

"My...my name is Chance Wilcox. I am here to plan a ball," Chance stuttered as the mouth of that oily, black pistol studied every pore on his face. He felt like an idiot...a small, scared idiot, afraid of the schoolyard bully.

"Well, Chance, who wants to go to the ball, why don't you let the ladies out of their bolt hole...it's just there, by that little painting."

The gun moved to the left a bit and Chance turned around to look. Sure enough, there was a sort of door inset into the wall's paneling. One push, Chance thought, and the hidden doorway would sag open.

Turning to face the man in the chair again, Chance knew there was no way in hell he would expose the ladies in his care to this awful killer, unless it was over his own dead body. "No, I will not." He replied in a flat voice.

The man smiled. "Oh, so the boy who wants to dance has teeth!"

Chance felt his fear turn into anger and he was glad. If he was to die here today, he wanted his death to be hard-fought, and achieved with some sort of dignity. "You bet I do, Mister, and you'll feel my bite if you harm a hair on those women's heads!"

The man stopped smiling and stared up at Chance with solemn eyes. "Yes, Mr. Wilcox. I believe you would do your very best. Where is your papa today?"

Chance was, once again, shocked to his toes. *Who is this man who knows me and my Pa?* he thought. "What does he want? Oh Pa...what should I do?"

"That's none of your business, sir." Chance snarled. "Now, who are you and what do you want?"

"My name is Timothy Farnsworth, Chance. I was sent here today to assassinate my oldest and closest friend. Where is Stephen, do you know?"

Chance shook his head. "No, I don't know where he is. The only people here today are innocent!"

Farnsworth barked in laughter. "Innocent... you? I guess if hunting down and destroying the Trinity is the act of an innocent man, you and your father are as white as the driven snow! Now, call Fanny out here right now. I want to speak with her for a few minutes before I go."

Chance was steeling himself to die, after he denied the man a second time, when he heard the double snick of the hidden door behind him. Keeping his eyes on Farnsworth, Chance held one hand in the air behind him and said, "Mrs. Castle, no! Go back inside, where it's safe!"

Ignoring him, Fanny saw Timothy Farnsworth, her husband's oldest and dearest friend, sitting in her favorite damask armchair. "Timmy! What is happening, my friend?" The old woman rushed to her uninvited guest in a rustle of taffeta and lace and knelt by his feet. Chance stood still, mouth agape, as the two older people embraced.

Hannah and Annie came to stand by his side. Chance looked down at his new love and saw that she held her small .22 pistol in her hand, and Annie had somehow gotten her hands on a long, silver letter-opener. None of their weapons seemed necessary, though.

Grasping Hannah and Annie's elbows, Chance pushed them gently out into the hallway. "Go now! I don't know if Farnsworth brought any men with him, but it's not safe here...GO!"

For a moment, it looked as if the women might argue, but Annie grasped Hannah's arm and dragged her out the front door. "We'll call the police, right away!" Annie cried as she left the house.

For some reason, Chance felt that the police were unnecessary. Of course, the murderer inside of Fanny Castle's tea-room needed to pay for his crimes...needed to be stopped, but Chance didn't think the police would help matters.

Stepping back inside the small tea room, Chance sat down and watched as the two older people talked. Fanny held a lace hankie to her eyes, trying, in vain, to stop tears from falling, while Tim Farnsworth held her left hand and spoke in a tone too low for Chance to hear.

Fanny shook her head in denial and at one point her voice rose enough for Chance to hear her say, "No, Timmy, don't!"

Chance fingered his pistol again, wondering whether he should just put the old man down when he heard

Farnsworth say, "I have no other choice, Fanny! Surely you know how I feel about Stephen."

Fanny nodded her head, and Chance thought she said, "Yes, my dear, and he loves you too, with all of his heart."

Then, before Chance had the time to make a decision —one way or the other—Farnsworth leaned forward, kissed Fanny Castle on the cheek, picked his pistol up and put a bullet in his own temple.

Chance stood up in shock as Fanny Castle cried out in mourning.

## 26

## A SORRY AFFAIR

Fanny Castle's butler rushed into the room. He stared at the body on the floor for a moment and at his mistress' blood-soaked gown and horrified face. Then he led her, gently, out of the tea room. Chance, like most witnesses to suicide, felt shocked, angry and nauseated.

On one hand, Farnsworth was clearly a dangerous man and had done many terrible things for the Trinity and his friend, Edward Branson. He should have stood trial and, hopefully, rotted in jail for his many misdeeds. He should have answered for his crimes!

Instead, some terminal point within the man's soul had been breached. He had been asked to perform a crime so heinous that his heart had broken in two. He had been asked to choose between his two oldest friends and, in the end, had chosen to terminate his own existence, rather than harm either of them.

Filled with pity, Chance walked over to where

Timothy Farnworth lie on the floor between a toppled chair and a high credenza by the wall. Blood had splattered everywhere, and Chance felt rage take over again. The man's ruined face was, thankfully, turned down toward the Oriental rug, but that hadn't stopped a spray of gore from covering—and ruining—a six-foot radius of Fanny's fine tea room.

"What a mess..." Chance murmured, feeling equal parts shame and horror at his own callousness and fury for Farnsworth's selfish immolation—not only did the man perform his final, bloody act in his best friend's house but he did it right in front of a woman he clearly loved!

"Prick..." Chance whispered, and looked up as a number of policemen filled the room. "Put your gun down!" one of the officers cried.

Chance stared at the pistol in his own hand and placed it, carefully, on the credenza. Then he put his hands in the air as he saw a number of police-issue firearms pointing his way.

"Step away from the body, sir," one of the policemen said. Chance took two long steps backward, out of the line of fire.

"Take your guns off my son!" a familiar voice rang out and Chance saw his father standing in the doorway. Matthew looked him up and down, and said, "Are you okay, son?"

Chance felt tears sting his eyes, but he nodded stoically and said, "Yes, Pa. Mr. Farnsworth decided to put an end to things right here in Mrs. Castle's tea room."

"I see that," Matthew replied. "...and Mrs. Castle, is she alright?"

Chance nodded. "Yes sir. Shook up some, but unharmed."

The sheriff in charge listened as the two detectives spoke and decided that they...and the frantic phone call from Annie Thurston...were on the level. "You can put your guns down, men," he said, watching as his deputies holstered their pistols.

Turning to Matthew, the sheriff said, "So, this can be written down as a domestic dispute and simple suicide?"

Although this was much, much more than a domestic dispute or a simple suicide, Matthew was not prepared to involve the Seattle city police in this case. Not only did he, himself, have an unfortunate history with the King County sheriff's department, but the sheriffs tended to run their own program and agendas, despite a civilian's experience or knowledge of the case at hand.

Nodding in agreement, he said, "Yes sir, I think so. My friend Annie Thurston, my son here, and his young lady friend were simply planning a ball with Mrs. Castle, when this man burst in. Luckily, Annie was able to escape and call you for help." Looking the older, grizzled lawman in the eye, Matthew added, "Thank you for arriving so quickly, sir."

"Well, we will need to speak with Mrs. Castle now, and the rest of you at some point in the future...probably within a day or two," the sheriff warned.

"Absolutely, whatever you need," Matthew replied, respectfully.

Turning back to his deputies, the sheriff barked, "You

two…wrap that body up and take it downtown to the mortuary. Pete, you take down these men's addresses and phone numbers and Hal…you come with me to interview Mrs. Castle!"

Turning back to face Matthew, the sheriff said, "Miss Thurston told me that you two are private detectives?"

Matthew wondered if the legal shoe was about to drop. Nodding in the affirmative, Matthew said, "Yes, Sir…the Wilcox and Son Detective Agency—out of Spokane—at your service."

The sheriff harrumphed. "Well, I'm sure you are aware that you need a special license to operate in King County, right?" The old man's eyebrows rose querulously over inquisitive, brown eyes.

Matthew grinned, and lied through his teeth. "Yes, sir. Honestly, we are not here for work at all. Chance and I are simply here to visit with old friends and attend a ball…"

Green eyes met brown in a silent standoff and then the sheriff stepped back. "Okay then, please don't leave town without calling the sheriff's office first, and try to stay out of trouble this time, Mr. Wilcox, while you are visiting our fair city."

The sheriff gave a small, knowing grin as he turned away and Matthew suddenly realized that this man knew exactly who he was—despite the years that had passed since he, himself, had put the King County sheriff's department through the public and legal grinder for conspiracy and graft.

Oh well, Matthew thought, at least he's going to let us

go on our way, rather than hold us on some sort of trumped-up charge, for revenges' sake.

Looking at his son, who was watching as the two deputies rolled Farnsworth onto a police-issued tarp, Matthew said, "Let's head back to the Thurston's house, Chance."

The young man started and then, looking a little ashy, he said, "Yeah, let's get out of here!"

---

A few minutes later, Matthew and Chance drove back to Clyde Thurston's home in a borrowed car. The day was still sunny, although Chance could see fog rising up like a large, gray ogre over the downtown area. He shivered as if the fog's clammy embrace had reached out to touch him, personally.

Matthew glanced over at him and murmured, "Death is never an easy thing to witness, Son. I would worry about you if you weren't a little bothered by today's events."

Chance sighed. "Yeah, it was a close thing, I think. I have no doubt that Farnsworth would have killed every single one of us if Mrs. Castle hadn't have been there…"

Matthew nodded in agreement. "I have seen it time, and time again. Even the most hardened criminal has a weak spot and, believe me, lawmen know how to use those weaknesses against them. I'm just shocked that

Branson is so ready to turn on his own men…it's going to make a messy situation even messier."

They rounded a corner and turned onto one of the wide, tree-lined avenues leading to Thurston's home. The houses and shops in this part of town were glossy and opulent, befitting one of the cities preeminent neighborhoods.

Matthew grimaced. "Now I have some answering to do to the lead man in Clyde's security force. Also, I'm not sure whether Mrs. Castle will still want to host this ball, now that her husband's crimes have come home to roost."

"I bet she'll want to do something- if it means protecting her husband." Chance replied. "Annie was right, Pa. Stephen and Fanny Castle are still real close. If this dance helps to keep him safe, Fanny will do her part."

Matthew stared at the road ahead of them and saw that some sort of disturbance was taking place a few, scant blocks from Thurston's house. His heart constricted in worry. Had Branson's men somehow breached Clyde's security… had yet another fire been set to burn them out?

Indeed, smoke was rolling down the road toward them. Automobiles, carriages and freight wagons were stopped in the middle of the street and many people had gotten out of their vehicles to stare at whatever was taking place in the distance.

Matthew and Chance glanced at one another with worried expressions and got out of the car to see for themselves what was going on. Walking toward a black carriage that was parked, haphazardly, about fifty feet away, both of them covered their mouths against the plumes of black smoke rolling their way.

Stepping up to a man in fancy livery, Matthew said, "Hello! What's going on, do you know?" He coughed a little as a particularly noxious finger of smoke stung his throat and eyes.

The old man started a little and said, "Well, it sounds like somebody put dynamite, or something in a judge's car!"

Matthew felt a chill of misgiving...surely it wasn't the same judge he had visited with just last night? "Do you know which judge it was, sir?" he asked the coachman.

The man shook his head. "Nah, I wouldn't know one judge from t'other, and I wasn't told a name. You might have better luck with those folks there in that fancy car, though..."

Matthew followed the man's pointing finger with his eyes and said, "Thank you, I will." He and Chance walked another twenty feet and saw the car's inhabitants clustered by the side of the road.

They were quite rich, apparently, in their fine clothing but also quite shaken up. The man of the family scowled as Matthew stepped up. "I don't know what happened!" he barked.

Matthew was taken aback but Chance said, "Sir, we are friends of Clyde Thurston. We were just heading back to his house and wondered if you know what has happened?"

The cranky gentleman stared past them and studied Thurston's fancy, black automobile. Deciding, apparently, that they were legitimate socialites rather than newspaper journalists, he nodded once and said, "It seems that Judge McKinley decided to pay a call on Clyde and his daughter,

Annie, today. While he was inside the house, having tea, someone put a bomb in his car..."

Then, he stopped speaking and stared in offended amazement as the two rude fellows took off running toward the still burning car.

## 27

## THE PLAN FALLS APART

Matthew and his son ran up the street and stared, aghast, at the smoldering ruins. One car was completely demolished, just a blackened husk, really, with small tongues of flame still rising up from the rear end. Another small black car was parked close by. It had not been bombed, as far as Matthew could tell, but the front window was smashed out and a number of dents and dings marred the front-end and bonnet, presumably from falling debris.

Looking closer, both Matthew and Chance saw withered human forms in the lead car. In the front seat, the dead driver still clutched the steering wheel with wizened, leathery fingers. The man's face had, literally, melted away and bits of bone and skull could be glimpsed through his shriveled, burnt flesh.

Queasy, Matthew heard Chance groan slightly and turn away, gagging. Then, he looked in the back window. The passenger had tilted to the side, and Matthew took off his hat in respect, and regret. Judge McKinley's suit had been blown away, although, incongruously, his familiar, gray derby was still in place on his ruined head.

Hearing a series of horrible cries, Matthew stared past the bombed-out automobile and saw that a carriage and two horses had also been caught in the blast. One of the horses was screaming in panic and trying to break free of the harness that held it captive to its partner which had, apparently, caught the brunt of the blast.

The horse that had been closest to the car was lying dead now, its glossy, black coat was pocked and bloody from the force of the explosion and one of its long legs had torn completely away. A number of men were trying to sooth the surviving animal and untie it from the carriage traces.

Looking closer, Matthew saw Ian Revell working alongside the other men. The front of Ian's shirt was back with soot and Matthew saw that the young man was bleeding from a number of cuts and scrapes on his face and arms.

"Let's go lend a hand, Son," Matthew said. He and Chance waded into the fray and within a few minutes, the surviving animal was led away to safety, leaving only human witnesses behind to ponder the horrible attack.

Ian had glanced over at Matthew at one point and nodded in recognition. Now, though, as he gazed about, trying to spot McKinley's nephew in the crowd, the man was nowhere to be found. Sighing, Matthew stepped back and removed his hat to wipe sweat and dirty soot out of his eyes.

Sheriff's deputies, ambulance drivers, newspaper journalists and photographers mingled with random citizens and many people who had come to gawk at the victims. Chance had gone to find water.

"Mr. Wilcox..." Ian Revell said.

Turning around in surprise, Matthew saw the younger man standing behind him on the street. Either Ian had a spare shirt handy, or someone had loaned him one. Most of the blood and dirt on his body had been washed away... Ian still held a damp washcloth in his left hand.

"Mr. Revell... I'm so glad to see you well! At first, I thought you might have perished along with your uncle." Matthew said. Ian stared up at him and Matthew could see tears forming in the younger man's eyes. Ian blinked them back, though, and stood up straight.

The look that came over Revell's face made Matthew blink in surprise and he studied the young man's face as he replied, "We almost always travel together, Mr. Wilcox, but in separate vehicles. Often my uncle would ask me to stop here or there for important business. We found it much more convenient that way...today, that habit saved my life."

Matthew extended his hand, and murmured, "I am so sorry for your loss, Ian. I did not know Judge McKinley well, but I found him to be a man of honor."

Ian shook Matthew's hand and replied, "He was an honorable man, Mr. Wilcox; kind, honorable and very, very intelligent. In fact, we were working on your case today..." Revell had finished washing up and was polishing the lenses of his spectacles.

In truth, Matthew had really only noticed the man's slight frame and large, round eyeglasses when they met for the first time two nights earlier, but now he saw how beautiful Ian's eyes were. Large and luminous, his eyes were as blue as the ocean on a sunny day. His face was pale, but handsomely put together, and although his hair was thin it was a rich gold color. All in all, although the man seemed rather frail, he was quite handsome.

When they first time met, Matthew had thought Ian a lackey... a subservient, public servant. Now, though, studying the cold calculations on Ian's face, Matthew realized that McKinley's nephew looked nothing short of frightening. Those blue eyes were as cold as ice and his golden eyebrows were drawn together in a fierce frown.

"I am glad you happened by, Mr. Wilcox. The bombing took place about a half an hour ago, and I have had a chance, by now, to collect my wits. You were not at Clyde Thurston's house, earlier, when Judge McKinley and Mr. Thurston agreed upon a change of plan, but now that you are here, I wonder if you could join me for a cup of coffee..."

Chance walked up to where the two men stood, and handed his pa a cup of water. Matthew introduced Revell to Chance and said, "Ian, do you mind if Chance listens in? He is not only my son, but my partner in this endeavor."

Ian smiled, although there no humor in his expression. "Certainly," he answered. "We will all need to be in on this plan, if we hope to pull off a coup of this magnitude."

Two days later, Henrietta (or, Henny, as she was commonly called) McKinley sat alone in her drawing room, listlessly picking apart the embroidery she had started on her unborn grandchild's baptismal gown. It was her third attempt to finish the garment in the last day and a half, a half-hearted endeavor she had assigned herself to keep her mind occupied against the demons of grief and sorrow that threatened to overwhelm her senses.

She had hardly slept since she heard of Ash's death, and even now she found it almost impossible to believe. But, every time she thought she must lie down before she fell down, she would make her way to her bed chamber and lie awake, eyes wide open, fingers clutching at her bedclothes in nervous agitation.

Her husband Ashley was gone! Blown to bits by some unknown assailant; probably a criminal who had been sentenced harshly by Judge McKinley...a man who was known to be strict, but fair. Henny took a deep breath, trying in vain to keep the weight of his loss from crushing her heart.

Looking up, she heard one of her grandbabies laughing in childish glee from the other room. Both of her children were staying with her—her daughter, Bonnie, eight months pregnant with two little ones, a three-year-old boy and a one and a half-year-old daughter already clinging to her skirts, and her son, Lance, morose and moody as usual...more so now that he had been called home for his father's funeral.

Henny sighed. God knew she loved her children but by now Henrietta wished everyone would just go away. She had spent more hours drying her daughter's tears and soothing her son's temper than she had dealing with her own loss, and she was tired...of the unrelenting sorrow, the "widow's weeds," the never-ending list of funeral details and the non-stop line of callers at her front door.

At that precise moment, she heard the doorbell chime. A few moments passed and then her butler Morris stood in the doorway. "Ma'am?" he said.

Frowning in fatigue, Henny said, "Yes, Morris. What is it?"

"You have visitors Ma'am...your nephew Ian, and two other guests...Mrs. Francis Castle and a man named Matthew Wilcox." Looking scandalized, Morris added, "That man is a private detective!"

Fanny? she thought. Why, I haven't seen Fanny Castle in ages! Henny looked forward to seeing her beloved nephew, Ian, but who was this private detective and why would he be in the company of her own family and friends?

Intrigued and awake now for the first time since she heard the news of her husband's death, Henrietta sat up in her chair, ordered Morris to arrange for tea to be brought and asked him to show her guests inside.

Three hours later—three excruciating hours of tears shed, truths revealed and plans for revenge mapped out and plotted, Henrietta begged her son and daughter's leave and made her weary way to bed.

And, for the first time in days, she slept well and dreamlessly, a small smile of grim satisfaction on her face.

## STEPHEN CASTLE

Stephen Castle slammed the phone into its cradle with a snarl of rage and winced as his aching head reminded him of his losing bout with a bottle of brandy the night before. The desk clerk at the Portland Hotel stared at him with reproachful eyes—he was subservient enough to know that he could never admonish a paying guest—no matter how unruly they might become. Still, this phone had only recently been installed...a fancy, long-distance capable device that had cost management the moon and stars!

Castle winced in apology and muttered, "Sorry...bad news."

The stuffy old clerk said, "That is quite all right, sir. Is there anything we can do for you?"

"No...wait! Tell maid-service that I won't require a turn-down today. I don't want to be disturbed."

"Very good, sir" the clerk murmured, but Castle had turned away and was already making his way up the stairway to his room.

Closing and locking the door behind him as he entered his suite, Stephen sat on the side of his bed, eyeing the scant two inches of brandy left in the bottle on the nightstand. Sighing in disgust, he unscrewed the cap and took two, deep pulls...a little hair of the dog, he figured, to pull his thoughts together.

He normally did not drink to excess, but he had proceeded to imbibe yesterday afternoon after reading the newspaper article in the Seattle Times, stating that his dear friend Timothy Farnsworth had committed suicide in Fanny's tea room the day before. At first, he simply did not believe it. *There must be some sort of mistake!* he thought. *Timmy would not do such a thing to me...or Fanny!*

He had tried calling his wife but there was no answer, so he called his lead man in the Seattle area instead, and was assured the information was, apparently, correct. That was when he ordered a bottle of brandy brought to his hotel room and proceeded to get stinking drunk.

He had awoken to a raging hangover and an unfamiliar body in his bed. Groaning, he sat up and stared at the woman who, in the harsh light of early morning, looked far older and much more used up than he had thought the night before in the hotel lounge.

Shaking the blonde-haired strumpet awake, he gave her a few bills and ordered her to leave. He was splashing cold water on his face and trying to deal with the pain of losing his oldest friend to suicide when there came a knock on the door.

Thinking the prostitute had returned for more money

he stormed to door and flung it open. "What do you want, now?" he demanded.

A bellhop stood in the hallway and the young man took two steps backward in alarm at Castle's disheveled appearance and fearsome visage. "I...there is a long-distance phone call for you, sir, in the concierge's private office!" he stammered.

Stephen growled in exasperation but disappeared into his room—emerging a couple of minutes later with his hair combed and a light suit jacket on. Following the bellhop downstairs, he entered a small office behind the check-in desk, closed the door and picked up the phone receiver. "Hello?" he said.

"Hello, Stephen," Branson answered.

Castle sat down in a chair next to the desk. His knees had grown weak with shock. He was already hung-over and trying to get his bearings...how had Edward tracked him here...and what did the old bastard want?

"Hello, Edward? How did you find me?" Castle asked.

"Tsk, tsk. Honestly, Stephen, do you actually think that I don't know where my friends are and how to reach them if need be?"

Stephen shook his head. "I always suspected you had me and Timmy followed—great friend you turned out to be," he snapped.

"Now, now..." Branson murmured, "This is not the time for you and I to quarrel, is it? You have probably heard, by now, that our mutual friend is dead?"

Stephen's throat closed with grief for a moment and then he replied, "Yes, Edward, although, I must say, you don't sound too broken up over it!"

"Of course I am, you fool! Just because I don't beat by breast and wail out loud doesn't mean I didn't care for Timmy!" he thundered.

Sighing, Stephen answered, "Why did you call, Edward?"

There was a silence on the other end of the phone line for a moment or two and then Stephen heard the words that would change his life forever.

"The official story is that Timmy blew his brains out in your wife's parlor, Stephen," Branson said softly. "But, I know what really happened...Are you interested?"

Stephen had been imagining the look on Fanny's face when Timothy shot himself. The image was so clear he almost missed Branson's query. "What did you say?"

Branson snarled, "I said...are you interested in what really happened to our mutual friend, or not?"

Stephen sat up straight. "Well, of course I am! Tell me..."

"Okay, then." Castle could almost hear the satisfaction in Edward's voice. "One of my men was watching over your dear wife, Stephen. He told me he saw Mr. Matthew Wilcox, along with two other people, knock on your wife's door. For some reason, she let them inside. A little while later, according to my witness, Timothy came to call as well. That was when shots rang out."

Stephen's heart was pounding hard by now. "Are you saying that Wilcox shot Timothy in cold blood?" he gasped.

Branson's voice was smooth, too smooth maybe, but he seemed to be sincere in his beliefs. "I wasn't there,

Stephen, so I can't say for sure. All I know is what my man heard from his source after the police came."

There was a slight pause, and Branson said, "I just didn't want you to be misled by what you might have read in the paper. Timothy's death was no suicide, my friend. It was homicide, plain and simple. Now...when are you coming back home to finish what Timmy started?"

Stephen had ended his phone call with Branson and made his way to his room, where he sat now, brooding over his own poor decisions. He had misjudged Matthew Wilcox. He had thought the private detective a man of honor, and Timmy had paid the ultimate price for his own foolish trust!

*Taking the last swallow of brandy in the bottle, Stephen wiped his mouth and glared at his image in a fine mirror on the far wall. I offered Branson up to Wilcox on a silver platter, he thought. The only thing I asked is that Timmy not be harmed. Instead, the first thing Wilcox did was set a trap for Timothy...in my own house!*

"Bah..." he shouted, throwing the empty brandy bottle at his own reflection. He was only half-aware that the mirror had shattered into a thousand pieces...and that some of those broken shards reflected his own tortured image as he plotted revenge against the man who had murdered his oldest and dearest friend.

*First thing first, he thought. I need to call my men in Seattle and arrange to have Wilcox and his son put down...permanently!*

Branson hung up the phone and grinned. *Sometimes*, he thought, *I am too clever, by half!*

Edward had also been shocked to hear of Farnsworth death. He was not grief-stricken, however. He was actually appalled and disgusted that Timothy would take his own life rather than kill Stephen. Nothing but a weak-willed fool! Branson had thought, savagely, when he first heard the news. Still, he knew that with some quick thinking, he might be able to turn this unfortunate incident to his own advantage.

It took some doing but he had tracked Stephen down in Portland, Oregon. It was easy enough to twist the truth...if Stephen had been canny enough to question the facts in the newspaper, Branson only need remind Castle that Wilcox and Thurston, the newspaper man, were working hand in hand.

Stephen hadn't asked though, which made things even easier. Knowing Castle, Branson figured that Stephen's small army of men were already on the move against the Wilcoxes. All he needed to do now was sit back and wait, like a spider in its web, for events to unfold to his satisfaction.

He glanced down at the formal letter on the table. Picking it up, Branson studied it again. His men had told him, a few days ago, that Judge McKinley might have been compromised...that Matthew had met with the man at the Hunt Club, and that the judge had set up a meeting with Thurston the very next day.

This was definitely worrisome. If Judge McKinley set his formidable resources against him, Branson and the Trinity might go down in flames...not to mention the fact that his hard-earned levels and his good standing in the

Masonic Lodge would be compromised for good. He had acted fast.

Branson had no idea what Wilcox, Thurston and McKinley had discussed, but now he didn't care either. He had made a snap-decision and now McKinley—and whatever knowledge he possessed—was silenced forever!

What Edward hadn't counted on was his sudden promotion to acting Grand Master of the Seattle Masonic Temple. The formal notice and invitation read,


Dear Mr. Branson,

Due to the unfortunate demise of the dearly departed...the right-Honorable Ashley McKinley, and due to unexpected health-related issues concerning the reigning incumbent, Frederick Thompson (who has resigned his seat), you—Edward Branson—have been unanimously voted in as Grand Master of the Seattle Chapter Masonic Temple.

In accordance to tradition, a masked ball will be held in your honor at the Mason's Lodge, basement level, in one week's time, May 18th at eight o'clock in the evening. Black-tie, please.

Sincerely, your brothers in perpetuity~~~

Secretary, Ian Revell

Seattle Chapter, Masonic Temple Lodge


Folding the letter in half, Branson smiled again. His star was finally rising, as he always knew it would. It took a firm and steady hand, sometimes, to grab what one wanted in life and a stout, fearless heart.

But, once Stephen had done the dirty work for him by getting rid of the Wilcoxes and those pesky Thurstons and, subsequently, found himself in an early grave, Edward Branson knew that he would be nothing less than a king!

## 29

## CASTLE'S RETALIATION

THREE DAYS AFTER FARNSWORTH'S SUICIDE AND McKinley's murder, Matthew, Chance and one of Clyde's security guards climbed onto a large freight wagon in order to accompany the cook's assistant to the public market. Normally, the cook and her young assistant went shopping two times a week for fresh produce, fish and meat but there was nothing normal about the Thurston's household now.

For one thing, their number had expanded from four to over fifteen people—from Clyde and Annie Thurston to their many guests and now, the men in the security detail stationed about the premises. The normally abundant stores were depleted to the point of having nothing to serve but porridge, red beans, salt crackers and last year's wizened apples.

For another, the houseguests were in danger and no one was allowed to leave without permission and/or in the company of one of the security guards. Although the cook usually liked to do her own shopping, she had reluctantly conceded to Matthew's orders and sent her assistant to do the deed.

She had warned Matthew to keep an eye on her young helper, "who has more of an eye for the lasses than on the shopping list!" and added, with a glint in her eye, "and this list is important since there's more's a'coming, everyday!" He had meant to ask what she meant by that, but she was carried off by her own duties.

Sitting in the back of the wagon with Chance, Matthew studied the list now and sighed. He had offered to pay for the supplies but Clyde refused, saying it was the least he could do in repayment for all Matthew, Chance and the security detail had done (and were still doing) to keep him, Annie and the others safe from harm.

Still, he thought, this list of foodstuff is going to cost a small fortune. I will pay for it, whether Clyde likes it or not!

Pulling his leather pocket book from his coat jacket and studying its contents, Matthew noticed that Chance was also counting the bills and coin in his wallet. "Do you need to pick something up, Chance? I can make sure the wagon drops you off before we reach the market, as long as the guard goes with you."

Chance shook his head, smiling. "No, Pa. I can pick up a trinket at the market. Just a little something, you know…"

Matthew grinned. "You got it bad, don't you?"

Chance shrugged. "She is beautiful, don't you think? And smart and funny…she's brave, too, Pa!" He studied Matthew's face. "You don't mind, do you, if I ask Hannah to step out with me? I know her people aren't real high and mighty…"

Offended, Matthew sat up straight and said, "When did I ever aspire to high society, son? I just want you to be happy. I have had a chance to talk to Jacob Lindsay and his family and they seem like fine people. Money does not make character, Chance. Actions do…and so far as I can tell, the Lindsays are the best sort of folks."

Chance placed his hand on Matthew's sleeve for a moment. "I knew you wouldn't mind, Pa. I just thought I would let you know my intentions, that's all."

Matthew said, "Just get to know Hannah before you make your intentions clear, alright? Sometimes life events make strange bedfellows. Times of trouble and shared disasters bring people together who ought not to be together, you see?"

Seeing the look of dismay on his son's face, Matthew said, "On the other hand, fortune sometimes smiles on the unwary—and the willing!" He added gently, "Just be careful, with your own heart as well as Hannah's, okay?"

"Will do, Pa," Chance replied and stared ahead at the giant outdoor market located on one of the city's piers. The smell of saltwater taffy, fish, peanut-oil and the murmur of the large shopping crowds drifted toward them. It was a sunny morning and promised to be a warm day. For a moment, Matthew felt a swell of contentment settle over him.

It was beginning to look like they might just have a handle on Branson and his Trinity. Ian Revell had promised to bring action against his uncle's murderer.

Matthew assumed the young man's revenge involved the Freemasons, but he knew better than to ask.

The dangerous Mr. Farnsworth had taken himself out of the picture for good, and Mr. Castle was probably long gone...he had promised to return, if necessary, but only after Branson was neutralized.

Matthew had been concerned when Farnsworth ended his own life—he had, after all, vowed to keep Farnsworth safe when he struck his deal with Castle, but Clyde had put an end to that by ensuring the suicide notice went to print two days earlier than usual. If Castle read the paper, and Matthew was sure he did, he would know that Matthew had not broken their agreement.

In addition, a series of articles had hit both the PI and the *Seattle Times* over the last few days. Clyde was practically rubbing his chubby hands together in glee with the sheer volume of op-eds and letters to the Editor both papers were receiving from the veiled accusations. "It's democracy at work, my boy!" he had crowed just this morning.

Matthew couldn't help but smile—between Clyde's smear campaign and Revell's planned denunciation, Branson was in for a few uncomfortable moments...and that was before he was marched off to jail for murder, conspiracy, and whatever other crimes the man had committed in his life.

Suddenly, the big draft horse pulling their wagon whinnied in panic and bolted. A second later, a loud percussion filled the air. Startled out of his reverie, Matthew pulled his son down into a crouch and stared about in shock as Eric, the cook's assistant, and the driver shouted out in fear.

The carriage careened dangerously through the crowded streets and Matthew could hear men and women shouting in alarm. Then the horse stopped screaming and came to a stop, shaking in its traces.

"That horse is shot, Pa!" Chance yelled.

Looking at the horse's hindquarters, Matthew saw that his son was correct. Blood was streaming steadily from a number of buckshot wounds. No sooner did Matthew realize that he and his company were under attack, another volley of gunshots filled the air.

Young Eric howled in pain and fell off the front bench to the street below. Matthew pulled his pistol out and crawled on his belly to the sideboards of the wagon. Peering over the top rail, he ducked just as quickly when his brand new hat sailed off his head and flew to the opposite side of the street.

"Chance! Stay down!" Matthew shouted and heard the guard on the front bench curse. "They are coming up the street from the east! I can see 'em!" he cried.

Thinking quickly, Matthew realized that that the west side of the street was probably clear. If they could use the wagon as cover and make it to that building... "Chance, slither down out of this wagon and run over to that door-way! Hurry, and for God's sake, stay low!"

Chance nodded and disappeared from sight. Matthew scooted backwards and saw the boards he had been hiding behind shatter from the repeated gunfire. A couple of splinters broke away and imbedded themselves in his forehead and left cheek.

He heard another pain filled shout, and saw the guard slump forward on the bench. The man's body fell and he died with his head and arms draped across the rein stays. The old, wounded horse made to take off again, but Mathew tried to settle its panic. "Whoa, horse. Steady now..." he crooned.

The gunfire had ceased for the moment, and the horse seemed to take comfort from Matthew's words. It stood still, ears pinned back, while Matthew tried to climb off the wagon but fell instead onto the cobblestones. He grunted as his right wrist bent backward under his body's weight and then tried to shake the pain off as he saw Chance gesture to him from the building's doorway. He struggled to his feet and took two steps toward his son when the world blew up behind him.

Matthew was propelled six feet forward by the force of the blast. Ears ringing, he turned around and saw the conveyance lying on its side, most of it in flames. Someone had apparently thrown a stick or two of dynamite into the back of the wagon.

For the second time in four days, Matthew could smell the odor of burning horseflesh and he turned around, retching, as the dying horse fell down on the street with a crash. Gunshots filled the air again, and Matthew tried to run toward the building where his son hid but he was disoriented.

Realizing that he wasn't sure which way to go and that the moisture trickling from his nose and ears was his own blood, he peered through the smoke, looking for Chance.

Suddenly, a small hand grasped his left arm and he

heard a boy say, "Come on, Boss. Me and Chen Li found a sewer we can hide in…"

"Tom…Tommy? What are you doing here?" Matthew stammered.

"Never mind that now, sir," Matthew's newest hire, Tommy O'Roarke, said, "We get to get going a'fore we're all gunned down!"

## 30

# UNDERGROUND

MATTHEW'S EYES WATERED, HIS EARS RANG AND THE BACK of his head and neck tingled painfully. He felt nearly deaf and blind, and his heart pounded anxiously at being so vulnerable during this latest attack. "Chance? Are you there?" he called out.

"I'm here, Pa," Chance said, close to his ear. "I'm with Chen Li. Take my hand, we're heading to an underground tunnel..."

Matthew's hand was seized and he followed along blindly, hoping the boys knew what they were doing. Tommy said, "It's just over here, we think."

They came to a stop and Chen Li said, "Mr. Chance, could you lend me a hand?"

Matthew heard a scrape of metal and Tommy whispered, "These are underground steam tunnels, boss. Just like what we got in Spokane. Some say these here are also Shanghai tunnels, although I don't know about that. Seems like too good of a neighborhood to me..."

"Come on, Pa," Chance murmured. "There's a ladder

leading down...looks like we might be getting wet, though."

Matthew blinked fiercely, trying to clear his vision, but the blood and soot, smoke and shock of the blast still blinded him. Stepping forward, with Chance holding on to his right arm, Chen Li grabbed his left hand and said, "Turn around, sir, and step down. I'll hold on to you 'til you get your bearings, okay? There are...five rungs on the ladder. Tommy is going first—he'll be there to meet you when you step down."

Matthew did as ordered, feeling around with his right boot until he found standing room on the topmost rung. Then, with help from both Chance and Chen Li he moved as quickly as possible (for a blind man) down the ladder until he felt Tommy grab his left arm. The boy pulled him to the side of the ladder as Chance descended, joining them on a metal catwalk.

They waited while Chen Li pulled the metal cover back over the opening and darkness descended upon the tunnel. It was in the darkness that Matthew's eyesight returned. The sunlight had proven too much for his sore and dazzled eyes but now Matthew could make out vague shapes and deep shadows.

"Sirs...we better get a move on. I don't think we were spotted but, since this looks to be a working steam tunnel, there's a chance those guys know about this underground too!" The urgency in Chen Li's voice was unmistakable.

"Okay," Chance said, "Lead on..."

Chance took his father's hand again and the four made their way down a narrow catwalk. Chance said, "It doesn't look like you're too injured, Pa, but it's pretty dark in here. How are you doing?"

Matthew took stock and said, "I'm okay, I think. There might be a few burns on the back of my head and shoulders, but my eyes are clearing up and I can hear better now."

"That's good, sir. You had me scared there, for a minute," Chance replied.

"That makes two of us," Matthew quipped. Turning to Tommy he said, "Now, how in Sam-Hell did you two just happen to show up here? I thought I told you to stay home!"

He saw both of the boys flinch, then Tommy filled Matthew in on how he and Chen Li came to be in Seattle. "We were doing all right back home, boss, and keeping our noses clean, when Mr. Fulbright came down sick. The newspaper office is closed down, as you know, or we would have gone back there to stay. But, when Marty's sister came to take care of him, we decided to make ourselves scarce."

"There weren't no room in Mr. Fulbright's little flat, see, so we sent a wire and asked Miss Annie if it would be okay to come here. It's funny, in a way, Boss. We'd just left the train station and were about to call the number Miss Thurston gave us when we spotted you in back of that wagon."

Matthew had used his handkerchief to wipe most of the blood and dust from his eyes and face, and he could see the look of excitement in Tommy's expression—as though to him this whole thing was a big, fun adventure. His eyes rolled as he contemplated how much more difficult it would be to keep the two youngsters safe, along with Chance, in this latest confrontation.

He wondered why Annie hadn't filled him in on the boys' imminent arrival and then, with shame, realized that he had spent most of the last two nights either patrolling the grounds with the security detail or holed up with the menfolk in Thurston's den. He couldn't remember seeking her out at all since Judge McKinley was murdered.

Feeling like a heel, Matthew knew he'd been alone for far too long. He had not forgotten that Annie was there, but he was so intent on keeping her and the others safe she had, for the last couple of days, become an assignment in his mind rather than a friend—and possible lover!

Also, he thought, why should she go out of her way to inform him that she had extended an invitation to Tommy and Chen Li? It was her house, after all! Sighing in exasperation with himself, Matthew tuned in on what Tommy was saying.

"…We were trying to follow you when we saw a bunch of men watching your movements. They seemed like a rough bunch and we didn't like how they were all pulling iron, so we followed them first…"

Chen Li interrupted, "Sorry, Mr. Matthew, we didn't get to you sooner. Tommy and I never thought those men would fire into a big crowd in the light of day like that… much less use explosives on you!" He shook his head. "There's a lot of injured people back there, Sir!"

"There is no need to apologize, you two…you saved our lives, I think." Matthew murmured.

Chance said, "Yes you did, and I want to thank you

too. By the by, in case you didn't know, I'm Matthew's son, Chance. Pleased to make your acquaintance…"

Tommy grinned. "Well, we figured that, sir. You're the spit o' your Pap!"

The boys stopped long enough to shake Chance's hand and then Chen Li said, "Let's keep going, okay? It's not far, if I remember right."

"Have you traveled these tunnels before, Chen Li?" Matthew asked.

The youngster nodded. "Yes, sir. I was born here and lived most of my life around here… but that was before my parents and little sister were killed in a riot. Still, this tunnel is unfamiliar to me, although I believe it comes out close to the trolley station. If we can get there, I think we can ride the trolley to wherever we need to go."

"How much further is it?" Matthew asked.

"About two blocks from here, I think." Chen Li answered.

Matthew heard Chance sigh and remembered his son was still recovering from a broken ankle. They had already traveled close to four or five blocks, he figured. This protracted walk was probably crippling Chance with pain. Turning to ask, the young man forestalled his question.

Holding up his right hand, Chance grunted, "I'm all right, Pa. Let's just get this over with, okay?"

Looking up at a sudden shaft of sunlight, Matthew noticed that, in some places, a person could stare up (or down) through large, square holes in the second floors of buildings that were open and in business. There was sunlight streaming through shop windows and, in some of the shops overhead, actual stairs that led down and into the rushing water close to where they trod. Here and there, citizens could be glimpsed emptying slop buckets into the water or stoking stoves and steam-powered furnaces just above the tunnel walls.

Shop owners and customers were visiting and transacting business, their voices echoing down into the tunnel and off the slow-moving water. At one point, Chen Li turned around and placed his raised finger over his lips. They moved swiftly past a small bar (the odor of beer, whiskey, and unwashed bodies was a dead giveaway). They moved past the drinking establishment and Chen Li stopped, turning to face his companions.

He whispered, "I don't think it happens much here anymore, but this used to be known as a Shanghai tunnel. Sometimes, if a sailor got too drunk to watch his own back, the barkeep would throw his body into the water below their bar. Kidnappers would pay the bar owner a percentage for these men and when that happened, the sailor would find himself onboard some ship—far out to sea and under indentured service...free man or not...and by then it was too late!"

Matthew shuddered and said, "Let's get out of here!"

"Yes, sir!" Chen Li replied and scurried ahead.

They traveled another block or two and then Matthew saw the youngster pause and look up. Coming to stand by Chen Li's side the four companions stared up at the metal covering. Just then, they heard the distinct clang of the trolley bell. Tommy grinned and said, "Let me go up first. I'm bigger than Chen and can help pull you up better if need be."

Matthew nodded. "You be careful now and look sharp…" but Tommy had already lifted the metal grate up and to the side. The kid stuck his head up and Matthew saw the terror in his eyes just as he heard a gunshot.

Tommy's head jerked sideways, accompanied by a red shower of blood that painted the dirt and brick tunnel walls red and splattered their clothing. Chen Li groaned as Tommy's body fell back down the ladder in a lifeless heap and then gasped as Matthew shoved him down and out of the line of fire.

Then Matthew and Chance both started shooting. Side by side, the man and his son stood on the underground catwalk and shot up into the sky. They heard a sharp cry of pain through the gunfire and saw the shadows of people running back and forth in panic overhead.

Telling Chance to stay below, Matthew climbed the rungs leading topside with his pistol held high. He saw a man lying on the cobblestones next to the tunnel entrance. The gunman struggled to get up, despite a large patch of blood on his upper chest that was slowly staining his shirt crimson.

The wounded man saw Matthew looming over him and lifted his six-shooter with an evil glint in his eye, but Matthew shrugged and shot him in the arm. The gunman screamed as his pistol fell to the ground and stared up at Matthew with hatred even as he groaned against the pain of his shattered arm.

The detective knelt on one knee and put the barrel of his gun on the shooter's left cheek. "Who sent you?" he snarled.

The man winced and jerked his face away as the hot

gun kissed his cheek. "I ain't sayin' nothing, lest you get me to a doctor!"

Matthew said, "If you don't talk right now, you'll never see the inside of a doctor's office. Now, who do you work for?"

"I'm dying, you son of a whore! If I tell you, will you fetch me a doc?"

Matthew wanted to drill the man right here and right now, but he took a deep breath and said, "Yes. Tell me who sent you boys, and I'll make sure you get medical attention...was it Branson? Tell me!"

The man's eyes got big and tears of pain began to streak his face. "Branson? Hell no! I'm one of Castle's men! He sent us to kill you for what you done to his friend Timothy Farnsworth!" Letting out a small moan, he added, "Won't you call the doctor now?"

Matthew was shocked to his toes by the news but he nodded and looked up. Calling a doc would not be necessary, he realized. Police whistles filled the air and a horse-driven ambulance was cutting a wide swath around the corner of the block, heading their way.

"Chance," he called out. "Better come on up now...and be sure to drop your pistol. It looks like we're about to be arrested."

A number of citizens had come to see what was going on. They were whispering in excited horror but grew quiet when they saw the older man with burns and blisters covering his suit-coat, neck and head step back from the wounded man and place his pistol on the ground by his feet.

They watched him put his hands in the air as a small

army of city police ran up with their guns drawn. Then they saw a weeping Oriental boy emerge from the underground tunnel, followed by a handsome young man who was carrying a dead boy in his arms.

Seeing the look of grief on the young man's handsome face and spilling from the Oriental's eyes, more than one of the watching citizens, people who had no truck with policemen or the outlaws they pursued, vowed to tell the truth if asked...and swear it was the fallen gunman who had shot into the tunnel first.

## 31

## MATTHEW AND THE LAW

MATTHEW SIGHED AND STOOD UP FROM HIS CHAIR TO stretch his legs. He and Chance had indeed been arrested on the spot, and they had been detained at the King County sheriff's office for more than four hours. He was getting fed up with the Seattle lawmen who were breathing down his neck.

Staring through the glass at an adjoining office across the hallway, he met his son's eyes and shrugged in frustration. Chance nodded slightly and immediately turned his attention back to the two deputies sitting on the opposite side of a long, scarred table.

This back and forth interrogation had been going on for hours and Matthew was ready to kick the wall in frustration. He had told his son to tell the truth and, knowing Chance, that was exactly what he was doing.

So was he, for that matter. By now, Matthew's reluctance to share his case with the King County sheriffs was a moot point. Blood had been spilled in the city streets and the police were involved...whether he liked it or not.

The sheriffs, however, seemed disinclined to believe either of them, which was one of the reasons for Matthew's initial decision to keep the police out of the investigation entirely.

Matthew had learned over his many years as a lawman that municipal entities like the sheriffs, hospitals, fire departments, even banks depended, in large part, on charity and ample donations. Police departments could not operate without money—and most of that operating cash came not from taxpayers but from those who possessed it...in other words, the wealthy.

He had made an educated guess when he and Chance came to Seattle and surmised that Edward Branson was probably one of the King County police department's biggest benefactors. And, it appeared that he was right. His honesty was being questioned, as was his son's, simply because the sheriffs refused to believe their biggest cash cow was as dirty as they came and twice as evil.

He had learned that Castle's man, Mike Lowry, was likely to survive his wounds, which let Matthew off the hook for murder. Unfortunately, now that Lowry was stitched up from his arm and shoulder wounds, he was refusing to talk to the sheriffs until he met with his law firm—the prestigious Castle and Castle, Attorneys At Law.

This is the problem with the super-rich, Matthew thought. They can get away with murder by hiding behind their mountains of cash! No one wants to challenge them...for if they do, their own fortunes may dry up in the process!

Which was another thing that made Matthew burn up

in anger. His young friend Tommy had just been murdered in cold blood, right in front of his eyes! But the way things were looking right now, Tommy's death would not be avenged legally, because the sheriffs were too afraid of incurring the wrath of his murderer.

Thurston knew this, and so had Judge McKinley, which was why they had tried so hard to bypass the authorities while trying to bring Branson down. Edward Branson, who had more money than God, had hidden behind his wealth so long and so skillfully, there was simply no proof he had done anything worse than sneeze in public.

What Matthew and his allies needed, instead of a police presence, was a jury of Branson's peers to judge him and find him wanting; men and women who could fight fire with fire or, in this case, meet and match the man's funds with equal wealth and power. Stephen Castle had all but promised this would happen, but now, despite the newspaper's accurate accounting of Farnsworth's demise, he had turned coat and was doing Branson's dirty work again!

Looking up as a shadow darkened the door glass, Matthew glanced over at the office where Chance was being questioned and saw the room was empty, except for his son. Chance raised his eyebrows with a slight shrug and then the door opened. The sheriff and two deputies walked in, accompanied by Clyde Thurston.

"My boy," Thurston exclaimed. "I'm so sorry for the delay! Sheriff Walker wanted to speak with me, privately, about what has been happening in his fair city and time just got away from us!"

Thurston's small eyes searched Matthew's face as he added, "I have truthfully told the sheriff everything I know, Matthew. Once I found out that little Tommy was killed, I thought it was high time to enlist in some help."

Matthew had already told this sheriff—the same sheriff he'd met in Fanny Castle's tea room after Farnsworth's suicide—everything he knew, but he knew that Thurston was seeking absolution, which he was happy to give. The waters were murkier now, for sure, than they had been just this morning, but now that Stephen Castle was moving against them again, they needed all the help they could get.

"I'm glad you did, Mr. Thurston," he said. "I had originally thought that this whole affair could be settled without having to involve the sheriff's department but it seems that Mr. Branson is setting us up."

Sheriff Walker sat down in a chair with a grunt of fatigue. He removed his hat and wiped his face with a large red kerchief before telling Thurston and the two deputies to sit down, as well. Finally, he turned to Matthew and said, "Every damn time you come to my city things go to shit, Mr. Wilcox!"

Matthew blushed. He had dealt with a different sheriff the last time he'd come to the Seattle area, but apparently, this man knew all about him. Still, he had done nothing wrong then, and was doing nothing wrong now! As far as he knew, it was not illegal to decline help from the law on a private matter...

Clearing his throat, Matthew said, "Excuse me, Sir, but have we met before? This is the second time you have cast aspersions on my character."

Walker grinned. "Oh, I'm sure you don't remember me, Mr. Wilcox. I was just a lowly deputy the last time you blew into town and put my department through the wringer...during that skin-trade operation you helped bring down. It just makes a body reluctant to lend a hand now, you see,"

"Now sheriff, surely you don't mean to..." Thurston blurted.

Clyde was interrupted when the sheriff stared hard at Matthew, adding, "Still, I got no love for the super-rich in this city. If nothing else, your little shake-down of my department taught me that money only talks so loud. Bribes are not tolerated now, Mr. Private Detective, or graft or any other type of corruption... not as long as I'm in charge!"

Matthew felt the sting of the sheriff's words but, looking into the man's wise old eyes, he also knew that he was dealing with an honest sheriff...a rare and welcome breed these days, especially now that an army of killers had apparently been loosed on him, his family and his friends.

"So," Walker continued, turning to face Clyde Thurston, "tell me again what your plans are. If my men and I can help out, and if it's all on the up and up, we would be happy to take a bad man out..."

Sitting back in his chair, he smiled. "I personally don't care if he's as poor as dirt or as rich as Midas... if he's a crook and a murderer, we got room for him in our jail!"

Just as Clyde and Matthew got into Clyde's car to drive home from the sheriff's department, Ian Revell hung up the phone in his auntie's parlor. He was shaking like a leaf and wondering whether he had done the right thing... or if he had just made a colossal mistake.

He had spent most of his adult life following in his beloved uncle's footsteps. He had studied hard and become a fine lawyer. He had also studied the Freemason's rules of order...from cover to cover.

He knew that the step he had just taken was something that could not be taken back. He also knew that he had done it without prior approval from the rest of the ranking Masons in his lodge.

But this decision would not—could not—go to a vote.

Although Ian was not a drinking man, he made his way to a beautiful maple credenza and poured himself a stiff shot of whiskey. Gulping it down in one large swallow, Ian stared out at the falling dusk of early evening.

Secrecy and surprise were the only tools he had left with which to take Branson down. He would give Mr. Wilcox a chance to bring the Trinity down his way but if that failed, well... Revell and his secret allies would do the deed.

Gritting his teeth, Ian thought, Uncle, you were the father I never had and I loved you more than I could ever say. I hope you approve of the wheels I just set in motion.

You used to tell me that a man, whether he be rich or poor, had only one compass he need follow...honor.

Well, my sense of honor will not let me rest until your murder is avenged. So, if you're sitting at the judge's bench in Heaven above, please smile on me now, as my justice is meted out.

Revell was unaware of the tears that streaked his cheeks as he stared out into the dark.

## ANNIE

ANNIE THURSTON STOOD ON HER BEDROOM BALCONY, staring down at the garden. The sun was setting, casting her roses into shadow and painting the lawn a gloomy shade of gray. Fitting, she thought. She had been in a gray funk most of the day.

It started when Matthew and Chance left this morning for the third day in a row, without saying goodbye. She was no clinging vine but, honestly, it seemed to her as though Matthew was a different man from the one she had met and fallen in love with last autumn. No longer was he the handsome, charming man she thought she knew, but a stranger with cold, dangerous eyes.

Then, to make matters worse, she had found out that young Tommy was killed in the street, right after arriving on the train from Spokane. Her chest hitched with grief and remorse...it was her fault the child was dead! Oh, she knew her hand had not done the deed, but Tommy and Chen Li would not have been in danger at all, had she not insisted they come!

Sighing, she allowed thoughts of Matthew to fill her mind again. She had sworn, after she became a widow over a decade ago, that she would not fall in love again, or let a man—any man —influence her heart. She had been in an unhappy marriage once, and had no intention of letting it happen again, thank you very much!

Her first husband, Andrew Gantry, was an Army man and Annie had known that going in. Still, she was young when he asked her to be his wife…young and in love with the dashing young officer. He had told her, honestly enough, that he was going to make a career out of military service and that he needed a presentable wife to support the civilian side of his life.

Annie understood his words and agreed to play her part but the reality of his commitment did not really sink in until years had passed. Andy was never, *ever* home. As soon as one conflict or war ended, he would sign up for the next. He was a soldier's soldier, never truly at peace with his unruly heart unless he and his troops were engaged in combat.

In Andy's mind, Annie was simply a means to an end. She was the respectability he needed to present to his commanding officers at military balls and parties, the gentle representative of a personality long ago honed to the sharpest edge by his love of fighting and the art of warfare.

When Andy was killed in the Spanish-American war, Annie held up remarkably well after hearing the news. Of course, to her, it was like hearing that a near total stranger had lost his life to war, a sad but remote statistic…for by then that was what he was to her—a stranger.

They hardly ever talked or enjoyed one another's company, but Andrew felt that it was his duty as a husband to have as many children as possible, and he set his mind and body to that task with rough enthusiasm whenever he came home.

Annie was unable to fulfill that simple requirement, which turned an already cool husband as cold as ice in his disappointment. The last time she saw her husband—almost a year before he was finally killed—he had not spoken to her at all.

She had sworn to herself, after Andy was killed, that she would never bring another man into her life. She did not need or desire one. She had plenty of money, she had her beloved father...and she had her work as a journalist. The fact that Matthew Wilcox managed to sweep her off her feet was a curious and unwelcome surprise to her.

Unfortunately, the fact that Matthew was turning into another version of her husband Andy was no surprise. She had known, instinctively, that she did not trust men, and now she remembered why. Growling under her breath, she stepped back inside her bedroom, closing the glass doors behind her.

Angry, Annie walked briskly to her vanity table and dried her cheeks. The next time she saw Matthew Wilcox, Annie vowed she would tell him that she was no longer interested in pursuing a relationship.

She would turn her nose up and lift her right brow in scorn. She would...she would tell him to go jump in a lake! Tears filled her eyes again...she had held such high hopes!

Annie jumped when she heard a knock on her door.

"Come in!" she called out, wrapping her dressing gown tightly around her body and standing to walk to the door.

Matthew stuck his head inside, and for a moment Annie thought about throwing him out on his ear. She tried raising her eyebrow in scorn but the look of heavy sorrow on his face undid her anger and she dissolved into tears. Matthew took five quick steps and put his arms around her miserable, shaking body.

"Oh Matthew," she sobbed against his chest. "What happened? How did Tommy and Chen Li get mixed up in this?"

Matthew sighed. "It was just a horrible coincidence, Annie. Tommy and Chen Li had no sooner got off the train before they saw me and Chance drive by in the wagon. They only thought to track us down, but ended up right in the middle of a planned assassination attempt. I am so sorry!"

Annie shook her head. "No! It was me...it was my fault they came!" she wept. "You thought it best if they stayed home in Spokane, where they'd be safe, but I went against your orders and brought them here!" She stepped back and stared up into Matthew's eyes. "You know, Marty is a Godsend but I've met his sister and she's a horrible woman...I thought to keep the boys safe from her sharp tongue...and now look what's happened!"

Her body shook with the force of her sobs and Matthew picked her up and carried her to her bed. "You lie down now and rest for a while, okay? I just came to see how you were doing and to apologize for not paying more attention to you over the last few days..."

Annie stared up at his face for a moment and then her

left hand sought his. "Matthew, do you still want me in your life?" she blushed. "I know we have never spoken of the future, but I…well, I guess I thought you were interested in something more than a few dinner dates?"

Matthew smiled and, keeping his eyes on hers, kissed the top of her hand. He murmured, "Yes, I do and I am. In fact, I was going to ask if you would consider being my wife, but things have been so tense the last few days and weeks, it seemed like poor timing on my part. Still, there is no time like the present…Annie Thurston, will you be my wife?"

Annie's solemn face went slack for a moment and she gazed at the room's far wall in silence. Matthew had the sickening feeling she was about to say no. But then a smile broke through the misery on her face and she sat up in bed.

Taking both of his hands in hers, she said, "Of course I will, Matthew. But first, I think we should get through this mess we're in, don't you?"

Nodding, he agreed. "Yes, that's exactly why I held off asking. There is too much at stake right now to let added distractions cloud my mind…" Matthew thought hard for a second or two and then he heard himself say, "Annie, I told you about the things that have happened in my life but, in many ways, you don't really know me as a man, yet."

Annie gazed at him, waiting.

Clearing his throat, he continued. "I don't believe that I am a hard man, but I am careful…very careful when it comes to criminals and the people I hold dear. My loved ones have been used against me, more than once, so if I tell you…or Clyde or Chance to stay back, to stay safe, it's only because I love you all, and need to keep you out of harm's way."

He sighed, adding, "I have been preoccupied the last few days, as you know, but that's no excuse for keeping you at arm's length. I think that you will need to teach me how to not be afraid to love, okay?"

Annie smiled and said, "I will, I promise." She put her hand on his cheek and traced his lips with her fingers. "Come here, Matthew. Let's seal the deal with a kiss, please?" He grinned and leaned down to place a chaste kiss on her cheek.

Annie, however, had no intention of being chaste. She was a full-grown woman who had ceased being a virgin when she was nineteen years old. Her heart was broken by the news of Tommy's death, and her mind was filled with equal parts joy for her own future with this fine man and terror at the thought of losing him in this dangerous game they were playing against the powerful Trinity member, Edward Branson.

Most of all, though, she was filled with desire. It had been years since she had felt a man's hands on her body. Annie turned her lips so that they met Matthew's and, within moments, their polite and formal kiss went from being soft and dry to red hot.

At one point, as Annie threw Matthew's new hat into the corner of the room, he protested. "Annie! Your father!" He gasped as her fingers fumbled at his buttons and she peeled his shirt from his body.

"Shhh!" she murmured softly, "What my father doesn't know won't hurt him…" and then, Matthew was lost to all sensation except for that of the beautiful woman beneath him.

He ran his hands up and down her body, weighing her heavy breasts and exploring the soft folds of her most private parts while she shuddered and writhed with excitement. Then, as she gasped with frustrated desire, he penetrated her fragrant warmth and they moved together, as one.

Heart pounding, Matthew put his hand over her mouth to stifle the cry of her passion and then he felt his own release overwhelm him.

Thus, Matthew and Annie, still clutched together as one, celebrated life the way so many other human beings do when faced with sudden death. Although their hearts ached with grief at Tommy's untimely demise, the two lovers pledged their hearts and bodies to each other with desire and in hope of a second chance at love, life and happiness.

## 33

## THE BALL

TWO NIGHTS LATER, A MASKED BALL...TO MANY OF THE city's luminaries, the social event of the year...was about to begin. Cars and fancy carriages made their way through the blue and violet shadows of early evening toward one of the most beautiful and exclusive structures in Seattle.

Built to resemble a medieval church, the four story stone structure was glittering brightly with Edison light bulbs. Most of the large wooden doors were shut tight, as usual, but one small door had been left open to the public.

The arriving guests craned their necks at the Masonic Lodge in excited anticipation. Normally, the public was never allowed inside these hallowed walls. Indeed, only a scant few Master level Masons were allowed full access to every room in the building. The fact that the ball was being held in the basement level was no surprise to most of the invitees.

In truth, many of those folks would have been subtly disappointed if they were invited to view those secret rooms and hallways. Even the city's elite felt that the mystique behind the tightly-drawn curtains of the Mason's Grand Orient was too titillating for normal human beings to gawk at like crass voyeurs.

Many off-duty Seattle deputies patrolled the grounds against unwanted intruders, and a score of Fellow Crafters, at all levels, were playing the part of Tyler (or doorkeeper) for this evening's festivities. Invitations were scrupulously studied and many a mask lifted, so the Tylers could ascertain the guest's identities. This only served to thrill the lucky attendees further.

Ian Revell was one of the temporary Tylers. Normally a man at his level would never stoop to such a task, nor would he have been asked to. But Ian had volunteered for the job. There was a good reason for that, of course. Matthew might have been granted admission…his standing as a low-level Mason would have sufficed to get him and his plus-one in the door.

But his son Chance was not a Mason, nor was Clyde Thurston, who had long since disdained becoming a Mason. There were six more men coming tonight, as well, who would have never gained entrance without a thorough investigation… and a good deal of alarm. Ian was well-placed to make sure these guests were present tonight.

Once inside, the guests were hustled downstairs, but many of them later told their friends and families about the softly gleaming solid oak wall paneling, and the electric chandeliers that graced the hastily glimpsed entrance hall. More than one person actually caught sight of a few of the heraldic crests which hung on the walls. It was rumored that many of the Masons in this particular lodge were members of French, British and Scottish royalty and (some days later), the rumor mills thrilled with credible evidence from their more reliable witnesses.

Stepping into the ballroom, people gasped at the magnificence of the room itself and the accoutrements of their hosts. Scores of large, marble-topped tables and chairs lined three of the room's four walls. Each table boasted a large, solid silver candelabra which flickered with the soft glow of a dozen white candles.

There was a raised stage at the back of the room where a full orchestra played softly, and behind the stage area a number of glass doors were flung open to opulent gardens, statues and water fountains on the grounds behind the main building.

On the room's left side, just beyond the entrance, was a full bar with a champagne fountain and food buffet that bustled with activity. Masked men and women helped themselves to some of the finest cuisine—the expense of the dishes enough to give even the richest guests pause.

There was fresh lobster, King crab legs, mussels and oysters on the half-shell. A suckling pig with an apple in its mouth and maraschino cherries in its eye sockets graced one end of the table, while a number of prime rib roasts turning slowly on metal spits above a steel basin filled with glowing coals took up room on the other end. Silver bowls in front of the meats were filled with gravies, sauces, horseradish and onion rue.

The next table groaned under the weight of fifty separate side dishes—roasted potatoes, piles of fresh salad greens, green beans with slabs of bacon, brilliant red tomatoes in vinegar, glistening ears of corn, bisques and fragrant soups filled the air with delightful odors.

A third table held piles of freshly baked and still steaming loaves of bread and dinner rolls with one of the most precious commodities available...sweet cream butter. No one knew better than the super-rich how dear butter was those days, and more than one of the guests briefly considered stealing a few pats on their way out the door.

The furthest table held sweets and was flanked by two French pastry chefs, whose haughty expressions dared complaint. Their concoctions were nothing short of works of art. Tiny bon-bons, cream-filled éclairs, fragile lace cookies and a towering twelve-layer cake sat in splendor on the lace tablecloth.

One elderly matron who had more money than common sense walked up to the younger of the two chefs and asked if he would like to work for her rather than the older man standing next to him.

She was met with a disdainful sniff and a nasally rebuff. "I am the owner of the finest French restaurant in Seattle, Madame. Claude is my assistant—not my employer, so thank you...but no! Now move along, please, there are others waiting behind you..."

The old lady beat a hasty, humiliated retreat, but she later told her friends and family that she would only eat at the little Frenchman's restaurant if she was forced to dine in public.

This was a masque rather than a costume ball, so although the guest's faces were covered by gorgeous, intricate masks, their tuxedos and ball gowns were on full display. If the necklines were too low, the cut too narrow, the colors too gauche, or the sheerness of the material "more air than there," this was one occasion that forgave the wearer and allowed the outlandish to be "stylish."

Matthew looked like a tall, dark shadow in his formal suit and tails. He wore a black and gray mask, styled to represent the horned visage of a "Death's Head moth." The mask's mottled gray and silver swirls and long, feathered horns were cunningly crafted and caused more than one lady to gasp and shy away in alarm when he approached.

Annie, on the other hand, resembled the moth's more beautiful cousin—the butterfly. Her multi-layered chiffon gown sported no less than fifty colors, from the palest cream underskirts to brilliant rose, salmon, scarlet and purple outer skirts. Her brilliant, spangled mask fell to an exotic point just above her painted, crimson lips and swirled a foot over her forehead into two long antennae.

Chance and Hannah had chosen to wear white— which, surprisingly, made them stand out, even in this glittering crowd. Chance's russet hair was brushed back and fell in glossy waves across his silver-white mask, almost to his shoulders.

Hannah wore a simple, white lace gown and shoulder high silk gloves, but she had defied tradition by wearing her long, black hair loose and unadorned. It fell in dark waves to her buttocks and seemed to glitter and gleam with a life of its own. More than one society lady squirmed with anger at the audacity of it...especially when they saw their husbands and lovers following the girl with their eyes...imagining, no doubt, running their hands through that dark mass of femininity.

Clyde Thurston took up the rear of their party. He wore a fine, black worsted and an equally fine silk mask but it was already bent and sitting askew on his brow. Clyde was no Mason but he was a very popular man in Seattle, and he had stopped to say hello and (after lifting his mask) shake at least ten hands since entering the ballroom.

He was immediately forgiven, though...Clyde had always been extremely generous with his charitable donations and ready to lend a hand to all men, whether they be rich or poor. That kind of man was a treasured commodity in Seattle's elitist circles...even the wealthy craved the friendship of a truly decent man (especially if that man had enough money to buy the moon).

Matthew and his companions stopped and stared at a large, rather battered but gaily-striped tent that sat (like a sore thumb) in front of the stage. A hand-painted sign at the apex of the tent doors read:

THE LITTLE GLOBE THEATER PRESENTS
A FOLLY!

Matthew couldn't help but grin, even as he noticed a large number of guests pausing to stare, point and titter in scandalized fascination in front of the tent.

His dearly departed wife Iris would have laughed out loud as well. Her father, Gerald Winters, who had passed away five years ago, owned and operated the Little Globe Theater for almost two decades. The theater was situated right next to the Seattle Opera House, and like an open sewer drain, it caught the run-off from its more exalted sister.

Burly-Q, stage shows, Can-Can and comedic farce were the Globe's specialty and, although no one here tonight would openly admit to patronizing the place, there was hardly a living, adult soul in Seattle who hadn't snuck in at least once to see a show.

The fact that the Globe had set up shop here for the guest's amusement tonight, though, was setting fire to the crowd's ever-growing sensation of impending scandal.

Annie took Matthew's arm and murmured, "Well, Mr. King made it, I see..."

Tom King, a long-time employee of Gerald's (and an old friend of Matthew's), had inherited The Globe when the old man died. A few days ago, being the perfectionist he was, Tom had howled at Matthew about not having enough time to pull off a good performance for tonight's show.

Matthew had soothed the younger man, telling him the performance didn't matter nearly as much as the message being reenacted in front of the audience tonight. Tommy had grumped and groaned but he and his fine troupe of actors were here as requested.

Matthew put his hand on Annie's and said, "Yes...and, as Caesar once said, 'Let the games begin!'"

## 34

## THE TRIUMPH

MATTHEW AND HIS PARTY NO SOONER FOUND AN EMPTY table and sat down, when a gentleman with a bright red mask and a dark goatee strode to the front of the large room and said, "Welcome to the ball, Ladies and Gentlemen! As many of you know, the Masons normally don't make our 'Level' promotions public, but we decided, in light of what has happened over the last week or so, to make an exception."

He paused for a moment, and the gaslights scattered along the walls shone off the red devil's mask he wore, casting an eerie shadow on the golden floorboards at his feet. "We felt that, at this time of grief over the loss of our beloved Grand Master, we should celebrate his life and his commitment to justice. Please, raise your glasses high to the memory of the Honorable Judge McKinley!"

Raising a champagne flute, the masked man drained his glass and cried, "Here, here!" Immediately, the guests raised their glasses and echoed his toast.

After the hubbub died down a bit, he continued. "This

is also a commencement celebration. Although the formal initiation ceremony will remain a private Mason-only affair, please give a hearty welcome to our new Grand Master, Edward Branson!"

A somewhat weak ovation rippled through the crowd as a bent and ugly old man was wheeled onto the dance floor. Matthew had heard that Branson, unlike Clyde Thurston, was not well-liked. He was too gruff, far too stingy with his many purse strings, and seemed to hold himself above everyone else, no matter their wealth or lineage. This was not a good way to endear oneself to the high society circles in the Seattle area.

A tall gentleman wearing a simple black mask and a long gray hooded cloak pushed Branson's wheeled chair. Matthew immediately knew who that man was, though his form was hidden. Stephen Castle was quite recognizable with his erect carriage and his silver mane of hair.

So did Fanny Castle, judging by the way she was staring in shock at the man she had thought was long gone. She shook her head in fear and Matthew saw the widow McKinley, who sat next to her, lean forward in concern.

Matthew had seen Mrs. Castle come in earlier, along with Mrs. McKinley. He also saw the police commissioner, a portly man named Homer Styles, Sheriff Walker, Seattle mayor William Womack, and a number of other luminaries. Crossing mental fingers, he hoped that these powerful citizens were enough to cast Branson into a pit of shame.

Glancing over at the police commissioner's table, Matthew realized that Castle's appearance had not gone unchecked by the sheriff, either. Walker was whispering fiercely into his boss's ear, and Matthew wondered if an arrest was imminent, but the host with the devil's mask spoke again.

"Our dear Mr. Branson has been a Freemason for over forty years now. He was not, at the time of Judge McKinley's death, second in line to be the Grand Master of this lodge, but circumstances have intervened to make it so. Ladies and Gents, please make sure to wish him well while you enjoy the ball, the good food, and the fine music... And, in addition to tonight's festivities, a special performance is planned for our intermission!"

The devil stood still for a moment, and Matthew could have sworn he grinned. "In approximately two hours, please be seated while the acclaimed Little Globe Theater players put on a performance for your entertainment!" The devil then bowed with a flourish and cried out, "Enjoy!"

There was a burst of delighted laughter and immediately the orchestra set to with gusto. Matthew was left to wonder whether the wheels he and his friends had just set into motion would be enough to roll over and crush Branson and Castle or if what was left of the Trinity would just dust itself off and walk away laughing.

"I want to go home now, goddammit! I made my appearance...what more do they want of me?" Branson grumbled querulously.

Castle wished they could all go home, but he said, "The Masons have thrown this ball in your honor as well as

Judge McKinley's, Edward. You must stay, at least for a few hours. You don't want to seem ungracious, do you?"

Edward sighed in exasperation. Although it appeared his triumph was a done deal, his gout was killing him and gas was building in his bowels. He knew, however, that Stephen was right. He had not been formally initiated yet...if he did something untoward now, he might not become Grand Master at all. "Oh, for Christ's sake, all right. But, as soon as that damn Folly is finished I want to go back home!"

Stephen pushed Edward's chair toward a table with Branson's name on it by the front of the stage. There were only two place settings there, which he thought odd, but apparently, Branson and his plus-one were not to be disturbed, which, considering the old man's flatulence, was just as well.

Stephen got Edward comfortably situated, and then sat down on the opposite side of the table. Gazing across the room, Stephen watched as the guests rose to dance. Ball gowns swirled and twirled around the room like so many bright umbrellas and the masks the dancers wore lent a mysterious, somewhat sinister glamour to the affair.

Stephen thought, *who can know what lurks behind those elaborate facades... friend or foe?* He still wasn't sure whether coming back to Seattle was the right move, or not. Branson had assured him, though, that no one knew that he was in any way connected to the death of that small boy.

Mike Lowry, the one man who actually could point the finger of blame, had been sprung out of jail on bail by

Castle and Castle Attorneys at Law. He had also been found dead, early this morning in his own home. He had, apparently, hung himself in remorse after killing an innocent kid in a skirmish by the city market.

Branson's doing, Stephen supposed, but he couldn't help but feel relieved that, once again, his name was staying clean. Stephen adjusted his mask so he could see the crowd a little better. The usual suspects, he thought. All the climbers in Seattle's society set were there, of course, plus many political movers and shakers. He gazed at the table where the sheriff, the mayor and the Seattle Police commissioner sat eating. They seemed tense, and it gave him a bit of a chill. Normally, Womack would be two sheets to the wind by now, cheeks red and eyes bleary with too much whiskey.

Stephen shook the chill off. As far as he could tell, everything boded well for him and Branson. Also, he thought, maybe now that Edward is being elevated to Grand Master of this lodge, the old man will finally lose interest in the gold and silver mines in north Idaho. God knows, he'll be kept busy by his new Masonic duties.

"Stephen, did you hear me?" Branson barked.

Castle jumped and said, "What? Did you say something?"

Edward glared. "Yes! I asked if you would go and fetch me some of those shrimps…and maybe some cake?"

Stephen stood up. "Of course. I'll be back in a few minutes."

Walking close to the stage to avoid the dancers, Stephen approached the food tables. He stepped up to a table filled with china and cutlery, and reached for a plate when he felt a soft hand touch his back. "Stephen...what on Earth are you doing here?" Fanny whispered in his ear.

Shocked, Stephen turned around and saw his wife standing behind him. There were a number of people queuing up behind her, so he grasped her hand and pulled her to a quiet corner. Facing her, he leaned close and said, "I might ask the same thing, wife! You never come to these types of affairs, not unless it's for a coming out. And, how did you receive an invitation to a Mason ball?"

Fanny glared. "I have been receiving invitations to all manner of parties since I was just a girl, Stephen!" Her eyes flashed indignantly, and then grew moist with unshed tears. "But to answer your question, Henny McKinley invited me." She pulled a snow-white hankie from her sleeve and dabbed at the make-up on her pale cheeks.

"Now," she whispered. "Pray tell, husband, why you haven't been returning my phone calls? I needed you!"

Stephen bowed his head in remorse. Nodding, he said, "Yes, Fanny, I know about what happened, and I am truly sorry. My men told me you were alright, though, after Mr. Wilcox attacked Timmy, and I've been kept very busy with my own affairs. Not the least of which is making sure that Wilcox pays for his crime!"

Fanny stared up at her husband's face in shock. "What in God's name are you talking about, Stephen? Timmy shot himself, in my own tea room, in front of my very eyes! Who told you that Matthew Wilcox had anything to do with what happened?"

Castle looked down into his wife's face, feeling the blood leave his own cheeks as the implications of her words sank in. Thinking back, he realized that he had taken Edward's words as gospel and, in his own sorrow, he had failed to do the proper research as to whether the old man spoke the truth or not.

Now, a young boy was dead in a failed assassination attempt, and his men were still scattered all over the city trying to finish the job on Matthew Wilcox and his son Chance, who according to Fanny, were innocent in Timmy's death.

"Stephen...answer me, please!" Fanny cried.

Castle spoke through frozen lips. "Branson did, of course."

"Branson!" Fanny hissed. "Branson was the one who started this, husband! Timmy told me, before he killed himself, that Branson wanted him to kill you...and me! Timmy couldn't make himself do it, Stephen. I think he came to the house, thinking you might be home. He came because his heart was broken."

Stephen staggered slightly and walked on weak legs toward a chair by the wall. Fanny followed and sat in a chair next to him. She took his hand and leaning close, she said, "Stephen, you must go...now! There is something planned for tonight—something we hope will expose Branson for the fiend he is."

Stephen looked at her sideways, and asked, "We? Who is this 'we,' Fanny?"

Mrs. Castle sat up straight. "Me, Matthew and Chance Wilcox, Ian Revell, and Judge McKinley's widow, Henrietta. We think we have landed on a plan that will bring Edward Branson down for good!"

"But," she went on. "You must go, my love. I fear that

you are too close to Branson to stay clear of this affair. Leave, please! Go to one of your hiding places and make yourself invisible for a while. Just give me a little time and I'll send as much money as I possibly can to ensure that you live comfortably."

Stephen felt the walls closing in on him. He had loved Timothy Farnsworth in his own way, just as he loved his fierce little wife. He wished he could take it all back...the Trinity, the murders, the all-consuming quest for wealth, the feelings of inadequacy he had always felt at being a relatively poor man in a rich man's world.

But it was too late, and he knew it. Fanny clutched his hand once more and raised it to her lips. "Dear, dear Stephen. Before you leave, just know how much I have always loved you...that will never change."

She stood up with tears sparkling like diamonds in her eyes, and said, "Go...now!"

Within moments, Stephen Castle stood up and fled the premises. He didn't realize it yet, but four very large and extremely deadly masked men left the building as well.

## 35

## THE WITNESS

IAN REVELL STEPPED INTO A PRIVATE BATHROOM SITUATED within his late uncle's office and shut the door behind him. He was shaking and his hands were clammy with nervous sweat.

He removed his red devil's mask and stared into his own reflection. The dark whiskers of his phony goatee itched miserably and he peeled that off as well. Then, he ran cold water from the tap and splashed his face, over and over again until he felt clean and calm.

Although he felt a thrill of vengeful excitement at what he had done, he worried that contacting the Knights Templar Order of the Red Cross was simply too much. He wondered whether his uncle (were he still alive) would have ever considered such a thing or if, even now, the judge was looking down upon his actions as something a common murderer might do.

Still, Ian had no intention of trying to stop matters now that they were in play. Ian had been raised (and trained) to navigate within the circles of wealth and power. He knew, as well as anyone, that the wealthy oper-ated under a different set of rules than regular folk. They could, and often did, get away with murder, theft, graft, blackmail and all assorted crimes most people would rot in jail for.

He knew that, unless something drastic happened, Edward Branson would not only get away with murdering his beloved uncle, but he would also take the judge's place in the Masonic Lodge in Seattle...a maneuver Ian himself had orchestrated in order to seek justice!

Shuddering at the thought, Ian studied his own scared eyes for a second and then grabbed a hand towel and wiped his face dry. Stepping back into his uncle's office, he made his way to a chiffonier and pulled out a snowy, white shirt and black silk suspenders. If he guessed right, he was about to have company and he wanted to look his best...calm, cool and collected, rather than the nervous, quivering pantywaist he felt like on the inside.

Turning to the credenza, Ian splashed two fingers of scotch into a glass and drained it dry. He considered another and changed his mind. This particular Order of Knights frowned upon alcohol consumption, and Ian didn't want their righteous wrath turned on him after they were finished with Castle.

He sat down behind his uncle's desk and laced his fingers together. He could hear the orchestra's music floating up the stairs...he wished for a moment that he could go downstairs and dance the night away with one of the pretty women he had seen in the ballroom.

Shaking his head at his own childishness, Ian took a deep breath and waited for the inevitable.

Stephen Castle had every intention of hailing a cab and heading to the train station and away from Branson for good. The grounds were fairly large, the size of a city block, but he knew the cabbies were out in force tonight, hoping, no doubt, to make a few coins hauling the rich party-goers home after the ball.

He didn't care to step out into the brightly lit street entrance so he hustled down a cobblestone pathway by the side of the building and out onto the back of the property. Peering through darkness, tall trees and shrubs toward the next block, Stephen let his eyes adjust. After a moment, he spied a fairly wide trail he could use to make his way to the back fence and onto the adjacent street.

He could see a few couples walking arm in arm through the shadows, and at one point he heard a barely-suppressed quarrel, but then he was in the clear. Picking up the pace, he kept his eyes glued to a flickering gas lamp on the street ahead.

He started slightly when he heard a branch snap to his left and he stopped to peer into a thicket. Staring into the dark, he saw nothing and shrugged. Probably a squirrel, he thought, or a night owl…

Suddenly and nearly silently, several huge, cloaked figures came out of the darkness to surround him. He only just began to shout out in alarm when his arms were seized from behind and a firm, heavy hand covered his mouth. He squirmed, grunting in fear, when he heard a whisper in his ear, "We do not wish to kill you, Mr. Castle, but believe me when I say we are prepared to do so if you do not cooperate."

Castle stood still, heart pounding in dread. A wadded up piece of material was shoved into his mouth and a long scarf tied over it to serve as a gag. Another piece of material was pressed firmly over his nose and a sharp odor filled Stephen's nostrils. Try as he might to keep from breathing in the noxious fumes, he had no choice.

Stephen felt his eyelids grow heavy and knew he was falling to the ground, but there was nothing he could do to stop it. He made one mighty effort to ascertain who his assailants were, and the last thing he thought before falling unconscious was *What on Earth are the Templars doing here... and why do they want me...?*

Then Stephen Castle knew no more.

Castle awoke slowly with a mouth that tasted sour and a pounding headache. His stomach roiled uneasily, and the electric lights scattered about the room hurt his eyes.

He blinked...there was a glowing white wall standing close to where he sat sprawled in a chair. A white glare with blood-red stripes...*Yes!* Stephen thought. *I remember... the Knights Templar Order of the Red Cross were the ones who accosted me outside.*

Stunned, Stephen shook his head. There were, to his knowledge, no Templars in Washington State—much less such a fiercely militant order—and he simply couldn't imagine what they were doing here in this room with him, of all people...he was, after all, one of the least religious people he knew!

Enunciating carefully, Castle said, "What the hell is going on? Wha…what do you want with me?"

"Silence!" one of the men barked as he stood up, and Stephen could see how tall he was. The man wore a white, floor-length robe with a red cross stitched on the front. His hair was dark brown with wide streaks of gray, his large hands were spotted with age and gnarly as old tree branches.

One of those mighty hands reached out now and slapped Stephen so hard that both he and the chair he was sitting in flew backwards to the floor. Stephen lay still for a moment tasting blood on his tongue and fighting against the shocked tears threatening to fill his eyes. *I will not weep like a baby,* he thought, even as his heart turned icy with fear.

The Knights Templar were a religious order within (and without) the Freemasons. An entity of its own, its members swore allegiance to no particular order but acted independently on its own to reinforce the Bible and its teachings. Almost all Freemasons were expected to swear allegiance to God above but the Knights Templar Order were fanatical in their beliefs and for centuries had been known to seek out and destroy those they perceived as sinners.

Who called them here? Stephen wondered frantically as his chair was hauled upright and situated in front of a wide, polished desk. A young, mild-looking man sat behind the desk, polishing a pair of spectacles. He finished cleaning his glasses and perched them on a dainty, almost feminine nose. Smiling pleasantly, he said, "Good evening, Mr. Castle. My name is Ian Revell."

Castle sat up in fury, and barked, "What do you want? Do you have any idea how much trouble you're in, young man? I'll own you for this...this outrage!"

Instantly, Stephen saw stars as he was cuffed hard over his left ear. The same old man who had hit him earlier leaned over and whispered into his right ear. "Mr. Castle, as I said earlier this evening, you have been accused of crimes against God such as theft and murder. Both things are cause for your immediate execution, but Mr. Revell here is offering you a chance at redemption."

Sitting down on the desk with a sigh, the old knight crossed his arms over his chest, adding, "Personally, I think you're irredeemable. I think that during your long life, you and your companions have committed crimes untold and you are only now—through God's grace—being called upon to be a witness to these terrible crimes."

Stephen's throat filled with bile. *Who is this religious fanatic to speak to me so...*But the spit in his mouth dried up in alarm as the old man drew a gleaming silver sword from his long white robe. Castle drew back in his chair as the knight stood up, but there was simply nowhere to go!

Stephen stared as the sword lifted into the air over his head and then he closed his eyes and started praying to the benevolent God he suddenly believed in with all his heart and soul.

"My Father, who art in Heaven,

Hallowed be thy name. Thy Kingdom come..."

"Enough!' a soft voice spoke from behind him and Stephen craned his neck to see who had spoken.

A man walked by him and sat in a chair by the side of the desk. He had removed his mask and sat still now, staring into Castle's face with wide brown eyes. Although the man was probably in his thirties or forties there was a childlike innocence in his expression.

He smiled slightly and said, "My brother knight believes that some sins are unforgivable, and that nothing short of death will atone for them." Gazing up at the old brute still seated in front of Castle, glaring down at him like Beelzebub, the younger man said, "Thank you, Geoffrey, that will be all for now."

The old knight stood up instantly and moved to the back of the room, leaving Stephen alone with the bespectacled pretty boy and the Knight Templar.

Stephen cleared his throat and whispered, "What do you want from me?"

Ian smiled and shrugged. "We want you to confess your sins, Mr. Castle...loudly and at length."

The knight smiled as well. "Do that, Mr. Castle, and my brothers and I will let you live. Refuse, and you will die—right here and now."

## 36

## THE FOLLY

Approximately an hour later, a brassy trumpet squawked and the orchestra members put their instruments away so they, too, could watch the show planned for tonight's intermission.

Edward Branson hardly noticed. When Stephen had disappeared into the teeming crowd to fetch him back some shrimp and cake, Edward had sat comfortably alone. Then, minutes passed and he grew impatient and alarmed. *Where the hell is that man?* he wondered, irritably.

One Mason after another came to sit at his table. To a person, they congratulated him on his new position, flattered him and whispered hopeful plans in his ears. At one point, he asked the men surrounding him if they had seen where Mr. Castle had gotten off to and complained about his lack of refreshments.

One fellow—the man with the red devil's mask, who had opened tonight's festivities—answered that Stephen

Castle had been detained by his wife, Fanny, and that he would be joining them shortly. He also offered to bring Edward some shrimp and cake, which brought a smile to the old man's face.

While that man left to bring Branson some dinner, even more people joined his table. Although, normally, he didn't appreciate crowds, Edward was having the time of his life. Every person there seemed to be swearing fealty to him, as if he was a newly-anointed king!

A plate full of shrimp and cake landed in front of him and Edward set to with gusto, looking up as a trumpet sounded again with a noisy wheeze. The curtains on the player's tent swept to the side and a tall, rather stout gentleman cried out, "Ladies and Gentleman, sit up straight now and pay close attention to the Little Globe Theater's presentation of a "FOLLY!"

There was a round of applause as people tried to peer through a sheer inner-curtain that hid the makeshift stage, but they didn't have to wait long. The sheer curtain was pulled to the side by unseen hands and many of the guests murmured in surprise as they spied a large, hand-painted sign that read, OREORNOGO SILVER MINE —IDAHO!!!

Three or four filthy-looking men were dressed up as miners and tapping away at silver and gold-painted rocks. One of the actors managed to chip a piece of fake gold away from the large boulder by his feet. The actor let out a whoop of joy and began prancing around the stage and crowing with delight. "Gold!" he cried, "I found me some gold, and now me an' my family are gonna be rich!"

There was a polite round of applause as all of the miners on the makeshift stage hugged one another and the sheer curtains closed. People turned to one another in confusion... "What on Earth is this all about?" they wondered aloud.

A couple of minutes later, the curtain swept aside again and the actor who found the large gold nugget had apparently come home to his family and was showing them his wonderful find. "We can buy a real home now, darling wife and maybe now that we have some money, take our daughter, little Suzie, in to the doctor to fix her poor lungs!"

The wife and children cheered and wept with joy, hugging their Pa tight in celebration. Then, three large men with black hats, black bandanas, large fake pistols and paper mâché knives crept onto the back of the stage and, amidst the squeals of the titillated crowd, murdered the whole family.

The actors must have been holding bags of red-dyed gelatin, because suddenly the stage area was dripping with what looked like gallons of blood and gore and more than one spectator stood up with cries of disgust. Their loud complaints were silenced, however, as the three black-garbed men stood up from their bloody chore and, after facing the crowd with evil sneers, turned their backs on them.

Gasps and scandalized whispers filled the ballroom as the ball-goers read the names on the men's backs. One sign read, BRANSON, one read, FARNSWORTH and one read, CASTLE! Underneath each name the word, MURDERERS! was written in large, red letters.

Edward's jolly smile had melted off his face as soon as the curtains opened. The Oreornogo mine was long since dismantled but the whole, North Idaho mining region was much too close to home for comfort.

He stared from side-to-side, peering suspiciously at the masks surrounding him to see if anyone at his table was in on the joke but he couldn't see past their strange facades. He murmured under his breath, "It's time to go home now…someone go and fetch Stephen Castle back here!"

There was a small ruckus behind the curtains and the guests craned their necks to see what new thing was about to present itself. The three men with the damning signs on their backs stepped to the side of the stage and bowed their heads as if in prayer. Then Stephen Castle himself stepped onto the platform.

As Edward watched, Stephen took a kerchief from his back pocket and wiped sweat from his face. He stared, dazedly, out over the crowd and, finally, his gaze landed on Branson. The same, gaudy trumpet blared once and silence fell over the ballroom.

Stephen cleared his throat, and swept his handkerchief over his face again. He looked like an animal with its paw stuck in the steely jaws of a trap. He started to speak, stopped and opened his mouth to speak again. He had no sooner said, "Ladies and Gentlemen…I am here tonight to…" when his wife Fanny stood up and cried, "Stephen, what are you doing?"

He turned to face her, and the sorrow in his eyes was unmistakable. "Fanny, I am sorry but I really have no other choice! Go home now, please! I have been promised that you and the rest of the family will be safe, but you must leave!"

The delicate, middle-aged woman looked as if she would argue, but a tall gentleman with beautiful red hair and a silver-white mask stepped to her side and whispered in her ear. She listened to the man for a few seconds and then she removed her mask, bowed her head, and wiped tears from under her eyes. Taking the man's arm, she swept through the doors of the ballroom and out of sight.

Most of the guests paid little attention to the woman's exit and focused, instead, on what Castle had to say. He turned to face Branson, and then he said, "Edward, I have been caught out, and I need to confess my crimes. Please forgive me—everyone—for letting my greed dictate my actions."

Branson sat up straight, and put his hands on the wheels of his chair but, somehow, he had become lodged in close to the table. At least a dozen men and women stood directly behind him so he was unable to make a fast getaway without running someone over in the process. "Excuse me, but I need to leave…EXCUSE ME!"

A man in a black and gray feathered mask, fashioned to look like a moth, leaned close to his ear and whispered, "You need to hear this, Mr. Branson. Stay still!"

Ignoring the moth man's orders, Edward still tried to back way but no one moved so he was forced to sit like a fool and listen as Stephen confessed in a loud voice, his part in the claim jumps over the last six months, or so, in North Idaho. He talked about the murders of landowners around the assorted mines in North Idaho, the assassination of a certain Chloe Brazil and the recent, murder of a young boy named Tommy O'Roarke.

He talked and talked until Branson wanted to scream in frustration! The whole time Stephen spoke, he stared at Branson as if he was urging Edward to confess as well, but Edward would no sooner do that than he would attempt to fly to the moon! Glancing around, Edward saw that the city sheriffs had stood up from their table and were making their way to the stage.

By now, many people in the crowd were booing softly and hissing their displeasure. The sound of their scorn sounded like angry waves agitating still sand in a rising storm. Edward groaned softly and, once more, tried to back his chair away from the table.

Stephen's words finally came to a stop and he held his wrists out for the Seattle deputies' handcuffs. He looked and acted like a whipped dog as he was led off stage by the policemen but, apparently, there was one more thing the man in the moth mask standing behind Branson wanted...

Matthew called out, "Is there anything more you need to get off your chest, Mr. Castle? You have implicated Timothy Farnsworth and yourself, but was anyone else involved in your schemes...anyone at all?"

Castle stared into Edward's eyes with almost superstitious fear. The two men faced one another as the attending audience held bated breath. Edward held his head high in arrogant disdain, while Stephen studied his old friend with equal parts love and dread.

Then Edward said, "Take this man away and clap him in chains! I had no idea what Tim and Stephen were doing behind my back! You must believe me...besides, I know you have no proof of wrongdoing on my part, or you would be arresting me too!

Matthew saw the defeat and raw sorrow in Castle's eyes and knew that their gamble had not paid off. He, Chance, Clyde and the King County sheriff had counted on Castle to implicate Branson during his confession so they would both be hauled off to jail but Castle had, apparently, lost his nerve.

Looking at the flat, cold hatred in Branson's eyes as Castle was escorted outside by the many lawmen who surrounded him, Matthew couldn't help but sympathize. The minute Castle implicated Branson would be the exact same moment Branson arranged for Fanny's demise.

Stepping back from Edward's wheeled chair, he bent down and murmured, "We will get you yet, Mr. Branson...rest assured."

To which Branson replied, "I have no idea what you're talking about, sir. Now, let me pass!"

Matthew watched as Branson wheeled his chair through the throngs of people attending the ball. Many people stepped back in loathing at Branson's passing but, it seemed to Matthew, just as many people stepped close and seemed to whisper encouragement in the old man's ear.

Chance, who had just returned from escorting Fanny Castle to her car, stood next to his father. "Any luck?" he asked.

Matthew shook his head. "No, he didn't implicate Branson at all...dammit!"

Chance stared over at Branson's table, where a number of men and women still remained after Branson had fled. Most of their masks had been removed by now and he saw the look of anger and disgust filling their faces. Ian Revell stood amongst them, and Chance was sure he was telling the bystanders that Branson would not be sworn in as Grand Master after all.

Both he and his father knew that the ball was just a ploy to get Branson accused as publicly as possible. Although the public accusation had never taken place, he had the feeling that Branson's place in society was now severely compromised. He bumped Matthew's shoulder and said, "Pa, I doubt that Branson will be able to continue his claim-jumping with one of his men dead and the other one rotting in jail!"

Matthew sighed. "Yes, I suppose you're right about that. I just wish..." He was interrupted by the arrival of Annie and Hannah.

"Well," Annie said with a smile. "I guess we have done our part, Matthew. Shall we go home? I think the ball is over and done with now, anyway."

In fact, many of the party-goers were starting to file out of the ballroom and the musicians seemed disinclined to pick up their musical instruments.

Matthew felt some relief...Branson was probably making his way home by now, and Castle was acquainting himself with the inside of a jail cell. He figured this was as good (and safe) a time as any to make their way back home to the Thurston mansion.

He would contact Revell and the King County sheriff's office tomorrow morning and try to make a new plan to finally put Branson out of business for good. For now, he was tired to the bone and ready to call the night over.

Taking Annie's arm he said, "Absolutely, let's head home."

# THE KNIGHTS OF DARKNESS

Edward Branson was met outside the Masonic Grand Orient by his lead henchman, Donnie McPhearson. Donnie had been forced to cool his heels outside, since he was not a Mason and now, as Branson rolled, unescorted, toward the car, he looked at his boss in alarm. Branson's face was red as a beet and the man seemed apoplectic with fury.

Sighing internally, Donnie thought, *Uh, oh!* Normally, working for the old man was a piece of cake as long as you bowed your head at all the right times and ate large slices of humble pie, but when Branson got in a rage, no one was safe...not even loyal employees!

Donnie ran to meet Branson and, taking ahold of the chair handles, he asked, "What happened, sir? Are you okay?"

Branson barked, "No! I am far from okay. Take me home—immediately!"

"Yes, sir!" Donnie replied, and whisked Edward and in

his chair into the back of the car in record time. They drove the miles to Branson's home in silence, but Edward was already scheming his revenge. On the morrow, he would arrange for Fanny Castle to meet an untimely death and, while he was at it, he would arrange for a number of Castle and Castle partners to suffer as well. A small smile twisted his lips as he thought about the damage he could do to that prestigious law-firm!

When they reached the house, Branson said, "Go and park the car and then meet me inside. How many men are here tonight, do you know?"

Donnie thought about it for a few seconds and said, "All of 'em, I think, boss."

Branson nodded, "Good, I want to meet with all of you within the hour!" Staring at the front porch, he said, "Where the hell is Trask? He should be here to help me inside!"

"I'll do it, Sir! Just hold on a sec…" Donnie cried.

He hustled around the back of the car, plucked Branson's wheeled chair out onto the graveled driveway and then helped Branson into it. As Donnie pushed the old man up a slight incline to the front porch, Branson muttered, "Looks like I might have to remind some of you men how things are done properly! The next time Trask forgets to meet me at the front door will be the last day he works for me!"

Josiah Trask, Branson's old Negro butler was always on hand—always—but Branson seemed to have forgotten that in his current furious state. Rolling his eyes, Donnie said, "Yes, sir!"

Panting with exertion Donnie pushed the old bastard

toward the house. The driveway was steeper than he had thought, and he was sweating under his dress coat. Reaching the porch he pushed Branson to the front door, which was slightly ajar.

"Sir…" Donnie started to say in alarm, but Branson cut him off in mid-sentence.

"What the hell are you waiting for, McPhearson?" he snarled. "Go and park the car! I want every man that works for me in my office in one hour!"

*Donnie stared through the slightly open doorway to the dimly-lit interior of the house. As he backed away, he couldn't help but think, Trask should be at the front door and this house should be lit up like a torch! Something bad has happened here in the last couple of hours and I want no part in it! If the old man is too stupid to see that, it's on him—not me!*

Tipping his hat, Donnie said, "I'll be right back, sir," and then he took off running past the automobile and into the night.

Branson, meanwhile, was still too filled with anger to pay attention to his surroundings. He used the wheels of his chair to bully the door open and rolled into the front entrance hall of his home. "Hello…where is everybody? Trask, Jonesy…get down here right now or you're fired!" he roared.

Suddenly, the front door slammed shut with a bang. Branson jumped in his chair and turned around to look but no one was there. Shrugging, he thought, *The men must be out on the back veranda.* There is always a draft in here when both doors are open.

"Still," he grumped under his breath, "Someone should be here to greet me upon my return!"

Wheeling himself along the hallway toward the back of the house, he stopped and sniffed the air. The whole place reeked of a privy house and he thought, Trask is sure being lax about cleaning the bathroom! Wrinkling his nose in disgust, he grumbled, "and why is it so damn dark in here?"

Angrier than ever, Branson came to the kitchen area and ground to a halt. His mouth opened and he gasped in shock as he observed the carnage in front of his eyes. Every single one of his men, besides Trask and young Donnie McPhearson, was lying dead on the kitchen floor!

There was very little blood and, moving his chair a little closer, Branson saw why. All of his men had been garroted and a few of them had voided their bowels and bladders at the moment of their deaths. The kitchen door was open and, despite the late hour, flies were finding their way inside the house.

Their steady drone filled the air and for the first time, Edward Branson took a deep, shuddering breath and screamed out loud. Instantly, his head was seized and a smelly gag was stuffed into his mouth. Grunting and quivering in fear, Branson bucked in his chair. "Numph!" he cried.

Someone seized the handles on his wheelchair, saying, "Shush now, Mr. Branson...this will all be over with soon." His chair was hauled backward down the hallway, and although Branson writhed and fought to break free, something soaked into the fabric of his gag was making him feel horribly sleepy. His head nodded on his chest and he allowed his eyelids to close. He flew far away for a moment, allowing himself to let go of the horror his reality had just become, but then a felt a light slap on his cheek.

He jerked awake and peered up at a number of men who were milling around his parlor. The strangers wore white robes with red crosses on them and Branson's eyes grew wide with alarm. *Templars?* he thought in disbelief. *What are these religious freaks doing in my parlor?* He bucked and wriggled in his chair again but, to no avail.

One of the robed men leaned over and said, "You can do one of two things, Mr. Branson. You can sign this written confession, acknowledging your part in the activities of the so-called Trinity over the last year or so in North Idaho. These charges include murder, theft and graft, and will result in your incarceration and eventual hanging."

Branson glared over the top of his gag at the gentle-faced man with wide, brown eyes thinking, *or else what?* The first choice was, of course, no choice at all! "Orrrr-aught?" he growled, thickly.

The Templar knight smiled and said, "You will die without atonement." Staring deeply into Branson's small angry eyes, the knight said, "We take our duties seriously, sir. Every man, no matter how evil, has the right to make his peace with God before he dies. We are giving you that chance now."

Branson's claw-like hands clutched at the arms of his wheelchair and the knights watched as he grimaced and spat into the gag over his mouth. Of course, the fluid had nowhere to go but back down his throat, and Branson hunched over, gagging and coughing. The Knights watched impassively while the old man heaved.

Finally, Branson quieted and tried to speak through the gag. Someone standing behind him loosened the cloth and Branson said, "Who are you? I will see all of you shot! You are nothing but criminals dressed up in fancy robes!" he squawked, hoarsely.

Shaking his head, the tall knight in front of him said, "Will you sign this confession and make peace with God… or not?"

Branson tried to lunge up out of his chair, but strong, heavy hands held him still. "I won't do a thing, damn your hides! You don't know who you are dealing with…I'll see you all hang for this!" he howled.

The knight shook his head and said, "Do it, Geoffrey."

Suddenly, Branson's head was seized again and his mouth forced open. Bucking and lunging, Branson tried to turn his mouth away but a small vial was pressed to his lips. Try as he might, he could not stop the bitter liquid from trickling down his throat.

The smell of almonds filled his nostrils and lungs and Branson realized he had just been poisoned. Shaking his head back and forth in fear, Branson grew weak and his stomach convulsed in agony. Staring up at his tormentors, Branson whispered, "I'll see you in Hell, Knight!"

The older knight who had forced the liquid down his throat stepped backward, out of sight, and the younger Templar stepped into his place. Bending over, he murmured, "I seriously doubt it, sir. You had your chance to repent…now the only thing you will ever know are the enduring flames of Hell."

Branson's eyes filled with sudden, terrible fear, and then he knew no more.

Staring down at Branson's dead body, the Knight sighed. "A pity," Looking up, he added, "Now, we should be quick. Mr. Trask, you can come out now."

An elderly black man stepped into the drawing room. His large, brown eyes were filled with sadness but he couldn't keep a small smile from lifting the corners of his mouth. He had been given to Edward Branson almost fifty years ago and had never been granted his freedom—not even after the War and the Emancipation Act.

Trask had never known another master, and he would not have left Branson's service after he was freed, but Edward had sworn that would never happen. He had even gone so far as to say, "Try leaving, Boy, and I'll have you shot down like the dirty, black dog you are!"

Any loyalty Trask might have felt toward his old master's son had died that day, and this afternoon, when the Templar Knights had shown up at the front door, Trask finally had a means to exact his revenge.

The old butler stared at the Knights, and nodded in agreement when the priest known as Father Adams said, "You four, please remove the men's bodies from the kitchen and take them to consecrated ground. Bury them and say prayers over their immortal souls."

Putting a hand on the oldest knight's sleeve, he said, "Geoffrey, you and Mr. Trask stay with me, please, and help me make this look like a natural death."

"As you wish, Father," Geoffrey replied.

Three and a half hours later, Branson's men had been buried and prayed over in a mass grave close to the Seattle cemetery, and Branson was sitting in his wheelchair, having died peacefully in front of a cold fireplace.

All evidence of ether and poison had been wiped clean and Branson was now dressed in his pajamas and silk robe. The following day a Seattle coroner talked to the old man's butler and, after hearing that Trask had found his employer sitting dead in his parlor early that morning, he signed a report of death by natural causes, with no foul play suspected.

The Knights Templar Order of the Red Cross disappeared like smoke on a breezy day.

## MATTHEW AND CHANCE
## HEAD HOME

THE NEXT MORNING DAWNED COOL AND CLOUDY. THE curtains stirred and a soft breeze ran caressing fingers over Matthew's shoulder. He awoke with a snort of alarm. *What time is it?* he thought in confusion. Peering over at the small mantle clock by the fireplace he was shocked to see that it was already ten-thirty in the morning.

Sitting up on the edge of the bed, Matthew ran his hands over his face. He had slept like the dead and felt guilty over the fact. It had been a long time since he had slept so soundly, but there was no time for that kind of rest—not yet, anyway!

Despite everything, Branson had managed to wriggle away from the long arm of the law. He was free and that meant trouble as far as Matthew was concerned.

Cocking his head, Matthew noticed how quiet the house was and for a moment, he felt a thrill of alarm. Like a boogie-man in the night, Branson had cast a shadow of fear over everyone and everything he held dear. Even now, knowing Branson was out in the world, instead of behind steel bars made Matthew jump to his feet to search for his loved ones.

He strode to the washbasin and splashed water on his face. Then he smeared some cleaning paste on a mouth brush and scrubbed his teeth. He studied his face and decided that shaving could wait. He pulled a clean, white shirt from a clothes-horse and was just starting to button up when there was a knock on the door.

Matthew opened it and saw Clyde's butler standing in the hallway with a cup of coffee on a silver platter. "Good morning, sir. Miss Annie thought you would like to join the others in the front parlor. We have company... Mr. Revell has come to call." The old man smiled. "I think you might be pleased by what he has to say..." he added, mysteriously.

"What? What is he saying?" Matthew blurted.

The butler pursed his lips and said, "Forgive me, sir. I have already spoken out of turn. Please, have some coffee. There is a full breakfast laid out on the warming tables, downstairs." With those words the man spun on his heels and walked away, leaving Matthew to stare after him.

Calming down now that he knew that all was well in the house, at least for the moment, Matthew finished dressing, combed his hair and walked downstairs. Sure enough, he saw the rest of his family and friends listening intently to their houseguest, Ian Revell, in the next room. Grabbing a couple of pastries, he walked into the parlor and sat down.

Ian Revell stopped speaking and stood up to shake Matthew's hand. Matthew stood as well, and said, "Well, it was a good try but I guess we need to come up with another plan, right?"

Matthew had not really noticed the expressions on his friends and family's faces but he saw the twinkle in Revell's eye as he sat down and said, "It's all over, Mr. Wilcox. I, and a couple of other Masons traveled to Branson's house earlier today to inform him his candidacy had been revoked. That's when we found out that his butler, Mr. Trask, found Mr. Branson dead in his own parlor early this morning."

"Dead?" Matthew echoed in shock.

Revell nodded with a look of satisfaction on his face. "It appears that the man expired from a heart attack. We called the coroner and he has written Branson's death off as an act of God."

Feeling relief sweep over him, Matthew murmured, "Amen to that!" and then he gazed about the room and apologized for his uncivil tongue. "I am sorry, but I won't pretend to be sorry."

Clyde grinned and said, "No need to apologize, my boy. We would all like to dance on that man's grave!"

Ian said, "Mr. Wilcox, I was just telling the others that the City of Seattle will be launching a full-scale inquiry into Mr. Branson's activities in the North Idaho area mines. Stephen Castle has learned of Branson's death and is now implicating Branson as the ringleader in multiple claim-jumps, thefts and murders in Idaho, Spokane and here in Seattle. If the city can prove Branson's culpability, his properties will be seized and sold for cash.

"Also," Revell paused to grin for a moment. "Fanny Castle has offered full compensation to any and all affected citizens. This will do nothing to bring back the dead, of course, but she promises to be generous, just so long as her husband is treated kindly in jail. What do you think about that, Mr. Wilcox?"

Matthew sat back in his chair and sipped his coffee. Being faced with a moral dilemma was not his forte, but Ian was asking him—as a direct complainant and witness —to sign off on Castle's incarceration. On one hand, Stephen Castle had done plenty wrong, and Matthew would never forgive the death of young Tommy during Stephen's revenge-filled assassination attempt.

On the other. hand, Stephen had tried to set thing right. It was far too little and way too late, but Matthew knew the man had really tried to put an end to Branson's murderous schemes. Plus, if Fanny Castle was actually ready to award financial compensation to Branson's victims, who was he to take that away?

Glancing up at Annie's face, he saw her give him a slight wink. He knew that she would not try to sway him, one way or the other, but he also realized she was giving her tacit approval of Mrs. Castle's offer.

Turning to face Ian, Matthew said, "I will cease my investigation and withdraw my complaints, Ian. As long as there are no further problems in my town, I am willing to let bygones be bygones."

Ian smiled. "Oh, trust me, Mr. Castle will not be going anywhere...not for a long time. But, this way, Fanny can visit her husband in jail and perhaps make his life a little easier. He is, after all, standing as State witness for more than two dozen accomplices'!"

"What about you, Mr. Revell? Will you be stepping in as Grand Master, now?" Annie asked.

Ian looked horrified. "No! I am nowhere near ready to step into those shoes! The Masons will have a valid vote in due time and swear in the best candidate available."

Standing up to take his leave, Revell bowed slightly and said, "I am pleased that this sad affair has come to a satisfactory conclusion. Will all of you be heading back to Spokane now?"

Chance spoke up. "Yes…just as soon as possible!"

"Well," Ian said, "Perhaps I could call on you sometime? I have heard that Spokane is beautiful…"

Matthew said, "Yes, we would welcome you anytime… and thank you, Ian, for your help."

The young man suddenly looked close to tears and his frail hand trembled slightly when he shook Matthew's hand in farewell. Studying Ian's face, Matthew knew that there was more to Branson's death than met the eye and he wondered, for a moment, if he should look into it…

Then he decided that he would not even give it a second thought. There were some things that were better left alone.

Three weeks later, Matthew and Chance stepped off the train in Granville, Washington. They had gone to Spokane to see the Lindsay's back home to their land claim in Idaho. After that they went to their little office, answered a few letters and paid some bills. They also picked up a number of realty sheets. Annie, who had stayed behind at the Imes' ranch, wanted to rebuild the

Thurston home in Spokane, but closer to the downtown news office and not until next year.

It was full summer now, and the sun's heat pressed down on them from a pale blue sky. Chance seemed slightly morose, and Matthew grinned. "You'll see Hannah again soon enough, son…"

Chance started and grinned. "Oh, I know, Pa. She and her family had to get back to their claim, especially now that their new equipment is about to arrive. I just miss her, that's all."

"I know, Chance. I miss her, too," Matthew replied. "Hey, what do you think about maybe planning a double wedding come autumn?"

Chance had asked for Hannah's hand in marriage about a week ago and received joyful permission from Hannah's family. The happy couple were planning on getting married in October.

Chance stared at his father now, though, with his mouth hanging open in shock. Matthew wondered if he had overstepped. Young folks shouldn't have to share their wedding day, and he had just put Chance on the spot!

"Hey, never mind, son." Matthew mumbled. "I was just killing two birds with one stone, but I wasn't thinking straight. Of course, you and Hannah want your own special day…don't give it another thought!"

But Chance grinned and said, "Well, you might have given me a little warning, Pa…I didn't even know you and Annie were planning on getting hitched! But, nothing would make me happier, sir, than to get married with you by my side!"

Matthew and his son smiled at each other, and then turned to watch as Annie rode up on the wagon to fetch them home. Turning back to Chance, Matthew murmured, "Maybe we ought to ask the womenfolk what they want first, eh?"

Chance just grinned and said, "They'll love the idea, Pa. I just know it!"

# A LOOK AT THE PISTOL MAN'S APPRENTICE

## BY LINELL JEPPSEN AND JEB ROSEBROOK

Scarred by the Civil War, now a loner by choice, Missouri-born Jack Ballard rides the West in search of trouble. Sometimes he's able to stop it from hurting innocent people—and sometimes he causes it.

It can't be helped, though. He is a good man with a fast gun, and in West Texas in the late 1800's, trouble lies around every bend.

Only he and his filed-down .44-40 Colt can stop it.

*AVAILABLE NOW ON AMAZON.*

# ABOUT THE AUTHOR

**Linell Jeppsen** is a writer of science fiction and fantasy. Her vampire novel, *Detour to Dusk*, has received over 44-four and five star reviews. Her novel *Story Time*, with over 130 4-and 5-star reviews, is a science fiction post-apocalyptic novel, and has been touted by the Paranormal Romance Guild, Sandy's Blog Spot, Coffee time Romance, Bitten by Books and 64 top reviewers as a five-star read, filled with terror, love, loss, and the indomitable beauty and strength of the human spirit. *Story Time* was also nominated as the best new read of 2011 by the PRG. Her dark fantasy novel, *Onio* (a story about a half-human Sasquatch who falls in love with a human girl), was released in December 2012 and won 3rd place as the best fantasy romance of 2012 by the PRG reviewers guild. Her novel, *The War of Odds*, won the IBD award for fantasy fiction and boasts 18 5-star reviews since its release in February of 2013. It also placed 2nd, as the best YA paranormal book of 2013 by the PRG.